What Happens

What Happens

John Herrmann

*Fiction
Herrmann*

Introduction by Sara Kosiba

Hastings College Press | Hastings, Nebraska

Introduction © 2015 by Hastings College Press

This book was denied copyright registration by the U.S. Copyright Office in 1926. It is not subject to copyright protection.

Production Staff

Dakota Anderson
Emilie Barnes
Kaitlyn Baucom
Allie Belitz
Hannah Currey
Razvan Dobrin

Kaitlin Grode
Rachel Jesske
Alex Kreikemeier
Brooke MacLeod
Holly Wolfe

ISBN-10: 1942885105
ISBN-13: 978-1-942885-10-8

Note on the text: This edition has been reset from the first (1926) edition. Original spelling and grammatical conventions have been maintained, except in the case of publishing or consistency errors in the first edition. The original punctuation has been maintained but updated using modern conventions (e.g., eliminating spaces around dashes).

Manufactured in the United States of America.

Text is printed on acid-free, chlorine-free paper with 30% postconsumer recycled content. Cover is printed on 100% recycled paper.

Contents

Introduction

Sara Kosiba

I first heard about John Herrmann's novel *What Happens* while I was writing my dissertation. I had never heard of the author or the novel before I came across a reference to the book during my work on Midwestern writers from the 1920s and 1930s. There wasn't much to the reference but enough to convey the idea that the work had been deemed obscene and that copies in the United States were destroyed. Obscenity charges toward literary works have always interested me, both as a reader and as a scholar, as I always wonder about who has the power to make those decisions and the impact those decisions have on writers and readers. So, I set out to learn more about John Herrmann and this "scandalous" book.[1]

John Herrmann's literary fame, such as it is, has always been as a passing reference in the biographies and stories of his much more celebrated friends. Born in Lansing, Michigan, in 1900, Herrmann grew up in an upper middle-class, fairly conservative household. His family was well respected in the Lansing community, as his grandfather had established a successful tailoring business in town and Herrmann's father and uncle carried on the family business. Upon finishing high school, Herrmann attended George Washington University in Washington, DC, for a short time, before transferring to the University of Michigan. In 1922, filled with wanderlust similar

---

[1] Part of this research was funded the Andrew W. Mellon Foundation Research Fellowship Endowment from the Harry Ransom Center at the University of Texas at Austin. Special thanks as well to Robert W. Trogdon and Bill Castanier for their assistance in clarifying elements of Herrmann's life and publication history.

to other Midwesterners of the time, Herrmann left for Europe
and studied art history at the University of Munich for a year. By
1924, he was in Paris and hanging out with the expatriate literary
circle that included notable figures such as Ernest Hemingway,
Robert McAlmon, Nathan Asch, and the woman who would
become his future wife, Josephine Herbst. It is likely that he
composed *What Happens* during 1923 or 1924.

While *What Happens* does not have the pacing of a
suspenseful page turner or the cliffhangers of an edgy murder
mystery, the novel is a notable representation of teen life and
moral standards during the 1920s. Customs officials and judges
deemed the text obscene due to mentions of masturbation and
implications of teenage and premarital sex, but Winfield Payne's
story contains truthful representations of the awkwardness
of adolescence and the struggles of burgeoning sexuality that
resonate even among today's youth culture. Winfield is not a
saint, but his sins are not irredeemable. In the early scenes in
the novel when seventeen-year-old Winfield is contemplating
situations like his fear of having gotten Ruth Potter pregnant, he
is also weighing the mixed signals of adolescence, aware of his
parents' beliefs and potential disappointment and yet mindful
of "what ... boys talk about in highschool" (2). As he faces the
loss of his high-school friend Harold to illness, Winfield both
uncomfortably notes the "amazing, frightening, unnatural"
appearance of the dead body and spends time obsessing over the
potential gossip of Harold's fraternity brothers at the funeral (55).
This contrast of the seriousness of confronting death firsthand
and yet feeling as if the most important details are the opinions
of one's peers is very characteristic of the conflicting concerns
adolescents face as they mature. Later in the novel, Winfield's
romances are all tinged with the question of permanence, as
any hint of seriousness in each relationship makes him question
whether he is ready to settle down or marry. It is clear from his
behavior that Winfield is not ready for that level of commitment,
but he continues to look for it just the same. He comes the
closest with Mary, a girl he meets in book six of the novel, when
he thinks early in their relationship, "God, I wish I could marry

her. Settle down into anything, business. Marry her" (171).
Winfield's emotional impulsiveness is the very picture of youth,
even if his actions are often misguided.

It was this honest, realistic quality that made the novel
attractive to fellow writer Robert McAlmon and his Contact
Publishing Company. Herrmann had tried shopping the novel to
American publishers upon his return from Paris in 1924, but he
was largely unsuccessful. The novel was presented to prestigious
publishers such as Boni and Liveright; Thomas Seltzer, Inc.;
Harcourt, Brace, and Company; and Alfred A. Knopf. It was
consistently turned down. A few did compliment some aspects of
the novel but expressed concern over publishing the novel while
it still contained words such as "masturbation." Other publishers
found *What Happens* to be too amateur and adolescent. When the
attempts failed among American publishers, Herrmann sought
help from a literary friendship made during his time among the
expatriate literary circle in Paris. Robert McAlmon's small Parisian
press had already established itself with a reputation for publishing
avant garde and unconventional works by authors as diverse as
William Carlos Williams, Ernest Hemingway, and Gertrude Stein.
McAlmon had earlier shown a favorable interest in Herrmann's
work by including a portion of what would become book five
of the novel, simply titled "Work in Progress," in his *Contact
Collection of Contemporary Writers* (1925) alongside writers such as
Djuna Barnes, James Joyce, Ezra Pound, and Dorothy Richardson.
In his 1938 memoir, *Being Geniuses Together*, McAlmon remarked
that "*What Happens* was not startlingly great, but it was a direct,
and authentic picture of American youth and not marred by
idealized 'love' scenes." He added the caveat that the novel "would
have been improved by a touch of wit, no doubt, but it would
have lost the gangly, awkward, fumbling-bewilderment of its
youthful quality" (McAlmon 165). Three hundred copies of the
novel were printed, and it appeared around July 1, 1926.

That truthful quality in the novel was likely due to the
heavy use of autobiography. *What Happens* clearly falls into the
category of a *roman à clef*, a French term for a novel about real
life with a fictional veneer. There are several places within the

novel where it is apparent that Benton, Michigan, is a veiled reference to Herrmann's hometown of Lansing. Like Herrmann, Winfield Payne attended George Washington University and the University of Michigan, although there appear to be some deviations in the amount of time the author and the character spent in attendance at those schools. There are similarities between other characters in the novel and real people, as well. Herrmann noted in a December 9, 1924, letter to his then-girlfriend Josephine Herbst that a woman he ran into while back in Lansing was the model for "the little Alice of my book." There are also implications that a gentleman named Paul Mixter, a high-school classmate of Herrmann's, played a role in the novel. Both Herrmann and Mixter were in Washington, DC, in the fall of 1919 when Herrmann was attending the university there, and with Mixter's newspaper background, he was likely a model for the Paul Pew with whom Winfield Payne associates in Washington, DC (book four). Mixter also wrote to Herrmann shortly after publication of the novel to note his displeasure with how closely the text mirrored real people and events.

When *What Happens* appeared in 1926, it received mixed reviews, although most critics found something to praise amidst the criticism. In an unsigned review in the *New York Times*, titled "Cautious Casanova," Herrmann's book was praised for its "photographic" quality, proclaiming

> this is a saga of the jazz age, couched in the pedestrian English which the "confession" magazines have made familiar. Mr. Herrmann is not concerned with interpretation; he merely reports what he sees and hears. He has given an astonishingly accurate portrait of the sort of youth who breaks into the tabloids, with his fervid drinking and callow love affairs, his search for new thrills, his utter aimlessness and his almost forbidding materialism. (7)

Babette Deutsch, in the *New York Herald Tribune*, contrasted the novel with Theodore Dreiser's *An American Tragedy* (1925).

In her comparison of protagonists Clyde Griffiths and Winfield Payne, she noted that the only significant difference between the characters, other than their backgrounds, was that Griffiths appeared more developed, and as a result, he earns more of the reader's compassion than does Winfield. Deutsch finished her review by praising the writing style while noting the detachment of the plot:

> What is refreshing here is the lean[,] hard, dry style, so infinitely preferable to Dreiser's tortuous verbosity. What is depressing is the lifelessness of so narrow a presentation, and the fact that there is not an individual in the book with whom one could bear to spend half an hour. The novel contains as little nourishment as an emetic, it leaves an equally nasty taste in the mouth and has, generally speaking, an equally debilitating effect. But emetics have their uses. (12)

A small review of the novel appeared in the November 1926 issue of the *American Mercury*, likely written by H.L. Mencken but unsigned, under the heading of "Biography." As this review was published well after the novel's seizure by U.S. Customs, it spent much of its brief commentary on defending the novel from detractors: "The thing is crudely done, but has sound observation in it and is plainly sincere. The book has been barred from the United States by the wowsers of the Customs Service. Stuff ten times more dangerous to Christian virgins, male and female, goes through the mails by the ton" ("Check List" 224).

Unfortunately for Herrmann and writers of his generation, the early twentieth century was not a particularly hospitable time for the publication of edgy or explicit literary works. Rachel Potter, in her study of literary publications in the United States and United Kingdom during that time, notes,

> In the period of 1900–1940, however, the claim that literary obscenity could corrupt the minds of

the young and impressionable fuelled the censorship
of a huge number of English-language texts and
made it one of the most tightly controlled periods in
literary expression. There were a number of high-
profile literary trials in the UK and the United States,
most notably the suppression of D.H. Lawrence's
The Rainbow (London, 1915), James Joyce's *Ulysses*
(New York, 1921), and Radclyffe Hall's *The Well of
Loneliness* (London, 1928). (1)

While *What Happens* never received the notoriety of many others,
it clearly became a victim of a suspicious literary climate. It is
likely that the association with Contact Publishing Company
got the novel into more trouble than any reputation it might
have established on its own. As Hugh Ford notes in his study
Published in Paris (1975), by the mid-1920s, in both the United
States and England, "books printed in Paris were automatically
suspect and often confiscated simply because they were believed
to be obscene" (65). McAlmon had issues shipping not only
Herrmann's novel, but also Gertrude Stein's *The Making of
Americans* and Emanuel Carnevali's *A Hurried Man*, among a
few others. Herrmann received a notification from U.S. Customs
on July 7, 1926, that his books had been held on charges of
violating Section 305 of the Tariff Act of 1922, which banned
the import of obscene material from a foreign country. The
penalty for such a violation was destruction of the material, so
a substantial portion of Herrmann's fledgling literary career,
as represented by those printed volumes, hung in the balance.
Herrmann almost immediately secured legal representation from
the firm of Greenbaum, Wolff, and Ernst in New York City, and
lawyers mounted a defense, attempting to appeal the decision
based on the novel's published reviews and testimonials written
by prominent literary figures and friends of Herrmann, including
H.L. Mencken, Edmund Wilson, Katharine Anne Porter, and
Genevieve Taggard.

In a counterargument to the initial appeals made by
Herrmann and his legal team, the Treasury Department vigorously

defended the Customs decision, as shown in a November 1, 1926, letter to Herrmann's lawyers. The letter cited the U.S. Supreme Court case of *Rosen v. U.S.*—an 1896 case involving an attempt by Lew Rosen to mail a paper containing lewd images—particularly part of Justice John Marshall Harlan's opinion[2], to note that their decision was guided by weighing "whether the tendency of the matter is to deprave and corrupt the morals of those whose minds are open to such influences and into whose hands a publication of this sort may fall; would it suggest or convey lewd and lascivious thoughts to the young and inexperienced?" (qtd. in Andrews). The letter also noted that while the entire text was deemed objectionable there were 62 pages in particular containing questionable content (roughly 22% of the original 273-page novel). In reviewing the listed pages, some do highlight words or scenes involving talk of sex or drinking. The worst language in the novel is the occasional use of the words "masturbation" and "whore." References to sex in the novel are highly veiled. For example, the Treasury Department letter selected a page describing Ruth Potter's behavior: "Some boys took her out riding and only kissed her and made love to her. She liked that too, but the other thing was better, it left her feeling better, more herself" (4). Another section alleged to be questionable occurs during a night of fun in West Virginia when Winfield, Dorothy, Gaston, and Justine are gathered at Dorothy's house. A page referencing drinking whiskey, telling dirty stories, and having a preference for loose women was flagged as objectionable (37–38 in this edition). However, other page numbers noted in the Treasury Department letter are questionable, as there is no similarity in the content of those pages with the subject matter or language flagged elsewhere. It appears Herrmann's legal team felt the same way, as several of the page numbers are circled in the original letter and correspond with seemingly harmless content. For example, on one cited page

---

[2] The *Rosen v. U.S.* decision and dissent can be read at http://www.law.cornell.edu/supremecourt/text/161/29#writing-type-1-HARLAN. Justice John Marshall Harlan would achieve notoriety the same year as the *Rosen v. U.S.* decision for being the lone dissenting voice in the historic *Plessy v. Ferguson* case.

the most scandalous thing that happens is Winfield tries to get a
kiss from his friend Harold's former girlfriend, Clara. While the
narrative also explains that Clara "didn't want just necking, she
wanted real affection," which perhaps could be read as a desire
for sex, it seems a stretch to imply that as the only way to read
that passage (59). A simple attempt at a kiss and a reference to a
desire for affection are hardly suggestive enough to cause moral
corruption.

To complicate Herrmann's life during this time, his lawyers
advised that he register his novel with the U.S. Copyright
Office. Since the novel had originally been published in
France, Herrmann had to make a separate application to secure
copyright protection in the United States. Herrmann filled
out the paperwork in the fall of 1926; however, he received a
January 12, 1927, response from the Copyright Office noting
that his application was denied. Herrmann had failed to meet
the required 60-day window for filing an application after a
foreign publication (Brown). I recently checked with the U.S.
Copyright Office and confirmed they have no listing for *What
Happens*. Ironically, when the Copyright Office returned the
submitted copy of his book along with his registration payment,
a handwritten notation on the letter to Herrmann by an office
clerk, Henry D. Gloyd, asked to purchase a copy of the book.
Whether Gloyd was tantalized by the rumors of the content or
simply was interested in the literary work on its own merits, the
evidence of a readership for his novel must have both encouraged
Herrmann and exacerbated the frustrations of having his
shipment of books held in limbo.

The case eventually went to a jury trial in New York City,
and the lead counsel in Herrmann's defense was Morris L. Ernst,
a lawyer who took a special interest in civil liberties cases. (He
would later serve as general counsel for the American Civil
Liberties Union from 1929 to 1955.) News of the case stretched
across the country, with papers in Ogden, Utah, for example,
including Associated Press coverage of the trial. It was clear
from the point of jury selection that the prosecution was not
necessarily interested in giving the book an assessment on any

literary merits. As Ernst cynically later wrote about the process
of defending books like Herrmann's, jury selection, much like
today, was a calculated process on both sides to lead to the best
result: "The prosecutor's game is to secure substantial citizens who
never read books. And this is not difficult. Persons who belong
to the book-buying public usually possess sufficient wealth or
political interest to keep their names off jury panels" (5). During
Herrmann's trial, potential jurors who were also readers of the
American Mercury were challenged by prosecutors ("Mercury
Reader"). This was likely due to some of the recent news
surrounding the *Mercury*, as it had itself gone to trial the year
before to challenge a post-office order banning the dissemination
of the April issue containing an article by Herbert Asbury titled
"Hatrack." The article was a chapter from a longer work by
Asbury and referenced prostitution. A judge later granted an
injunction against that decision.[3]

Not only was the jury carefully selected, but the
prosecution's case against *What Happens* also relied on reading
selected passages from the novel and making appeals to the
protection of "the hearth, and the family" in considering the
content of the book ("Book About Youth" 28). The federal judge
in the trial also, in essence, assisted the prosecution by dismissing
the defense's use of any testimony from the literary community.
Herrmann's defense had a panel of literary figures and prominent
critics ready to testify on his behalf, including Babette Deutsch
(writer of the *New York Times* review), Heywood Broun, H.L.
Mencken, Harry Hansen, and Genevieve Taggard. However,
Judge John C. Knox dismissed the need for any experts: "The
jury represents a state of mind of the community and we are
going to submit to them the question of whether or not the book
is obscene. On that point there is no necessity for the calling

---

[3] There is evidence in the Morris L. Ernst papers at the University of Texas
at Austin's Harry Ransom Center, in a carbon copy of a letter to Arthur
Garfield Hays, lawyer for the defense in the "Hatrack" trial," that Ernst and his
co-counsel consulted papers related to that case in preparation for the *What
Happens* trial.

of literary experts" ("Bars Book" 10). The judge also dismissed
the use of any other literature, including an example from
Shakespeare, as a comparative form of evidence. Herrmann's own
testimony was the only substantive evidence that was allowed
for the defense, and he testified that the book was "a truthful
description of what happens among high school and college girls
and boys in Michigan and elsewhere" ("Bars Book" 10).

The jury was unconvinced by the appeal to the realism
of the novel's content and wasted little time in coming to a
decision upholding the obscenity charge. Judge Knox publicly
commended their decision at the close of the trial: "He said he
had been on the point of ordering such a verdict before they
retired to deliberate" ("Book About Youth" 28). Morris Ernst
later wrote a book inspired by his defense of Herrmann's novel,
To the Pure ... : A Study of Obscenity and the Censor (1928). Ernst
noted the irony of the jury's responses post-trial:

> After convicting *What Happens*, by John Herrman
> [sic], in New York City in 1927, several jurors came
> up and shook hands with the defeated author. The
> jurors were in good humor for they had retained the
> exhibits, the copies of the condemned book. "And
> why did you vote against my book?" queried the
> author. The masculine answer was direct and typical,
> more honest than can usually be expected. "You see,
> that book wouldn't hurt me. I wasn't scared by the
> mention of masturbation. But then I felt it might
> hurt some other people." (6)

Herrmann's book was temporarily given a reprieve from
destruction by Judge Knox, pending an appeal, but it does not
appear an appeal was ever filed. Herrmann's financial hardships
were the most likely reason the process did not go forward. As of
1930, Herrmann was still in debt to Ernst's firm from the 1927
trial (Herrmann, Letter to Morris Ernst). The copies in the seized
shipment of books were destroyed, although Robert McAlmon
claimed in *Being Geniuses Together* (1938) that "the remaining

copies did get to America, ultimately, but by that time Herrmann was doing much better writing" (232).

The trial and its aftermath did not dampen John Herrmann's literary enthusiasm, although it did little to truly boost his reputation or success. A second novel that Herrmann was trying to circulate to publishers around the time of the trial, *Foreign Born*, never found a publisher. While Herrmann published a novella, "Engagement," in the *Second American Caravan* in 1928, the next full novel to appear in print would be *Summer Is Ended* (1932), a work that probably achieved its publishing success due to the efforts and support of some of Herrmann's more successful literary friends, including John Dos Passos, John Cowper Powys, and Ernest Hemingway. Hemingway's support appeared in an advertising blurb helping to promote that novel: "John Herrmann writes of the tragedy of the human heart as truly as any writer that ever lived" (*Summer* 8). Herrmann published a variety of other articles and essays through the late 1920s and throughout the 1930s that appeared in publications as diverse as *transition, This Quarter, American Mercury, Blues: A Magazine of New Rhythms*, and *Scribner's Magazine*. His moment of greatest fame came in 1932 when he tied with Thomas Wolfe for the *Scribner's Magazine* prize for short fiction for his story "The Big Short Trip," splitting the $5000 prize. Herrmann increasingly became involved in politics and the plight of the working class during the Great Depression, causes and concerns that slowly moved him further away from the literary world. There is currently no evidence Herrmann published anything after his last novel, *The Salesman*, in 1939.

Herrmann's book resonates with today's readership for a number of reasons. While it is an historic text providing insights into youth culture and censorship issues of the 1920s, those elements of its value to the past are also incredibly relevant in the contemporary world. With the contemporary rise of reality television shows or documentaries highlighting teenage sexuality and pregnancy and concerned editorials and discussions regarding adolescent morality, a book like *What Happens* demonstrates that those issues were alive and well in the early twentieth century and provides an opportunity to reflect on how attitudes may or may not have changed during the intervening decades. *What Happens* also provides an opportunity to talk about and reflect on the evolution of censorship in the United States. While standards of decency may have changed and far fewer people today are likely to find Herrmann's novel scandalous, we still currently struggle as a national and global society with issues related to free speech and what is fit to print. This first U.S. publication of Herrmann's novel, 89 years after its first appearance, gives readers an opportunity to use a literary text to reflect on our past, contemplate our present, and speculate on what role literature may play in our future.

Works Cited

Andrews, L.C., Assistant Secretary of the Treasury. Letter to John Wildberg (c/o Greenbaum, Wolff, & Ernst). 1 Nov. 1926. Container 233.6. Morris Leopold Ernst Papers. The University of Texas at Austin, Harry Ransom Center.

"Bars Book Experts at Obscenity Trial." *New York Times* 4 Oct. 1927: 10. Print.

"Book About Youth Is Found Obscene." *New York Times* 5 Oct. 1927: 28. Print.

Brown, William L., Assistant Register of Copyrights. Letter to John Herrmann. 12 Jan. 1927. Container 233.6. Morris Leopold Ernst Papers. The University of Texas at Austin, Harry Ransom Center.

"Cautious Casanova." Review of *What Happens* by John Herrmann. *New York Times Book Review.* 11 July 1926: 7. Print.

"Check List of New Books." Review of *What Happens* by John Herrmann. *The American Mercury.* Nov. 1926: 224. Print.

Deutsch, Babette. "An Emetic Novel." Review of *What Happens* by John Herrmann. *New York Herald Tribune Books.* 22 Aug. 1926: 12. Print.

Ernst, Morris L. *To the Pure ... : A Study of Obscenity and the Censor.* New York: Viking, 1928. Print.

Ford, Hugh. *Published in Paris: American and British Writers, Printers, and Publishers in Paris, 1920–1939.* New York: Macmillan, 1975. Print.

Herrmann, John. "The Big Short Trip." *Scribner's Magazine* August 1932: 65–69, 113–128. Print.

———. "Engagement." *The Second American Caravan.* Ed. Alfred Keymborg, Lewis Mumford, and Paul Rosenfeld. New York: Macaulay, 1928. 377–474. Print.

———. Letter to Josephine Herbst. 9 Dec. 1924. Box 13. Josephine Herbst Papers. Yale Collection of American Literature, Beinecke Rare Book and Manuscript Library, New Haven, CT.

———. Letter to Morris Ernst. 7 Jan. 1930. Container 233.8. Morris Leopold Ernst Papers. The University of Texas at Austin, Harry Ransom Center.

———. *The Salesman.* New York: Simon and Schuster, 1939. Print.

———. *Summer Is Ended.* New York: Covici, Friede, 1932. Print.

McAlmon, Robert. *Being Geniuses Together.* London: Secker & Warburg, 1938. Print.

"Mercury Reader Banned as Juror." *New York Evening Post* 3 Oct. 1927: 3. Print.

Mixter, Paul. Letter to John Herrmann. N.d. Container 2.11. John Herrmann Collection. The University of Texas at Austin, Harry Ransom Center.

Potter, Rachel. *Obscene Modernism: Literary Censorship and Experiment, 1900–1940.* Oxford: Oxford UP, 2013. Print.

Summer Is Ended by John Herrmann. Advertisement. *New York Times Book Review* 2 Oct. 1932: 8.

....

Sara Kosiba is an Assistant Professor of English at Troy University. Her research primarily focuses on writers from the American Midwest, including Ernest Hemingway, F. Scott Fitzgerald, Josephine Herbst, Dawn Powell, and John Herrmann. She is a past president of the Society for the Study of Midwestern Literature and serves on the editorial boards for *Middle West Review* and *The Dictionary of Midwestern Literature*, Volume II.

Original Foreword

Directness is not necessarily the best, or the most subtle, or intelligent, of qualities in literature, but it is a healthy quality. If we regard the few bigly productive periods in literature, English, Greek, or French, we find that underlying any stylisms, manners, or attitudes, exists a clarity, a directness of perception, that observing, see no reason for evading, refining, or idealizing experience. It was so particularly with fifth century Greeks, the historians of which were mainly, simply clear-minded and honest recorders. What beauty, what satire or irony, what drama they attained came out of the sheer healthiness of their observation. Then, of course, it was not deemed necessary to say that a writer was courageous, or fearless, if being honest. "Idealism" had not then come in so much to make smirkers, hypocrites, and visionaries believe that romanticism, mysticism, and "beauty-howling" were the only acceptable qualities in art.

Fairly much the same was true of the Elizabethans though they did take attitudes, and did "strut the tragedy and "stunt the beauty" or "pull the comedy" lines somewhat. They were "erudite." Rabelais had left his mark on "English literature," … Fielding was self-conscious as a satirist; Smollet was more so; Sterne rolled his tongue in his cheek, tickled at his own devilishness; but underneath they perceived directly, and very little mention of the much-later-day thing "beauty" or "spiritual value" was made. They had the sound, healthy, lively strain within them.

American writing, naturally, because of America's mixed race and pioneering-puritanical background, started out with a handicap and a derived impulse back of it. They thought in earlier America, if they thought at all about literature, that they knew what the novel, the essay, and poetry, were; as present day England is apt to think that they know what the novel and poetry are. Tennyson, Browning, Shelley, Keats, in being, gave lesser beings—as greater beings always have—discipled ideas of what is or is not literature in any of its forms. That in Russia, Finland, the Scandinavian countries, as well as the East, modes quite different were being developed, did not occur to writers in America, which believed itself Anglo-Saxon. About ten years after the beginning of this century, however, something happened to the complacent faith in the United States, so that the derived manner began to be doubted. English poetry seemed to some Americans somehow false, for them; French and Russian novelists were admired, but they too seemed not quite the thing. Whitman had written his poetry—if you will—and a few thought him the saviour of American literature, and his far-flung, loose impulsed, mysticism started a school, but schools are seldom satisfactory or really productive. Any particular piece of writing is more apt to have interest if it is individual, even if the individuality is limited, eccentric, precious, mannered, artificial, or even pompous, or pretentious, so long as it is any of these in its own way. More whole work however will probably be none of these; any more than it will be "old-fashioned" or "modern." Any reading person finally ceases to be surprised to find how much more "modern" some work done centuries or ages ago is than much contemporary work that essays the "modern" manner. It is probable that in all ages true "moderns" are simply wanting to steer clear of the stale, academically developed "values" that hamper, not literature, but the recognition of it, in any period. It is an affair of life against dust and mould. The same hampering will against active thought and sensibility functions in other metiers, no doubt; metaphysics, science, medicine, architecture, stage-designing, window display, and shop-keeping. The will is not against the new; it is against any bit of observation that cuts through sentimentalities and conventions that protect insular social habits.

The new generation in America begin to show signs of having emerged so that they don't revolt against the nonsense of puritanism; they simply don't bother about it. They have their drink; they love without being ashamed of it; they naturally can't see the legislation, and the social habits of the older generation,

and think seriously that the older ones really knew what they
were about. So much as life is life, that is that. Theodore Dreiser,
Sherwood Anderson, and some others have written novels
about people who were the hunted rabbits of—not fate—but
of economic situation, bad heredity, defective mentality, lack
of will,— just victims. Both of these writers give, at moments,
the sensation of having somewhat perversely, a little willfully,
like hurt boys, selected altogether will-less and ineffectual types
to write about when depicting American life. It is not all the
picture and not the interesting part of the picture. Escape from
environment, and from mere economic fate, is and has been fairly
possible in America. A look at the ad pages of any magazine in
the country will show that an up-and at-em, go-get-it philosophy
does exist, however vulgarly, in even the horde of the country.
The race is not a meek or humble one; and it is not a naively
trustful one. It is one very apt to want what it wants and to try
and get it, and to an extent it succeeds, as people do succeed.

This book of John Herrmann's is a very fair picture of
adolescence in America. It is no more grey or material in its view,
point than Fielding's *Tom Jones*. It may lack a mature sense of
humour which Fielding had, but the book was written when the
writer was twenty-two years old, and utterly regardless of the
writer's age, fairly manages to record an American youth's life
without blagi, gush, or bitterness. There is enough tenderness
in it, of restraint. The two death scenes, the first of the young
bon friend, the second, of the automobile accident, are handled,
expressing the frustrated, pitying, helplessness of boy before
death, with a dignity that older American writers often fail
to achieve. The love scenes—American love scenes, what
contemporary morality has inflicted upon youth—are hard, and
if cynical, or ruthless if you will, truthful. Nothing brutal or
sentimental is apt to be located in the book; much that suggests
tenderness, much that is youth trying to be hard enough to
attain detachment, it does contain. Judged for itself, apart from a
contemporary tendency to prefer "romance" or "life-interpreted"
or "god-seeking" or so-called "spirituality" and" beauty" in novels
and books, it might prove to have the modern quality which

any book of any of the big productive periods of any time has. That quality is more a kind of perception, a way, a directness of observation, a clear thinking, rather than it is a manner, or a way of putting words and phrases together. These manners are generally local only, or of a period. The underlying quality of emotion, of energy, of wit, of sense for and feeling about life, the "classics" had. The classicists don't so undoubtedly realize them, perhaps; and critics who talk of style may mean something stale, and would be upset by actual vitality of intelligence. But people resisted the telephone, the skyscraper, the automobile, the radio, and other inventions. All who talk about literature do not care for it, or even read it. This *What Happens* is worth reading, however. It is good, plain, simple, direct, and honest writing; young writing. It has a right to be young, since it is on the path of authentic research into the author's own style of writing. From a standpoint of popular or quick success that may be bad luck on the author, since "the artists who derive always get recognition before the artists they derive from," as derived artists are seldom very raw or very red meat. This book has the added disadvantage, as one publisher has said, of having characters who are "just like real ordinary people." That is a strange proportion, an unusual circumstance, in a novel. So the book cannot be a work of art. It is materialistic, and does not have the purpose of explaining life. But as many "works of art" that are purposeful, and interpretive, are fallacious, and dull, we sponsor this book for its plain easily read, direct and honest writing.

Contact Editions
29, Quai d'Anjou
Ile Saint-Louis
Paris

I

Winfield Payne was seventeen. His highschool course was almost finished, but not quite.

He wasn't in highschool then. He was in Cleveland, working in an icecream factory. They didn't tell him what they expected of him when they hired him. Nothing about the lifting of heavy blocks of ice back and forth, working all day long in a refrigerator. But he worked at it, he had to work at something. Five days at it and he looked like a ghost, felt like one too. Working in an icebox, carrying cakes of ice. No sweating to it, but plenty of hard work carrying heavy cakes of ice.

God this is the last one I can handle.

But he went on with it into early July. Just when work was at its hardest. In an icecream factory. Sweets for the little children. Fourth of July food. And he wasn't fitted for that kind of work. Should have been a salesman, could have been too, if he only half tried. But he was afraid to ask for a gentleman's job and didn't think he could hold it if he ever landed it. But he couldn't hold this kind either, no boy could hold it, and he had to do something. Back home a girl was walking the streets with a baby in her belly. Winfield's baby, she said. And what happens when girls have babies and boys are at fault? The boys go away sometimes and their parents wonder where they are. The boys are in Cleveland, or someplace two hundred miles away working in an icecream factory.

He couldn't stand it much longer. I got to get out
of this someway. Too scared to go back home and face
the music. People might do anything to a boy who got
a girl in trouble. Might make him marry.

Never catch me like that. God the disgrace. I
wonder if mother knows? I wonder if father knows?
Or, if the Jameses know? What would Mabel say?
No more decent girl's kisses. I should have married
her. But damn it I couldn't. Nothing but a lousy old
whore.

He worked on another day at the factory. Six days
shalt thou labor, etc. And then get paid, twentytwo
dollars and fifty cents a week, eight hours a day.

And the girl, Ruth Potter. Known to everybody
in Benton, but spoken to by few. Everybody knew
the older boys in highschool went with her and went
with her for nothing. Daughter of charity. Nothing
much in it. Go to a dance at the Moose Hall any
Saturday evening and then drive out in the country in
an automobile and she would open up. Nothing much
to it. Nothing much ever said about it later either.
You did the thing and it was done with. Winfield
knew all about this. What else do boys talk about
in highschool? Mrs. Brown's maid goes out with the
boys. Free stuff. Easy. Make her think you like her
and be quiet on the back steps. Don't even need a car
to get her. Toughy, the Potter girl, wasn't so easy, but
she wasn't hard by any means. One had to have a car
though. She liked the back seat of a big car. It worked
like champagne works on other girls. Turned her head
right away.

Before school started at noon Winfield and Paul Pew sat on the stone steps of the highschool building waiting for the bell calling them to classes. Let's get Toughy, Paul, what do you say?

—Nothing easier Winnie, if I can get the car tonight. Can you get away from home?

—Sure some way. I wish I knew what it was like. We'll do it. Had a chance once in Detroit. I'd do it now.

Ruth Potter was home then, just finished her lunch. Her mother was in bed, chronic invalid. The father worked in an auto factory and drank liquor. Nothing unusual about that, especially for Potter, the father. Mother Potter had always been more or less sickly doing the housework, bringing up a baby girl, and fighting with a drunken husband. She gave in.

—Oh hell, what's the use?

And she went to bed and stayed there. No more meals to cook. The little girl could sweep and make a breakfast. Much easier all around.

Toughy had to cook breakfast and pack up a dinner pail for her father and then she would sweep the house and get something together for lunch for herself and her sick mother. In the afternoon she would walk around the town, lingering in front of shop windows, wishing for that hat or that blouse or just anything nice. She wanted nice things. Like a little whore. And later she was going to learn how to get them. Not children or love, just nice things, and she was going to learn to get them. But first she must learn. And learning meant giving favors. Giving lots of favors just learning.

After Toughy was ten years old no more school.
Her mother needed her at home. A sick mother at
home was all she needed to stay away from school. She
made breakfast and swept and packed her father's lunch
pail from the time she was ten to fourteen years old,
and then she started doing something else.

It just happened that first time and she took it for
granted. One of the facts of her life like being made to
sweep the floors. Full firm hips at fourteen and boys in
highschool with newly awakened desires.

—Want a ride?

—Sure, wait for me.

Out in the country and no coming back the way
she went out. At home nothing said, just a little more
color in her cheeks, that was all.

The boy, her first lover, told others in highschool
and others picked the little girl up from the streets and
tried their luck, all with equal success. Then began the
dances, Moose Hall dances, where she met more men
and enlarged her circle and gave herself to more men.
Some boys took her out riding and only kissed her
and made love to her. She liked that too, but the other
thing was better, it left her feeling better, more herself.
She used to swear and curse and the boys thought
it quite a stunt to hear her. It was exciting to hear a
woman talking that way.

Paul Pew and Winfield drove to the dance in Paul's
father's car and danced with Toughy and took her for
a ride. She kissed them and showed her legs. Put them
way up on top of the windshield so anybody could
have seen them from the street.

—Ticklish business this. What if somebody should see us, somebody we know?

They drove quickly out of the city into the country, felt of her legs and kissed her on the lips with real kisses. And they wanted to do more but didn't know just how and she didn't seem to want to show them how.

—You've got nice legs, Toughy, I'd like to see you all undressed.

—Well it's too cold out here for that. Besides it's getting late and I've got to go home.

—Whew, it's twelve o'clock. We better be getting home Paul: Winfield came back.

The two boys took her to the corner nearest her home, said good night, kissed her again and then drove quietly home. Nothing to be said.

At last Paul ventured, Someday I'm going to get that little kid. She would make something nice.

—Did you ever have a girl Paul?

—No but I know how to do it, don't worry.

Winfield didn't say anything but he wanted her too. Would have to get his aunt's car some night and get Toughy to go out in the country. Couldn't do anything with another fellow along anyway.

He went to the dances a few times and danced with her. March came and he asked his aunt for her car for a drive to some friends in the country.

House party, birthday affair, he told her. Highschool girl daughter of a family friend and all that.

—Of course you can take the car Winfield, but do be careful. See that there is plenty of gasoline in the tank.

—All right, Aunt Mary, thanks. I'll be awfully careful.

Then the explanations at home and grudging assent, cautions to be home early and not be a bad boy. He felt like a bad boy already and nervous too, as if the thing had happened. Winfield was seventeen, senior in highschool.

Eight o'clock in the evening. Too early for the dances. Toughy wouldn't leave at this hour. She always liked to stay until eleven at least. Winfield drove to an icecream parlor, a drug store on a corner, a shop patronized by highschool boys and girls in the afternoons and by highschool boys in the evenings. He ordered a coca-cola and lit a cigarette from the burning stump of one in his hand. Uneasy and shy, afraid that some friend might come in and let it out that he wasn't really in the country at a party.

What the devil did I come here for?

He drank hurriedly, left the shop after carelessly dropping a nickel on the counter. Drove out Michigan avenue, turned around thinking and wondering why he was so nervous.

I should have taken Paul with me. He could have got another girl there. The Vorce girl. She's always in line for a ride. I hate like hell to go to that dance. Shall I go back home?

No, he would see it through. Toughy and the thought of her legs and lips, full and luscious, lips that cried for kisses, lips that had been kissed. He remembered kissing them. He recalled her tongue in his mouth. Not for long, but long enough to make him want her, to make him excited and passionate.

He let the car roll along three miles an hour, barely moving on the asphalt pavement. Click, click, click, went the generator. Electricity being used, not stored in the battery. And his electricity being used in thought.

Perhaps it's not so much. Perhaps I won't like it at all. It's rather messy, slimy. Losing his courage. He came now to a place where the lights were brighter and the street wider, lined with shop windows. Ninethirty.

I guess I'll go up there now.

He increased the speed of the car and drove to the dancehall, parked the auto, locked it, and trembling now more than before, walked into the dancehall. He had always been nervous, going into this place. So different from the respectable highschool dances. Always a fear of meeting some maidservant of a family friend, always afraid that his parents would discover that he went to these dances. Tonight more nervous though than ever before. He was going to get Toughy. This was his night. After tonight he would know what all this meant. All this sex, this love and passion, consummation of passion.

In the hall he saw some of the Catholic boys with whom he had fought in snowball fights. In grammar school at noontime coming home from school. Ten or twelve boys on a side. Protestants against the Micks, snowballs. These days left memories. He instinctively feared the northend toughs, these Catholic boys. But they feared him too, his family, his aristocracy, that something of pride unconscious snobbery which kept him even as a child a little above his most intimate playmates. It was hell that thing.

Here in the dancehall he wanted to go up to one
of these boys, shake hands and be friends, they were
better kids than he had thought. But something was
between them, the Catholic boys and Winfield, and
he was alone in the dancehall. He recognized some of
the town toughs, mechanics, factory workers. But they
were not his friends. He was alone and more nervous.

There was Toughy, dancing now and smiling at a
snake of a shoeclerk.

—May I have the next dance?

—Sure Winnie, I'll look for you when it starts.

Toughy knew that Winnie was worth playing up
to. Family, or perhaps just for Winfield and his clothes,
shoes, neckties, which were admittedly better, more
refined, respectable. He didn't belong in the dancehall.
Toughy was a woman, and saw in him a desirable man.
But she liked the other men better, she only knew that
he was better, and because she knew it she played up to
him. A little afraid all the time though.

—Toughy, I've got the car out here. A closed one.
You saw it once before didn't you? Let's go out for a ride.

—Oh, it's too early now. But I'll go out with you
later. You can take me home.

—All right.

He thanked her and then walked into the men's
smoking room, lit a cigarette, puffed a few times on it,
threw it away and went out to the dance floor again.
He saw a little girl. New to the towns, he thought.

—Can I have a dance?

She merely nodded assent. Not a word said during
the dance. He couldn't start a conversation. There was
nothing to say.

The next dance came. He stood watching, had waited too long to ask anyone to dance with him. Besides, he didn't want to dance with any of them. Not even Toughy.

Another dance.

—Can I have this dance?

The girl spoken to turned around. Deliberately looked at his feet, his legs, his waist, his chest, then his head, and then slowly down to his feet again. Said not a word. Turned slowly, deliberately away. Not saying a word. This tall office girl turned away from him without a word.

Winfield's face went red, his lips whitened.

Choking, he said, I'll send my dog around for you to dance with.

Then he walked away, mad, hot under the collar. Those damned girls. He knew he was better than they, but they scorned him like that. She wasn't the only one, others had done the same thing.

Thought it was awfully smart. He was such a nice boy, no guts, nothing. Winfield sat in the smoking room lighting one cigarette from the other for a halfhour before he dared return, he was so ashamed. This girl had hurt him unbelievably. He wanted revenge. To slap her or hit her or kick her. What was she? Why any girl in highschool would dance with me and be damned glad of a chance.

And they would have too. The middleclass highschool girls knew what men were desirable and knew that Winfield was one of them. A good husband, they thought. You will make a good husband. Girl's mothers even told him that pointblank, out of a clear

sky. You will make a good husband. And if I were
young I would love you, Winfield. But here in the
dancehall things were changed, different. Any mechanic
was better than Winfield, even for Toughy, though she
felt deep down somewhere that he was worth playing
up to. He danced with her a second time and talked to
her. Told her about this girl and how he hated her, how
Toughy was the only girl in the place and all that. He
felt it too.

They left after the dance together.

A quiet woods road three miles from town, lonely,
deserted. No danger here of passersby. The old road
was no longer a thoroughfare. Driving out to the place
Winfield slipped his arm around her waist, under the
arms and held her nervous like, talking with teeth
that shook, almost chattered. He had never been so
frightened. His voice was different. He scarcely dared
talk. His mouth was dry. Moving the tongue around
brought no saliva.

But Ruth Potter was not nervous, she was used
to this sort of thing. Natural. She was acting reserved,
playing up to Winfield, trying to be a lady. That was
it, trying to be a lady of his standing. But nevertheless
willing to give herself and almost anxious. She liked
the highschool boys. They were different than the other
men.

It was pain for Winfield to say it, and took seconds
that seemed like hours to get up the courage.

—Let's sit in the back seat?

Toughy was impatient, she was just about to take
things her own hands and run the affair in a more
systematic manner. She sensed his inexperience.

In the back seat, he said, Toughy, I've never been
with a woman in my life.

Well that's nothing. Lots of fellows never have
been with girls. What do you want from me?

He kissed her then but his mouth was awfully dry.

—Hurry up Winnie, I've got to get home
sometime. It was different now that he was alone with
her. But she was excited, waiting.

Oh, why couldn't she shut up. Why couldn't she
just be quiet a minute. Here I was getting all ready. It
takes a little time. Can't do something all at once, can't
do it at all I guess. I don't want her. I wish I were home.
What the devil did I come out here for?

Toughy was all excited, animal like now, but
Winfield was limp and nervous, impotent little boy
at the moment, and he wanted, oh so much, to want
her. If she had only let me kiss her a little. He wanted
to fight for what he got, wanted to be the aggressor.
The first time too. If Ruth Potter had been a virgin
highschool girl, unattainable virgin middleclass
highschool girl, Winfield would have kissed her and
been passionate. But to know this woman was waiting
and ready and wanted him, made him cold. How
awful it was to be cold like that. He held himself away
from her, kissed her, but kept his body away from her.
She mustn't know how he was. She mustn't know that
he couldn't take her. He ventured to touch her leg,
fleshy cool.

Clammy, he thought. Animal meat. Oh God, I
can't do it. I don't want to do it. I wish I were home.

Toughy, he said, with shaking voice. I can't do
anything. I want to really. I want to bad enough. I don't

know what it is Toughy. I think about you at home in
bed and get all excited. What is it Toughy?

—Well hurry up, do something. Most men are
ready when they first see me. Oh that is funny. Why
Winfield, whatever can be the matter?

—Oh, shut up Toughy. I can't do everything all at
once can I?

Nothing happened.

—Well, I've got to go home. I guess it's better
anyway.

Winfield didn't say a word, just got up and
arranged his clothes, climbed in the front seat, started
the car, still nervous and still shaking and ashamed.
God, I hope Toughy never tells anyone about this.

Ruth Potter had been angry but now she was
strangely glad. She took Winfield's arm and said, It's all
right Winnie, I know you're too scared. You're a good
kid Winnie, but you'll be glad.

She was soft, a little mother to him now, she
seemed to understand, no longer hurt. She kissed
him quickly on the neck. Winfield was again at ease,
cursing his luck. He felt warm after that kiss, he
thought of her legs that he had felt in the darkness,
the leg under her skirts that felt cool and soft, and the
breasts that he rubbed against, not daring to take in
his hands, and, the lips that he had kissed and found
cool and damp, almost repulsive they had been. Now
it was different.

—Gee, Toughy, let's stop again? Will you?

—Do you want to? We better not.

—Oh please, Toughy.

—All right, here's a good place.

They stopped, climbed into the rear of the car. Winfield was passionate, and Toughy was a good teacher.

Back in the front seat again. Toughy was still unsatisfied, just excited to a high point that was all, and Winfield finished with the thing, disgusted, like after masturbating, and frightened too. Now there was disease to think about. He felt strangely unnatural and uncomfortable. These Y. M. C. A. lectures with the lantern slides showing syphilitic women with big holes in their foreheads, and legs eaten away with disease. No woman was clean until she had been proved clean, the motto of the Y. M. C. A.

He hurried along home. Left Toughy at her corner, with a kiss that he hated to give, a kiss of duty.

I've had enough of women. Nothing much to the whole thing. At home he undressed, looked at himself carefully, washed in soap and water and worried. He was frightened. And the strange feeling too.

If I get anything from her I'll kill myself. No, I'll go to a doctor. They always say, go to a doctor right away. But what doctor? I can't go to our own doctor.

He went to bed tortured by worry and fear and thought and thought and thought until late in the night when he dropped off into a deep heavy sleep. Next morning he felt himself again, as if nothing had happened. The sunlight cut off his worries. He was a little elated in fact, proud too. He must tell Paul Pew all about that. Paul never was with a woman, and Winfield had learned mysteries.

Monday morning Winfield left home early. He wanted to see Paul before school started and tell him

the story. He waited impatient on the steps until Paul
came.

—Hello Paul. I had Toughy out the other night.

—Did you? What did you do?

—What do you think I did? She's good stuff Paul.
Knows how to throw a party. Lively too. I showed her
the time of her life. Can have her any time I want now.
She seems to like me pretty well.

—Well for God sakes don't be so cocky. What the
devil did you do? Tell me something about it. I don't
give a damn how much she likes you.

—Well I got her up at the dance and took her out
the Miller road. And put it to her, if you want to know.
You ought to see her wiggle around. She's damned
good stuff. Why don't you take her out?

—Oh, there are plenty of others. She's not so hot.
Any guy can get her. I got my eyes on something else
now anyway.

Winfield was a little frightened again. He wanted
Paul to have half the responsibility now that the
boasting time was past. He wished Paul also had taken
the chance he took. And here Paul was, talking about
somebody else now.

—Well, Toughy's as good as anything you'll find. I
can tell you that.

March, April, May. One more month of school,
or six weeks counting the examinations. Since the
night with Toughy Winfield had stayed strictly away
from dances of the shady sort and had returned to his
highschool girl friends with a new air of assurance.

Some of them thought he kissed differently, but that was only natural for a boy in his last year of highschool. Besides they all knew that he had played around with young college girls during the year and young college girls were apt to be, well, different from highschool girls anyhow. He avoided Toughy in particular, never wanted to see her again, spoke deprecatingly of her to his friends, and thought otherwise of her during the nights, at home in bed alone. When thoughts of her excited him too much he satisfied his desires as most boys do, then slept and forgot her.

Life had changed for him but not noticeably. At least it was scarcely noticeable to others. If his mother saw the change, she didn't move an eyelash, and his father, too much engrossed in work, couldn't possibly have noticed anything.

After school walking down Washington avenue toward a billiard parlor where the older highschool boys played illegally and in constant terror of being found by the truant officer, or asked to leave by the proprietor, he met Toughy. First time in over two months.

—Why, hello Toughy. Where you been? How are you?

And he looked furtively over his shoulder. If any highschool girls should see him talking to Ruth Potter. Whew. It wouldn't do to be seen.

—I got to hurry along to my father's store.

—Well say, you needn't be on your pins like that. I've got to have a talk with you. You did something awful to me, do you know that?

—Huh?

—Yes, I got a baby, you gave me. You've got to marry me too. I've been looking all around for you.

—Marry you. Got a baby? Marry you? What, a baby? Say, what are you talking about? That isn't my baby. What are you handing me? Go along, I'm in a hurry, I am.

Oh, but Winfield was terrified. Could hardly talk. A baby. Got to marry her. Hell, no, isn't my baby. And he was red and white in the face, lips trembled too, knees shaky. Got a baby, my baby. Go along.

—Don't you ever speak to me again Toughy. That isn't my baby. I didn't do anything.

—Well say now, see here, will you. That is your baby. I ought to know. I'm going to tell your father and the highschool principal too, and I'm going to show you. What the devil will I do? Tell me that. I got the kid inside me, you haven't. You aren't even decent. I can make you marry me. I know what I can do.

Ruth Baker walked past the two and Winfield turned away, couldn't look at this highschool girl.

Twice as ashamed and frightened.

Toughy kept on talking. Why Winfield you know as well as I do. I liked you, trusted you too. I let you do that didn't I? Well there, see what you did? We can go away. But say, you've got to do it. I tell you you've got to do it. There's no way out, I tell you, there isn't any other way. Come on, Winfield, I won't tell if you marry me.

—Get out of here, damn you. Get out. You're a liar.

—Winfield, come here or it will be bad. Come here.

Winfield was running along the street, to get away,
to get away. He was going home, he was in trouble.
Going home where things were safe. But he knew they
weren't safe, his mind knew things were not even safe at
home, not any more, not now. That was long ago when
things were safe at home. He had been young then, but
now it was different. After running a block he walked,
but with long rapid steps. Went into the house. It was
empty. Maidservant out, mother calling, father at work,
and the brothers, Lord knew where. Upstairs to his
mother's room first, where he stood a moment.

What did I come in here for?

He went to his own room, piled clothes together.
Back to his mother's room. Took his father's old suit
case, threw things into it, too much of some things,
too little of others. Money, good God. I almost forgot.
I got to have money. He pawed through the drawers of
his mother's bureau. Her pocket book, the big one she
never carried, was there smelling nice and leathery, like
a harness shop something. He took out ten dollars and
some change. Then wrote a short note. I'm going away.
Everything is all right. Don't worry. Love. Winfield.

Should have taken all that money, he said, but
didn't go back.

Out on the street waiting impatiently for a street
car. Then the ride to the station, and the three quarters
of an hour wait for the train. Furtive, brooding, half
witless, waiting for the railroad train. Waiting, minutes
creeping, mind wandering, waiting for the railroad
train. Oh, God, Oh God, Oh God, got a baby, got a
baby. No, no baby, baby, no baby, oh-h-h-h. And then
the long ride on the train, with snatches of sleep, half

crazy sleep, wild dreams, sweaty awakenings. Hazy, the whole thing, unreal. It can't be true.

And then Cleveland.

He stuck it out in Cleveland, the work in the icecream factory, not daring to leave. He had a cheap room and ate cheap food and led a cheap life talking to the laborers.

Men who came and went, men who worked at seasonal jobs, shoveled coal in winter, made icecream in summer. Here and there a daring spirit but mostly clods, these men. Men who ate and slept and drank. Winfield liked them though, they helped him forget Toughy and home and highschool and his friends. People whom he thought he would never see again.

He began planning a new life. He couldn't stick it out in the icecream factory, too much work, too tiring. He couldn't even read a book. No time for reading. Only work and sleep and talk with the men. He had to come down from his high falutin perch and be one of the men too, and this wasn't easy at first, because he simply didn't belong to them and they knew it.

They sensed the fact that he was not one of them, and when they talked to him it was always with condescension. Here was a boy who had been to highschool. Probably from a good family, and he had a poorer job than any of them. It did them good somehow, to see Winfield working at a job they wouldn't have touched.

Good for that kind of a kid, one of them said. Do him lots of good. These young fellows ought to have to get out like he is, get out and work. That is what they said about him at first. It was later that he became more

one with them. When he learned to chew tobacco and
spit in the corners. When he learned to curse with
rounder curses than the old ones, and when he too
became like the mechanics at home that he hated.

He went to a dance one night. Now he found it
easier to get dances with the shopgirls. The new life.
But he had had enough of it, couldn't stand the work,
that was all. He was just about to give up the job and
look for something else. He couldn't go home. He had
to stick it out some way.

A Sunday afternoon, a few days before the Fourth
of July, strolling along the lake front past beautiful homes
of Cleveland's wealthy he came suddenly upon Mr
Sturmer, assistant secretary of the Benton Y. M. C. A.

—Hello, Winfield, my boy. I heard you were in
Philadelphia.

—No, I'm here.

—Well, this is a surprise. I hope your sickness is
gone. I didn't know you had been sick till I saw your
father. Always told him you were a bit peaked. You
should have worked in the gym more. That's what you
needed. Nothing like exercise. I told your father he
should have sent you to us. We could have built you
up. But you look pretty well though. What are you
doing in Cleveland?

So they thought he was in Philadelphia, sick?
Father and mother must have told that story. Good
story. Nobody knew what was wrong. Hell, I thought
that damned Toughy would spill the whole thing. It's
lucky she didn't though. Good story for the folks to tell.

—I'm stopping here with some relatives for the
time being. Going back to Philly again though.

He would have to go somewhere now that this damned Sturmer had seen him in Cleveland. No good walking around the boulevards like this. Should have known better.

Sturmer, insatiable talker, went on. Do you go around to the Y? I'm stopping there. We're having a conference of the Business Men's Bible Clubs. I'm speaking tonight. You ought to come around, we're doing great things I tell you. The possibilities are unlimited, for good I mean. Now in Benton. Well in Benton for instance. Your father probably wrote you what we've done. Great things. Our bible class has over fifty members now, good solid men. I'm leader of it. These things should have been done long ago.

—Good work, Sturmer.

—Yes. Well, I mean. Now take for instance that street toilet. You know about that. Going to put it right on the main corners. We stopped that thing though. Imagine, with women always walking past. And they were going to have a place for the women too, right there on Michigan and Washington avenues. Call it indecent. The Y. M. C. A. put in a word I tell you.

—Really, that would have been handy though.

—Yes, that, but look at the morals of the thing. Walk along Winfield. You aren't going anywhere are you?

Winfield wanted to get away but he walked along. Sturmer was excited now that he had a listener, a quiet listener, who wasn't even thinking about Sturmer. Just trying to get away from him that was all.

—We cleaned out the Majestic too. Lots of highschool boys were going there playing pool and

billiards. Should have been at the Y. I know you never
went there, but some of those older fellows, they never
did come to the Y. Most of them Catholics I guess.
The morals were awful. We've done great things. What
you need is more exercise. Now I take mine every day
regular as a clock. That's what the young men need.
Instead of that. Say did you hear about Bob Armstrong?
He never came to the Y. Used to laugh. But he won't
laugh now I guess. Got that Potter girl in trouble. I tried
to get him to come around to the lectures but he never
came. You know Armstrong?

—Yes, I know him. Winfield was listening now.
Excited, waiting.

—Well it turned out that he was a regular
profligate. He was no good. Going with this girl out
in the woods. He had to marry her though. It's a good
thing she was a menace to our work in a way. He
deserved what he got. I always said that fellows like
that never amounted to anything. No parents. His
grandmother wasn't strict enough with him. He was
pretty sick though. Went to Detroit. Couldn't stick it
out. Good thing for him though. We're doing great
things there. I've got to hurry along now. Come down
to the lecture, seven o'clock. It'll be worth while. I'm
speaking tonight. Seven o'clock. It'll be in the gym.
Good speech. I wrote it before I came down.

All this on burning ears, deaf ears too. Married,
married. Toughy married Bob Armstrong. Married him.
I didn't do it. What? Oh, I didn't do it. Married him.
God, God, wonderful, God. I don't have to marry her.
I can go home. I can go home. I'm going home. I'm
going home. I'm going home again. The little devil, she

knew it wasn't me. I didn't do it. I might have known. It wasn't my fault. Not my fault. Going home. Going home tonight. Tonight I'm going back.

Good bye Sturmer, and Winfield hurried, almost ran to his cheap room in the cheap section of town. Threw his things together. Paid the rent.

Money, where is my money?

He opened the lower drawer of his bureau and took out a small, worn, leather wallet. Got fifteen dollars left. Going home. Then he hurried out of the house.

—Good bye, Mrs Mercer, good bye, I'm going home.

—Well bless me, what's got into the boy?

—I'm going home.

Then the wait for a street car, slow dragging minutes. Then the wait at the station for the train, one hour to wait. Dragging minutes. Then the long ride home, the excitement, the worry. What would he tell them? The snatches of sleep, dreams, nervous awakenings. What would he tell them?

And then Benton.

No one in Benton knew that Winfield Payne had run away from home, or even that Ruth Potter had accused him of getting her with child. The people all thought he had been taken suddenly ill and had been sent to a sanatorium near Philadelphia. Winfield's mother had invented such a good story that even the gossiping women in the church women's clubs had to believe it.

Now he was back home and he must tell the story when asked about his illness. He told girls that it was a rather delicate thing for them to ask, something to do with his stomach. He told the boys that it was kidney trouble, acute kidney trouble. This was the story his mother had told. As a young boy he had had such trouble, and his mother knew that if she mentioned a thing of that kind, a delicate illness, the people would ask fewer questions and say only, Oh, yes, I see. It's too bad for the boy. I hope they cure him in Philadelphia.

He felt ashamed seeing the women whom he knew had heard about his illness, but it was better than having them know the truth anyway. But why wouldn't his mother have thought of some better story, something like heart trouble would sound grander. She could even have called it lungs, that wouldn't be as bad as this. He thought the whole town must know. Really the people didn't care. Now that he was back they forgot it readily, and in a few days the matter was never even discussed.

It had been easy to fix things with the town. With his parents it had been difficult. His mother wanted to know whatever would make a boy with everything that her son had want to run away from home.

I think you have been very unfair, after all we have given you, she told him. And you have missed the last of your highschool. You didn't graduate. All the boys in your class will be in college, and here you are. Mr Page told me that you would just have to go to highschool another year. A whole year. When even the principal says that, then it means you've got to do it. Waste a year of your life that way. Don't you feel ashamed? There

must have been some good reason for your running off
like that. Tell me all about it. I'm your mother.

—Well mother I'll tell you. Promise you won't be
angry though. I loved you or I wouldn't have gone. You
won't punish me if I tell you? I hate to tell it all.

—Now Winfield just make a clean breast of it all.
I'm listening. Your mother knows. Just tell every thing.
I will find it out anyway.

—Well, it's that Potter girl.

It had been hard to say it. Now though, he felt
that he could tell it all. Once his mother knew he had
been mixed up with some woman he might as well
tell the whole story. He waited a minute. His mother
spoke.

—You surely don't mean that awful girl, that that
Armstrong boy had to marry. Why Winfield, have you
been a bad boy? You should have told your mother.
Tears formed in her eyes.

—Tell me it all

He told the story from beginning to end. His
mother wept.

—I didn't think a son of mine would do such a
thing. I have always watched you so carefully too. I
hope it's a lesson for you. I do hope it's a lesson. Oh
Winfield, you will break your mother's heart. I knew
it though. I felt it. You cannot deceive me Winfield. I
know. Don't tell your father. Don't tell your father. I'll
tell him something. He mustn't know. He would be
angry. He was very angry.

Winfield and his mother made up a story of a
milder order. They told Mr Payne that Winfield had
only made love to Ruth Potter and she had said that

was enough to get him in trouble, and so he had run away, afraid.

—If your father knew he would be very angry.

He might have thought his wife was somewhat at fault. It would look bad for her, a son running with a little tough girl like that. Winfield was his mother's son, she would protect him, even now, after all this. Mother and son conspired together and made up the lie. And from now on the mother had a weapon to use against her boy. She could warn him to do as she said or she might tell his father the real truth. And then his father might just send him away from home and never give him any more money. It was a good weapon and remained dangerous for many months.

II

A friend of Winfield, Donald Thorpe, who had
been in college for the past three years, was working
during the summer vacations for the L. M. Perry garden
seed company of Detroit, the biggest garden seed firm
in the world, the firm that did eighty percent of all the
commission garden seed business of America, the best
advertised seed company in the country, the seeds that
were known as pedigreed. Pedigreed like dogs, a long
line of ancestor seeds before them, the forbears of the
final perfect product.

Young Thorpe made good money during the
vacations at this job and he told Winfield that he
should try it too. They needed men. It was the first year
of the war and men were needed, so many had joined
the army. A young fellow like Winfield could get the
job if he tried.

After the experience with Toughy Potter and his
running away from home Winfield felt that it would
he more comfortable away than with his mother and
father, where he felt like an exconvict. It was not
pleasant for him around his home any more, and he
didn't want to go to northern Michigan with his mother
and brothers this summer. His mother would always
be telling him how wrong he had been to go with that
girl, and she would load him with odd chores, knowing
that he must give in to her will, she had him under her
thumb now. Could get him in a lot of trouble with his

father if she ever told the truth about that running away from home business.

Winfield decided he would try and get the job.

He went to Detroit, applied to the sales manager for a job. He had good recommendations from people in his home town, and he talked glibly. They hired him. He had to spend two weeks in a school for salesmen run by the company. There he learned the good points of his particular brand of garden seeds, and he learned how to take up the unsold seeds left in the commission seed boxes, to figure out how many packages had been sold and the amount due his firm by the merchant. Then he must collect this money and pack the unsold seeds in the boxes and direct the boxes to be sent back to Detroit, to L. M. Perry and Company. After this was done he must renew the order for the next spring, and go on to the next store, repeating the process. The checking up of the old seeds, the leftovers, was a difficult thing and two weeks were needed to learn how it was done.

L. M. Perry paid good wages to their men and gave them all of their expenses. That first year he made eighty dollars a month in salary with all of his expenses paid.

He was seventeen, but had told them he was twenty, they wouldn't have hired a seventeen year old boy for a job like that and he knew it.

When he had learned the technicalities of the work and was ready to start out, the salesmanager called him into his office. He wanted a talk with young Payne, wanted to instill in him the ideals of service of the company.

—Well Payne, I guess you have learned the stuff
from start to finish now. You'll be able to make a good
record for yourself this summer. It's a short job. Two
months. But next summer you can go out again if
you like it. You will. Our men all like it. Why we have
men, been in the game twenty, thirty, and more years,
and they go out every summer for us. It's one of the
best jobs. Now what we want, get an idea of the seeds
being used mostly in your territory. In that way we
can fill the boxes with the right kinds. Also see that
all the boxes get back to us. We lose a lot every year.
We do eighty percent of the commission garden seed
business. Let the merchant know that, it's important.
Try to get them to buy our seeds exclusively, that's
what we want. We got the best. Believe that and the
thing is half settled. The best in the world. That must
be drummed into them. The difference in radish
seeds for example is important. Our radish seeds are
better than any others. We test out seeds, that does
it. It's the same with all our seeds. But you learned
all that in the school these last two weeks. Now every
week send the reports and money in promptly. The
prompter the better. Our best men are that way.
Prompt. The money though. You can send it in every
day or so, drafts. You learned that too in the school.
I guess I can't tell you anything that wasn't taught in
the school. It's a great thing, the school. Remember
there are no hours in the game, work from morning
to night. Cover all the ground you can. We recognize
merit in our men. It's repaid. No hours. Work is the
thing that makes a man. You'll do well Payne. Good
luck to you.

—Thanks Mr Garlock, I am the man that can do it. I learned all that in the school. Yes. I am sure you will find me O. K. Where did you say you were going to send me?

—West Virginia. We can't send you anyplace else. All old men, you know. It's a good place though. Lots of the men like it. You'll like it. West Virginia is not so bad.

He knew it was the worst possible territory and the hardest. So did Winfield.

—Yes? West Virginia? I kinda wanted, well, I thought of something else. But well, West Virginia. Which part?

—Well, it's the southern trip. Now you see, you're going to have a little in Ohio and then a few towns in Indiana and then West Virginia. It isn't like making the whole trip there you see. You'll be down in Mingo and Logan counties. Around there. Lots of the men have liked that trip though. It's not half so bad.

Winfield listened to a talk by the vicepresident of the firm, on service, ideals, working for the right and the firm of L. M. Perry, and then he left to begin his work.

He worked at the job in Indiana for three days, in Ohio for four days and then went to the wildest part of West Virginia. Southern West Virginia filled Winfield with a feeling of loneliness, of danger and depression.

Such a waste. A barren dirty waste. But what activity. Mines, and all.

The first town on his route list was Milton, W. Va., a town near Huntington, between Charleston and Huntington. There were six stores in the little town for him to call on, six stores that handled garden seeds, and all stores do handle them in country villages. He had to work the country trade, call on the crossroad stores too, and this he must do with automobile or horse and carriage. Around Milton he could work with an automobile, and he hired a man to drive him from one place to another. Some of the roads were practically impassible. When he had finished working the territory around Milton he went to Logan, in Logan county. This country was impassible for automobiles. There was nothing for it but to work the territory travelling horseback.

He had never ridden a horse. After three days a vacation was necessary, his bottom was too sore and bruised for more of that kind of punishment. He decided to rest a few days. He fell sick with diarrhoea, grew weak. He thought the climate was at fault. Thought he might die. He couldn't eat and then this awful illness. Three days he stayed in bed, sick. The doctor was called for. On the fourth day his system was in order again, he was weak. But he went back to work. Horseback riding didn't trouble him now. He was hardened underneath. With saddle bags attached to his horse he went through the country, called on the country stores, settled their seed accounts, renewed orders for the next year's seeds.

At night he would sleep in country boarding-houses or smalltown hotels. He found bed bugs several times. Then all he could do was sit sleeping in a chair during the night. No where else to go. He wished the trip would come to an end. He wanted to finish as soon as possible. He worked long hours, as late as the

stores were open, in order that he might finish and get
out of that awful, terrible country. At the end of the
week he would go back to Logan and stay at the best
hotel there. He had a bath with his room, and he ate
good food. He had an unlimited expense account, and
could live well if the accommodations were only good.

He wrote letters home to his friends, to Paul Pew,
and to several girls. He wanted to get mail from people,
it was very lonely there. On weekends he went back
to Logan to this hotel, this city hotel where he got
everything that he could have gotten in a big city.

One Saturday night the clerk told him they were
having a dance there. He could come down. Had an
orchestra from Cincinnati and the best girls in the
town would be there. He might find a good girl. The
clerk knew that a young fellow like Winfield working
away from home would be lonely, and would like a
chance to dance with some nice girls.

—Say, that's great. I'd like to dance. It's been a
long time. What time does it start?

—Nine o'clock. I'll introduce you to some of
them. Don't need that though, just ask them for a
dance. They'll dance with you. Girls like to dance with
a good young stranger. Funny, they do though.

That night he waited expectant in his room, waited
for the music to start. After the first dance stopped he
went downstairs, rode down on the elevator, thought it
would be better to come down that way, casual like.

The first girl he asked to dance was Dorothy
Jefferson, daughter of Henry Jefferson, operator of
the Jefferson Amalgamated Coal Companies of West
Virginia, a big stockholder in the company. He liked her,

she looked like Margaret Perrin back home. Damned
goodlooking, got lots of form, that girl.

She hadn't bobbed her hair yet, but would have
it bobbed when the fad came to Logan. That kind
of a girl. Nice girl, goodlooking. A little too fat. Not
fat though, just nice. Not skinny, that's it. She's the
best thing here anyway, thought Winfield. Some
goodlookers though, but she's got more gogetem to her,
upandatem. I like a girl that way. Lots of spunk. Jesus,
I'd like a little loving party with her.

He danced with her and recited Kipling's Vampire
as he danced. She thought it fine, a young fellow
reciting poetry that way and asked him to recite some
more afterwards. He told her he could recite poetry all
night to a girl like her.

—You're a wonder, really you are. I know girls,
don't worry about me. I've been through the mill. I'm
working now though. Salesman for L. M. Perry and
Company.

—Oh, we always plant their seeds. Father wouldn't
plant any other kind.

—Well, they are the best. You see, they're tested.
Lots of other companies just send out the same seeds
year after year, don't test them. We do. You see they
grow, that way. That's the whole difference. We do
eighty percent of the commission seed business, if you
understand that. Big company, L. M. Perry, Detroit.

He was selling her his wares, just as he sold them
to the country storekeepers.

She liked him, listened to him with interest. Wise
little woman. She knew how to get a man. Be nice to
have a fellow like that.

You a college man? she asked.

—Oh, yes, certainly. Go to Michigan. We got
a good football team this year. Oh, yes, of course.
Michigan. Good university.

She liked him. It was nice having a college man
to dance with. Especially a Michigan man. It was a big
school, and she knew it. The other college boys she
knew went to the state university. That wasn't so much.
Michigan sounded lots better.

Let me take you home? he asked.

—All right. After.

Away, working as he was, Winfield had more
confidence in himself than he had at home. It had
always been hard to start a loving party at home. To kiss
a girl at home sometimes took days of effort. He had
first to convince her of his love, then slowly, carefully
work up to a point of kissing her.

Here in West Virginia, far from home, he had
confidence in his ability to get necking from a girl. And
Dorothy Jefferson looked as if she wouldn't put up a
fight. He had heard about southern girls. Passionate.
Make love to everybody. Like to be loved. Make good
necking. He thought he would try it out.

She kissed him hard on the lips when they reached
her home. She must wait until a girl friend came, the
girl was staying over night with her, her mother and
father were at White Sulphur Springs. Living alone in
the house she liked to have a girl stay with her. They
waited on the steps leading to the white Georgian
entrance to the house. Bushes in a hedge along the side
walk hid them from the street. It was dark and warm

sitting there. They made love. Winfield thought that he
really must love her, she made him very passionate.

Dorothy told him she loved him, Oh, I'm so glad
you are here. I like men tall, light hair. I like your eyes
too. Nice brown eyes. They sparkle so. I can almost see
them. I've been waiting for somebody like you.

This was sweet music to Winfield. He fell hard.
Forgot the work on the road, the horseback riding,
and the dirty country stores. The coal company stores,
and their rush and dirt. And he felt so far away from
home and ties. He forgot Benton entirely and forgot
other girls, all other girls, except occasionally when
the thought of Toughy Potter went through his head.
If he could get a girl like Dorothy Jefferson, it would
be all right if she asked him to marry her. He'd do it if
he had to. Her father would probably give him a good
job in the company. She was as unattainable as his own
highschool girl friends, but here away from home he
felt more confidence, and then not knowing her family,
not knowing her very well either, that made him see
possibilities if he went at it right.

Every girl will do it if she loves a man, he repeated
to himself. All you got to do is get them excited, tell
them you love them, and act as if you would suffer if
they didn't come across. Then, if you've done it right
and she likes you, there's no chance to fail.

Winfield knew the formula. Besides Winfield
had had experience with Toughy Potter and it was far
enough back of him now to seem quite to his credit.
He thought now that he had handled things in good
shape. Because he wasn't excited, there at first, was no
sign he was no good. Lots of men, older men, were that

same way. He got it later anyway. That was the main thing.

He had confidence and set about winning Dorothy Jefferson to him. He told her how he loved her.

—Never met a girl like you before. There is just something about you that no other girl has got, and that's what I like. You're you, that's it. Say, you're wonderful, Dorothy. I had a sister named that. She was a sweet girl. Dead now. I loved her. Same name as yours. Isn't that funny? I loved her. You remind me, Dorothy. Just to say the word makes me love you. I feel different all over. New life in my blood. It's great.

Winfield had never had a sister.

This was sweet music to Dorothy. He was a nice fellow. From Detroit, went to Michigan, to the university, Detroit. Big city. Big city man. You can see it on him. He's from a big town. Can tell. There's a way about fellows like that. It beats anything the other girls here have got. They'll be jealous. College boy. Detroit.

She kissed him and drew him close to her.

He's nice too. Big tall fellow. Strong too. How tight he holds me. I'd like to just let him pull and pull at me, till he hurt me. He is nice. Not to marry. Nice to go around with. He doesn't live here. I'd like to. Safe. He'll be away from town soon. Nobody know. It must be wonderful.

She kissed him again, rubbed her leg easily, surely against Winfield's. He was very excited.

The girl friend, Justine Bradley, walked up the narrow cement pathway leading from the sidewalk.

Charles Gaston, a University of West Virginia student,
who had been fired from the university because of low
grades, was with her. Gaston was a happy go lucky sort,
with a ready line of talk, the life of the party always.
From a good middleclass family. Drank whenever
booze was to be had. West Virginia was dry at this
time, but Ohio was wet, and Gaston got his stuff from
across the border. He had been half drunk at the dance.
He started a lively line of talk.

—Want to try this bottle, Perry's seeds?

Winfield objected to the flippancy, he was trying
to make an impression on Dorothy. But he took a long
pull at the bottle.

—Four Roses. Best whiskey, I know, Winfield
said.

He had seen the label, thought it would look well
to mention it. Make him in the know. The girls each
took little sips from the bottle after Winfield.

—Say, you shake a mean hoof. What's your last
name?

—My name's Payne, Winfield Payne, live in
Detroit.

—Payne, we ought to get up a little quartet
between the two of us for the benefit of the ladies. Get
a little harmony. Say girls, did you ever hear that story?

He told a dirty story. Winfield was surprised,
but pleased. He told one. The girls giggled, they had
probably heard the stories before but it was better
not to say that. Finally after a long preliminary one
of the girls told a story herself. It was a mild one, but
sufficient to make Winfield feel that his chances were
pretty good with Dorothy.

Loose girls? I like them that way though. More
genuine, you feel like you were with men. Best kind of
girls.

He was not at all disgusted at their looseness. He
enjoyed it. Would like to tell the boys back home about
the southern girls. Real girls all right.

Gaston asked the girls why they couldn't all go
in the house. Your folks are away. What's samalio? he
asked. Let Uncle Wiggley and the Blue Goose in.

Then in a deep voice he told a bedtime story of his
own invention.

—Uncle Wiggley and the blue goose went down
to the river to wash their feet. The blue goose fell in.
Oh, oh, oh, exclaimed Uncle Wiggley.

The girls laughed. They had heard his line, and
knew when to laugh. Winfield waited for the end of
the story, the point.

Then Gaston chuckled and said, I'm the dirty dirt,
I am.

Winfield saw the point now, there was none. He
laughed too.

That Gaston is a hell of a fine fellow. Knows how
to talk to the girls too. Got a devil of a line.

Come on let's go inside and rob the governor's
cellar, he said.

Dorothy Jefferson looked at her wrist watch.

—No, it's too late. It's three o'clock. People might
see light, hear noise. Better tomorrow. Come tomorrow
afternoon, both of you. Tomorrow night too. Do you
want to? Tonight's too late, really. Tomorrow.

Yea, I guess it's better, Winfield said. Tomorrow
would be better. Didn't know it was so late.

Gaston walked back to the hotel with Winfield. Say Payne, that Jefferson girl likes you. She's the best in town. All the fellows after her. I go with Justine regular myself. You did something when you got her. First time I ever heard of a drummer getting her. You're lucky. She's good necking isn't she? That's all though. Can't get any more. Wouldn't try anyway. Decent girl. Good family.

—I like her too.

He noticed Gaston was quieter, not so bubbling with witticisms, when he was alone with a fellow. His line's all for the women. Around women he's all pepped up. Guess I'm something like that myself. Only he's better than I am. Older, maybe that's it. College.

Gaston asked him some questions about Michigan. He could answer all of them. When asked his fraternity Winfield mentioned the name of his uncle's. Gaston belonged to another so he was safe.

Much better, let them think I'm in college. Highschool kid wouldn't have a chance. Anyway I ought to be in college. I would be too, but for those damned rules. They ought to let me through, only missing two months. Got to go a whole year to make up two months. Highschool is hell.

The next morning Winfield worked, making out his weekly reports. Adding up the sums of money collected, the new orders taken, and making out a report of the whole week's work. It was a hard job and a nervous one. If the amount of money he should have collected did not agree with the amount really collected he was responsible. If he lost money, it came out of his own pocket. This week he found that he should have

collected three thousand dollars. When he added up
his expenses and the money he had actually at hand, he
found himself short eightyfive dollars. A month's salary.
He was worried and wrote to the firm telling them.
Hoping there might be some mistake. It was awful to
lose that money. A whole month's work.

Gaston called for him at the hotel in the
afternoon. Let's get some liquor, Payne?

—All right, sounds good to me. Where we going
to get it? Winfield wanted to drink. Thought it would
help him forget his money loss.

—Why, that's easy. Punch the button, there. Get a
bellhop.

—Get it here in the hotel? I didn't know that.
Would have had some before.

The boy brought them a quart bottle of good
Kentucky whiskey, smuggled into the state from Ohio.
They took a few small drinks, felt warm inside. Then
they went to the girl's home. Winfield paid for the
whiskey, so he left the bottle in his room.

I can use her later, he told Gaston.

The Jeffersons lived in a beautiful house, large
and roomy, plenty of space to dance in three rooms
downstairs. Phonograph, piano, long bookshelves filled
with sets of books, eight to twelve volumes to a set.

Look pretty intellectual, all those books, Winfield
thought. Guess they're just for looks.

They were just for looks. The Jeffersons were
business people, making big money. Their house was
the house of a wealthy business family. Phonograph,
piano, fireplace, davenport, big leather chairs, reading
lamps, table lamps. Type A, the American home.

Winfield could have found his way about this house as easily as about his own, he felt easier now. Seemed like being back home. The girls he called on at home, like their houses, his own house too, just about.

They danced to jazz music on the phonograph. Justine Bradley played the piano. While she played Gaston started his tricks. Danced for them, shimmied. Some of the same stuff Winfield pulled in Benton. The two boys had a great deal in common. Winfield went out to the center of the floor, showed them how to shimmy all the way down.

Try it with me? Dorothy asked. Oh, Winnie, that feels funny. You make me feel funny. I feel funny here in the house with the folks away.

Dorothy felt a strange sensual feeling there in the big house, with her parents far away.

Gaston and his girl went into another room and made love on a davenport there. Winfield and Dorothy sat in the living room, where the phonograph was, and also made love. Dorothy was very passionate, and wanted to give herself. If it had been evening she would have done it.

They ate dinner there. The girls prepared a meal. The two boys walked out and bought icecream. When they came back they went into the cellar, picked out some fine old wines which Jefferson had imported from the Rhineland and from the Bordeaux regions of France. Also a bottle of sweet Spanish malaga wine.

Gaston remarked that that was the best stuff for the women. Makes them hot as the devil, malaga wine. They like it. Get loving from them with that stuff.

With their dinner they all drank wines, talked, smoked cigarettes. Winfield had some very good ones, but Dorothy brought some of her father's initialled, made to order, cigarettes, which were better. It was fun for all of them, and the wine made them very sociable. A few kisses were exchanged between Winfield and Justine. Gaston, following the example, kissed Dorothy.

After dinner lying on the davenport in the living room Gaston and Justine in another room, not within hearing of them, Dorothy scolded Winfield for kissing Justine.

—Was that nice of you Winfield? I have loved you. You shouldn't do that. She'll just think less of me. That isn't fair.

Winfield was glad that she was jealous of him. He said he was sorry.

—Wouldn't have done it. Thought, though, being a party like this, ought to kinda make a party out of it you know. No harm in that. I love you, not her. You know that. I'm sorry though. Wouldn't have done it. Didn't think, really.

They kissed, loved. Both were hot, perspiring with heat. Just loving one another for two hours, three hours. Both excited, wanting each other.

Neither Winfield nor Dorothy really knew what being together would mean. His experience with Ruth Potter had not increased his desire for women. Rather it had stolen something of his boyhood longing and made him look upon sex as more or less distasteful. With Dorothy his interest revived. He wanted to know what it would be like with a really nice girl, a girl that a fellow would be willing to marry if necessary. He wanted to take her. But something in him kept him from making too great advances. He and Dorothy had done everything to excite them to the highest point. He had felt of her legs, above the knees. He had pressed her tightly to himself and she had responded to him. The excitement of the two people finally reached such a pitch that neither could control themselves. They were together.

It was over very quickly. Tears. Dorothy was crying, hysterical.

Jesus, I've done it, Winfield thought. She was a virgin. I heard they always cried like that. I don't want her to cry.

He tried to comfort her. He kissed her, talked to her. Please don't cry. I love you Dorothy. Can't you see that? I love you. You're all right Dorothy. Don't worry.

She did worry though. The thought of a child, and the thought that perhaps her parents might know what she had done. And they away from home as they were.

—Oh, Winfield, I didn't think it would happen. What will I ever do? Suppose, oh, a child, Winfield. I loved you, Winfield.

He sent her upstairs. Told her to wash herself well. It eased her mind. When she came back she kissed him immediately.

—I guess it will be all right. I'm so worried. Winfield, love me. You've got to.

Just going upstairs like that for a few minutes had eased her mind. She was different now. Not so frightened, and yet she was too. Her will wouldn't let her show her fright. She thought, I'm glad I did. It's not so much.

On the way back to the hotel Gaston told
Winfield not to go too far with Dorothy. She might do
anything. Got to be careful with a girl like that.

—I hope you don't.

Winfield told him he never would. Not to worry.
He was a gentleman, knew how to treat girls too.

—Never worry about me.

Next night they were alone together in the
house. Winfield and Dorothy. They were again on
the davenport, in the living room. The same thing
happened. They fell asleep there together and slept
until the dawn came boldly through the windows that
faced the street.

—Oh, Winfield, you must go. What will the
neighbors say if they see you? You must go carefully. At
once Winfield, or it will be too late. I'm so afraid.

His mouth was dry, from smoking and drinking.
Half awake, he kissed her good bye. She clung to him
tightly.

—Winfield, if anything happens to me? Oh, what
then? I'm worried, we weren't careful enough. I'm
worried.

—It'll be all right. Never worry about me, Dorothy.
I love you. You needn't worry at all. It will be all right.

He kissed her again. Left the house then, cautiously
looking to right and left. It was too early for him to be
seen.

In three days he left Logan, West Virginia, and
went to another town on his route. He would write to
Dorothy, he wanted to know if everything would be
all right with her. He wanted to be sure she would not
have a child.

She wrote him a week later. Dearest Winfield.
Tuesday was a bright and sunny day and I was very
happy.

It relieved Winfield of a great worry. She was all
right now. He began to forget Dorothy. She was further
and further away from him. Only a hazy memory
remained, and he cursed himself for not taking her
upstairs to her bed that last night. It was foolish to
waste such a fine chance on a davenport. It would be a
long time before he ceased to regret this thing.

He was forgetting Dorothy, but there remained in
his mind an ideal girl, that he could have for his own,
for keeps. A girl that had come to him for the first
time. He felt grown up after it. When you can get a girl
like that, you're all right, he thought.

The highschool girls in Benton would be pretty
tame to him now. None of them were such girls as
Dorothy.

Think of it, everything so beautiful about it all.
She was wonderful.

But it wasn't Dorothy he thought about. It was
an ideal girl, that he had known for a few short days
in Logan, West Virginia. The only thing that made his
work in West Virginia pleasant, the one reason he was
glad of it all.

And Dorothy would also forget Winfield. She
would remember a lighthaired boy, tall and beautiful to
her, who came out of nowhere and disappeared.

The passion of her first letters died and they
stopped writing to one another in a few weeks. She was
glad it happened, now that there was no danger of a
child. And she had had her first lover.

III

Winfield went back to highschool. He felt ashamed, sitting there among people who had been in a lower class than his the year before. Now they were his classmates.

He needed only five credits, and could take his time getting them. Take the whole year to it, studying to get five credits to be graduated from highschool. The fellows in highschool seemed so young and the girls so silly. He was far above them. The teachers seemed to be younger even than he was. He couldn't respect teachers who had never even worked or been far from home, as he had. He felt that he knew more than any of them, and perhaps he did.

He read verse, Kipling and Laurence Hope. After his love affair during the summer the lyrics of Laurence Hope seemed as if written by him to express his own feelings. He felt very superior during this year and it wasn't long before he was looked upon as a snob not only by his classmates but also by the teachers.

He began to think there was no use going to college. He could get in some good business and make money and then everybody would have to look up to him. If he worked at it he could be a wealthy man before he was thirtyfive. Business was the thing. School was not much use. You didn't learn anything in school anyhow, and had to get your experience later when you finally went in business.

L. M. Perry and Company sent him a check for eightyfive dollars. He had forgotten to take it from a store where he had made a settlement, and the honest country merchant, after waiting to see if he would hear from the agent, had sent it to the company. They sent it to Winfield. He kept quiet about this. It meant extra money above his allowance, he could spend it as he chose. Now as he thought back on the summer's work it didn't seem unpleasant. He thought he would like to do it again, next summer. He had so many anecdotes to tell his friends, so many stories of life in West Virginia, of the coal fields, and for his more intimate boy friends he had a story of a love affair, more romantic than any story a highschool boy could tell. He enjoyed telling the story and added touches here and there that made it even more romantic than it was. The story of his love episode with Dorothy Jefferson took on great proportions and he managed to turn it into a story of how his heart was broken.

Paul Pew had been graduated from highschool the summer before and was now in Washington working on a newspaper. He told Winfield he should get the job of highschool correspondent for the Benton paper. Paul had worked at it the year before. Winfield got the job and wrote the sports news of the highschool teams for the paper, also general highschool news. It made the teachers show more respect for him, knowing that he was the person who wrote about their activities. They never could quite agree that it was safe to let a young man in highschool write the news, but since it was as it was they had to show a little more respect for the young man. He was somewhat of a power after all. He gave a great deal more attention to the paper than he did to his school work.

The police reporter on the Benton paper was a little nervous man, Ronald Weeds, about forty years old, who had worked on ten or twelve papers during his lifetime and who was a great admirer of Schopenhauer's philosophy. Winfield detested going to church, he was an embryo atheist, not yet daring to give up the thought of a God, a good God, all powerful. Weeds liked to talk with him because he would agree on every thing except that there was no God, no good God. Weeds gave him a cheap edition of the complete essays of Schopenhauer. During the study periods in highschool he would read this book and make notes.

That's just the way I always thought, and he would write down some epigram from Schopenhauer. It was his first real intellectual thrill and he could not restrain himself. He must tell people what he thought. He talked Schopenhauer to everybody who would listen, that was mainly to the girls in the school. They would listen but not heed his talks.

—Well you may he right, but that's awful to think about. I think it's bad for you to talk that way. It may be so, but wouldn't it be awful?

He felt contempt for them, went back to Weeds and talked with him. Weeds felt proud to have brought his young pupil to the truth. He felt proud of himself as an Evangelist feels proud when he gets someone to hit the sawdust trail.

This new learning of Winfield made him feel far superior to his teachers in highschool now. They were

all dumb lumps of dirt now, they didn't know the
truth. All of them, or nearly all of them, came to dislike
him and wished that he had been allowed to graduate
the year before. He disturbed them in their teaching
and was a bad example for the other students, his work
was so very careless and yet not careless enough to
warrant them flunking him out of school. He would
get through, but just by the skin of his teeth. They
would be relieved when he finished too.

He took very little interest in his highschool
fraternity. The boys couldn't talk about Schopenhauer
with him and so they didn't interest him. He found a
friend in another fraternity, one which Winfield had
always felt was far inferior to his own. But this young
fellow, Harold Eldridge, was a good fellow.

Eldridge should have been in my fraternity,
thought Winfield. Eldridge felt much the same way
about Winfield.

Harold Eldridge, because he had read too many
novels, had failed his last year and was compelled as
Winfield had been, to stay in school another whole
year. Both boys felt a grudge against the school, and
that with their atheism brought them closely together.

—Say, Harold, I never told you why I was away. I
wasn't sick. I got in trouble with a girl, Ruth Potter.

—Did you? Hell, I thought you were sick. What
trouble? What do you mean?

Winfield told him the story of Toughy Potter and
told it all, truthfully, from start to finish. He didn't
embellish his life story when he talked to Eldridge,
there was no need, they were friends. He told him the
truth about the West Virginia affair too.

Eldridge confided in him too. In November he
came to Winfield.

—Say I got the clap, I guess. It's running. I hate to
go to a doctor. I can't tell my folks. What will I do?

—Jesus. You don't mean you got the clap? God,
what do you do for it? Say, that's too bad. How did you
get it, Harold? That's too bad.

—Off that damned Vorce kid, she gave it to
me. She's out of town now though, nothing to do.
I'm scared. I got to do something. Do you think my
brother ought to know?

—Say, now that's it, your brother. He's old enough
to know. I heard once it's no worse than a bad cold.
You can get rid of it. Your brother probably knows all
about it. Most fellows, old like that, know. I'd go to
him, really.

Harold Eldridge asked his older brother, a married
man living in a nearby town, what to do for it. The
brother gave him the name of a patent medicine to take.
It was the thing, he had heard of a fellow got cured in
one month using it. Best cure.

The disease went on into December growing
worse. Eldridge caught cold, weakened the way he
was, and became very sick with tubercular gonorrhea.
He told his father the whole story. The best physicians
in the city were called for and tried to cure him. Mr
Eldridge spent several thousand dollars trying to cure
his son.

You ought to go to a doctor the first thing, he said.

—I was afraid.

He had electrical treatments, homeopathic
treatments, various injections, a doctor from New

York City was brought to Benton. They couldn't cure
the boy. He grew taller lying in bed, slowly dying
with tuberculosis. The gonorrhea was stopped, but
consumption had set in. They even tried to cure him
using Christian Science. In his weakened state, he
gave in and tried it, though he had laughed before.
But through all his illness ran the hope, never
slackening, that he would live. Every day he saw signs
that indicated to him regaining health. But he was
declining in health. Wasting away.

Winfield went every day to see him. Mr and Mrs
Eldridge came to love Winfield, because he was so fond
of their son. Mr Eldridge was a good hearted man of
Irish descent, he looked like a real Irishman.

—Well Winfield, how's your newspaper work?
Harold is getting along. We think he'll be cured. Never
do it, Winfield. Go to a doctor. Remember. I'll spend
every cent I've got on the boy. I'm going to make him
get well. He's a fine boy, Harold.

Mrs Eldridge was not so courageous as her husband.
She feared the inevitable. Her woman's intuition told her
that the boy could not get well. But she tried to keep up
courage, tried to make herself believe that he would get
well.

—Winfield, Harold is very fond of you. It's so nice
of you to come and see him like this. You have been
nicer to him than his fraternity brothers. Some of them
are nice though. That Carter boy comes too. You saw
him here yesterday. It's nice of you boys. Harold must
get well. Oh, I hope you boys will see. I am so thankful
to you, Winfield. We love our boy. If he should be
taken away. It's awful. We try every thing.

Harold had liked a certain pipe tobacco. Winfield smoked a pipe and this tobacco in his bedroom, so he could smell it. Harold dared not smoke himself, but he could smell of the tobacco. He thanked Winfield.

—I know you don't like to smoke that Prince Albert stuff Winnie, but it's damned white of you to do it. I'll be glad when I can smoke a pipeful of it. I think I'm getting better. That Christian Science didn't work. You could see I was getting worse. That doctor from New York, he's given me some good stuff. I feel better now. Weak though. He said I would be weak, maybe weaker. Then you begin to pick up. I'll get well. But damn that Vorce kid, damn her. I hope she's out of the working now. Be too bad, she give it to other fellows. If I'd gone to a doctor, that's the thing. Too damned scared, though Winnie. You know.

After Harold was in bed a week Winfield began losing faith in his recovery. But he always had hope. He would hate to see Harold die that way.

Think of it, dying of that, that's hell. He was the only fellow worth a damn in the whole school. That's just the kind of fellow that gets it, every time.

They ceased talking about Schopenhauer. Winfield couldn't.

Be better to believe in a God if you're going to die. He couldn't discuss his old theories any more.

Before his illness Harold had been going with a highschool girl, Clara Saunders. He took her to all of his fraternity dances and she took him to her club's dance. He told Winfield that he kissed her, but that was all he did, just kissed her and made love to her. Someday he would marry that girl. Then he had gone

once with the Vorce girl and his illness came on him. It
was known in the city that the illness was tuberculosis,
not the complicated disease that it really was.

Clara never knew, never would know. She loved
him, and now that he was sick, loved him more than
ever. He was so weak lying there. Her heart softened
and she loved him more and more. She could love him
now as she had once loved her dolls, he was so weak
and powerless there in bed. She came and sat by him
for hours, often when Winfield was there, and she held
his hand.

Mr Eldridge wanted Winfield to take Clara to
dances, now that Harold couldn't do that. Winfield
didn't like her very well. That is, he didn't feel love for
her, so he didn't like to take her to dances either.

But Harold asked him to. Show the girl a good
time. Winnie. I wish I could.

He took her to the Friday night dances at a
dancing school. When Christmas came, Harold asked
him to take her to his own fraternity party. He wanted
Clara to go, she had been there the year before. He
wanted her to go this year, and he couldn't take her,
sick in bed that way.

Winfield was more touched by this than anything
that Harold had said to him, or asked of him before.
To go to that other fraternity party with Harold's girl.
Harold must like him pretty well. The boys in Harold's
fraternity would all be jealous because Winfield Payne
was shown so much consideration. The best friend of
Harold should be one of his own fraternity brothers,
not a member of another fraternity, especially of Payne's
which was envied by the others.

Winfield was uneasy at the party, though the boys did try to make him feel at ease. They were not mean enough openly to show what they felt. He traded all the dances he could with fellows there. That would look best, he thought.

Harold's illness dragged on into the spring. In March he died. Winfield was asked by the parents to be a pallbearer at the funeral. The other ones were all to be members of Harold's fraternity. That was the custom.

I guess I was his best friend though. He was the only fellow I liked around the place. But I'll bet those fellows in his fraternity will be sore. They think they ought to be the pallbearers. I'd rather they were. They'll just be sore about it.

For the funeral Winfield borrowed a black coat and a black hat from his father. The ceremony was to be at the Eldridge home. He went there early, two hours early, because Mr Eldridge had asked to see him.

—Winfield, he liked you, you were good to him. I'm glad you are here. My wife and I feel it. We feel it Winfield. You have been good. The boy dying this way, it's awful. Do you want to go in and see him? What's left? He's in there. I can't go in.

Tears were in Mr Eldridge's eyes.

Winfield walked into the little room where the body lay in its casket. Harold was very tall, he had grown very tall during his illness. It was amazing, frightening, unnatural. And so pastylooking, wax.

God that's not Harold. It's awful, he thought.

An uncle of Harold walked in.

—Are you young Payne?

—Yes, Mr Eldridge. It's too bad. Can't understand why. Young fellow like that. Doesn't look like him.

—Here, feel of Harold's hands. So cold, aren't they? He was a good boy.

Winfield couldn't touch those hands. He broke into tears, though he had decided before that that was one thing he would not do.

—He liked you Winfield. I heard him say. It's too bad. Two young friends like you and Harold. It's too bad.

Harold lay there stiff, cold, motionless. Listening, it seemed to Winfield.

I wonder if he did like me best? I hope he did. I liked him. That's hell. What am I crying for? No sense in that. Leave it to his father and mother. They ought to cry. I am a man. Ought not to be crying.

He sobbed, aloud now.

Then Clara walked into the room, dressed in mourning. Seeing Winfield crying as he was, she burst into tears, went up to him, put her arm around him, her head against his breast.

—Harold liked you Winfield. He told me.

God, why don't people shut up? He liked me. I can't help it, I feel crazy, all this. But he was touched, softened by Clara's warm young body against his. She was weeping, silently. Her young love was gone.

Of a sudden he liked Clara. I want her to be happy. I want to help her, make her all right again. It's awful for her. He was a good fellow for a girl. All the stuff he did. I never did anything like that for a girl. Winfield wanted to help Clara come back to herself, and be happy as she had been before.

—Clara you'll be all right. I know how he felt about you. He loved you. He told me so himself. I know.

In the living room of the Eldridge home chairs were placed to accommodate the mourners. Many chairs were needed, for nearly the whole highschool student body turned out for the funeral. The coffin bearing his body was rolled silently into this room. Flowers were stacked from floor to ceiling, thousands of flowers, hundred of bouquets of flowers, piled up all over the room, giving out odor, nauseating odor of funeral flowers. The people were filing in, dressed in black and somber clothing.

Winfield seated himself on the front row with the pall bearers. Clara was sitting with Mr and Mrs Eldridge. Young highschool boys were muttering conversation back and forth.

—Too bad. Fine young fellow. Young. Jesus think of it. Mother and father all broken up. Clara must feel awful. How did Payne get in the mourners? He's in another fraternity? Good friend Payne. Kinda pushed himself into it, I guess.

All this talk around him. He felt that he should be back further. The fraternity brothers of Harold were a little angry because he had been chosen along with them to carry the body. Winfield didn't want to be butting in. Somebody had said that he was butting in. He had heard it said.

I wish they hadn't asked me to do it. It'll make the fellows all hate me for it.

The smooth snakelike undertaker slipped noiselessly back and forth, a sickly smile lighting his

face. Suave he was. A comforting pat on Mrs Eldridge's
back.

God, that snake. So smooth. Black like that.
Smiling. What's he laughing at? Makes me sick, the
fellow.

The Presbyterian minister delivered a short
address. Mr Eldridge had asked that it be short. Want a
service like the Episcopal. Short, to the point, beautiful
service. A woman in black with a rasping voice sang
about the sunset and evening star, and that stuff from
Tennyson about going over the bar.

Makes me sick.

Winfield was sobbing. He couldn't help it. He
noticed none of the other boys were doing it. Tried to
stop.

The minister's talk, about the wonderful Christian
qualities of Harold, made Winfield sob, he couldn't
help himself, didn't care who saw him. It was a lie. He
was better than they knew.

Clara spent a part of every day with the Eldridges.
They were almost as sorry for her as for themselves, and
wanted her to be happy. They thought it would be nice
if Winfield and she would go together. Harold would
rather she became Winfield's wife than the wife of any
other boy. They knew this, and tried to bring the two
young people together. Mr Eldridge would stop for
Winfield in his car and then pick up Clara and take
them for a ride. They suggested excursions and dances
to the young people. Clara rather liked the idea, but

Winfield didn't care for her very much. She wasn't the
type he liked.

A little too conceited and snippy. Grumbles too
much. I like a happier sort of girl.

But he did go around with her, because he felt
sorry for her and also because he knew the Eldridges
wanted him to.

One night driving with her in a car he tried to kiss
her. Just a little kiss was all he wanted, something to
give him a reason for showering attentions upon her.
He didn't try to force the matter, that would have been
the way to get a kiss. But he just gave up when she
drew herself away from him.

I'm sorry I ever tried. Just make her think less of
me. Harold's friend ought not try a thing like that just
two months after he's dead.

But instead of making her like him less, it made
her like him better. In a few days, if Winfield could
have shown the girl that he really was fond of her, he
could have had all the kisses he wanted.

She knew that he went from one girl to another,
and he had a reputation of making love to any girl that
would let him, so she wanted to hold herself aloof and
wait until he had proved that he really cared for her.
She didn't want just necking, she wanted real affection.
After the rebuff in the car though, Winfield was
through trying.

Hell with her, he thought. There are plenty of
others. She thinks she's so damned good looking she
can put on airs.

He never tried to kiss her again, and began to call
on her less often.

When Winfield saw Mr and Mrs Eldridge he noticed that they were disappointed, they had hoped that he and Clara would go together. But they saw that something was wrong and suspected it was Winfield who was spoiling their plan. Harold had told them how fickle Winfield was, he had had too easy a time of it with girls and now, unless the girl laid her snare very carefully for him, he evaded her. Clara had not cared to snare him in, she thought it was his duty to run after her, she couldn't chase after any man, especially so soon after Harold had died.

Winfield took other girls to dances, and now when he saw the Eldridges he felt a little guilty, but he couldn't help it. I can't waste my time on that Saunders girl.

He began to see them less often and worked back into the routine of highschool life.

A cousin of Winfield, a pretty girl of twenty years, was studying at the University of Michigan. She invited him to a dance at her sorority house. He was to go with one of her friends, a member of the same sorority. The cousin, Esther Randall, was engaged to a young man from Benton, Ward Howe. He was a student at the university and belonged to the same fraternity that Winfield's uncle had belonged to. Ward Howe asked Winfield to come down to Ann Arbor and stay at his fraternity house over the weekend of the party. His fraternity was rushing Winfield, wanting to make him a member when he came to the university.

The night of the dance, Ward Howe and Winfield sat in the fraternity house, waiting until it would be

late enough to go to the dance. Howe was very much
in love with Esther Randall and thought by being nice
to Winfield he would make Esther love him even more
than she did.

Some of the boys in the fraternity came in with
several bottles of bootleg whiskey. The state of Michigan
was dry and the booze had been smuggled from Ohio,
from Toledo. Winfield thought it would be good to
drink a little before going to the party. Howe objected
because he knew that Esther would not like it if the two
boys came to her sorority house drunk. However with a
little urging he drank.

Winfield, after the first drink, wanted more and
Howe drank with him. Both of the boys were tight in a
short time.

Winfield got up on a table. Told the Uncle
Wiggley stories.

—Uncle Wiggley and the Blue Goose went down
to the river to wash their feet. The Blue Goose fell in.
Oh, Oh, Oh, exclaimed Uncle Wiggley.

And then the Shooting of Dan McGrew,
accompanied by piano music.

Winfield was having a fine time amusing the boys
at the house. Howe sat in a corner a bit stupefied. He
had drunk too much.

At nine o'clock the dance was to start. Some of
the fraternity brothers of Howe helped the two boys
along the streets, half supporting them, urging them
to walk as fast as possible and get over the semi-stupor
the drink had put them in. It was almost ten o'clock
when they reached the dance. Ward Howe collapsed in
a chair on the front porch of the house.

Winfield's cousin, Esther, seeing him in this state,
went to her room, crying. Her fiancé drunk like that.

Oh, it's awful. What will the girls think of me?
And Winfield drunk too. I did so want the girls to like
him. I told them what a nice cousin I had. It's awful.
Those boys doing that. Might have known it would
happen. It's those fellows at Ward's house set them up
to it. None of the boys here like the girls, the coeds.
She stayed in her room the whole night. Some of his
fraternity brothers carried Ward home, put him under
a cold shower bath and then to bed. Winfield stayed at
the dance, drunk.

Between dances the girls made him walk with
them trying to sober him down.

—Let's just take a little walk. It's so nice out
tonight. Don't you like to walk, Mr Payne?

The girl that had invited him to the dance, through
his cousin, gave every dance she could to other girls.
She thought of the disgrace. Of what the chaperones of
the party would think of her.

Two days later Ward Howe was called to the
office of the dean of the university. He was asked to
bring the young man who was drunk with him along.
At the office he was told that he was expelled from
the university, for setting a bad example to a young
highschool boy by being drunk. Also because it was
against the rules of the university for students to
drink. Winfield was asked if he intended to go to the
University of Michigan.

He said he *had* intended to. Didn't know now
though.

They took his name and address. Found that he had applied to enter the university the next fall. Made notations on his application for admission.

I guess I'll never be able to get in here after this. They'll be watching me like blazes. It's too bad for Ward though. Getting kicked out of school. Gee Esther is sore.

Esther refused to answer the telephone when Ward called her, the day after the party. She was through with him. Sent his engagement ring back, his fraternity pin too. She couldn't be disgraced in that way. Ward getting her cousin drunk and then bringing him to a party. That was too much.

Winfield had to go to her and tell her that he had made Ward drink, that Ward had asked him not to drink. After a long apology, after his taking all the blame on himself, Esther softened, and in a few days she and Ward were back on their old basis, of love and order.

Ward had to go to work in Benton, but on weekends he drove in his car to Ann Arbor to see Esther.

Winfield was afraid to go to Michigan, but he didn't dare tell his parents the reason.

Perhaps nothing will be said to me though. They shouldn't say anything to me. I wasn't in college then. He argued with himself that everything would be all right at school in Ann Arbor. Decided he wouldn't mind going there, taking a chance on it.

When graduation time came he decided there was no use sitting in a theater and walking across the stage in order to get a diploma. He refused to attend the graduation exercises. His mother had to ask the highschool principal for his diploma. He wasn't going to sit up there with a lot of younger people than himself, all of them dumbbells, and walk up for his diploma as if he belonged to them. No, indeed not.

His mother couldn't understand.

—Winfield, why do you act so? Why don't you do as the other boys do? You just cause your mother and father trouble, that's all.

But it didn't move Winfield.

—No, I won't sit up there with that bunch of fools. The teachers are as bad as they are. Why, who wants to hear a methodist preacher talking about how the young people graduating today are the pride of their country? I don't want to. I know more than any of them do. They did me dirt making me stay another year in highschool. No mother, you don't understand. Tell them I'm sick if you want to. I won't go. That's it, I won't go.

Mrs Payne was very ill at ease. She didn't like to see her boy standing in front of her saying he wouldn't do something she wanted him to do. But she knew that he wouldn't do it, so she gave in to him. And she was very seldom willing to give in to any of her boys. But Winfield was so determined. It would be easier.

And too, she thought, my head aches. I simply cannot have all this strain on my nerves. I can't be the mother to him that I used to be.

After school was over, his father and mother told him he might go to their summer cottage in the north. He intended to work for L. M. Perry and Company after the first of July anyway, so he had better have a little vacation. He would start in at the University of Michigan in the fall.

He went north. The season had not started and all of the cottages on the lake were vacant. He sailed his sailboat, read books he brought with him, and fished in the lake. It was lonesome up there alone, so he wrote letters. He wrote to girls he had known, wrote to Paul Pew in Washington, wrote a letter to Weeds, and to Gaston down in West Virginia, telling him they would meet in a month or two.

At night it was so quiet in the woods on the shore of the lake, with only a fire in the fireplace and a book in his hand. But it was too quiet. He was afraid of the intense stillness, and he wrote letters. Several times he started a letter to Dorothy Jefferson, but each time he stopped himself.

No, I won't write to her. That's over now. She's probably got a fellow now.

He didn't want to know it if she had, so he just didn't write to her.

He heard from Gaston. Dorothy was engaged to a boy down there, son of another coal operator.

Glad I didn't write to her. There would have been no use.

He grew sentimental about Dorothy, and thought he was a little, just a little heartbroken, to hear that she was to be married. She was the best girl I ever had. Funny she was so much better than girls at home, and she was real. I wouldn't dare try it on girls at home. But with her it was different. Guess it's being away from home that way, makes the difference in how a fellow feels.

After the first of July he went to work for the seed company. They gave him a new territory to work in, up in the northern part of the state of West Virginia. The roads were better, there, he would be able to travel to his stores in an automobile. It wouldn't be necessary to ride horseback.

He had told them he couldn't ride horseback. It wasn't good for him underneath. Illness of some kind he couldn't stand horseback riding. So they sent him to the northern part of the state.

He hired a taxi driver with a four passenger touring car to drive him over his route. When Winfield told him that he thought there was no God the taxidriver was indignant.

—What no God? Why that's anarchism. You don't believe that? Of course there must be a God. Look at the grass growing there. Doesn't that prove it? Why that's awful, you'll go to Hell sure. That's terrible. There has to be a God. Look at the Bible!

Winfield looked at the Bible. At least he quoted things from the Book contradictory enough to satisfy himself that it was no authority. But the taxidriver was still unconvinced. Winfield wished he had hired someone else to drive him around. There was no use arguing with a plain dumbbell. He ceased talking with the driver about religion. One day in a country store when the work was done, the driver spoke to the merchant.

—That fellow doesn't believe in God. What'll happen to him?

That was too much. My driver speaking like that. Why he ought to be fired. Might make me lose a

customer, might not buy from an atheist. I'll fix that
fellow.

Out in the car driving to the next store Winfield
gave him a sound calling down.

—Say you'll lose me all my customers. That's
no sales talk for L. M. Perry and Company, telling a
merchant that your boss is an atheist. You ought to
know better than talk that way to those dumbbells. You
can't do that, that's all. It can't be. Why don't you see?
You'll lose me my customers.

They had an unhappy time together, after that.

Winfield thought it was too bad he and Gaston
couldn't see each other. He wrote to him. Gaston came
up to Clarksburg to see Winfield for a week or two. He
wasn't working then and could get away from home.

Gaston and Winfield went to dances in a park
near Clarksburg. The two fellows were a good team and
they had plenty of bootleg liquor and could easily get
any girls they wanted. Twice they got girls out in an
automobile and went all the way with them. Most of
the time though they were satisfied with only making
love to them, and kidding them.

Their line of talk was getting to be very similar.
The Blue Goose and the Uncle Wiggley stories were
told and retold by each of the two.

Winfield enjoyed his second year of work with
L. M. Perry and Company. He didn't work as hard as
he had before and he went to bigger cities whenever
possible, instead of stopping over night in country
boarding houses. Besides, with Gaston in Clarksburg
he always had a partner of his liking to go where he
would with. The summer went by very rapidly.

Paul Pew wrote to him three or four times and asked him to come to Washington. Paul had been his best friend in Benton before that last year of school, and Winfield wanted to see him again. He decided that when he finished his work in West Virginia he would make a trip to Washington and see Paul. It wasn't far and he could go home directly from Washington anyway.

I V

Winfield went to Washington. Paul Pew was working as a newspaperman, assistant correspondent to the Detroit Record Herald, interviewing senators and representatives, rewriting news from the Washington daily papers. He had written to Winfield, Come down to Washington. Best place to go to school after all. The college here is better and cheaper than Michigan and besides we can work together. Get a whole string of papers and send them carbon copies. The stunt should be a sure winner. You can live at the fraternity house, the boys will like you. It's a fine fraternity.

Winfield went to Washington. He decided he would stay there.

He was installed in the fraternity house, matriculated in the law department of George Washington university, went to classes in the morning, made briefs of law cases in the evenings, and during the afternoons worked with Paul, sending out letters to weekly papers throughout the country.

Pew and Payne, Washington Correspondents, a chance to have your own representative in Washington. A chance to receive the latest news each week, with special emphasis on news regarding your own district. This and more, and all for five dollars a week. The weekly news, an office in Washington, and two able correspondents. Three hundred letters were sent out. Three answers came back. Price is too much, we get all we need from the service we already employ.

Now Winfield must write home for money, and
tell the folks all about the university, how good it
was, and how later on he would be able to earn his
own living there, and besides, remain in school. They
wanted him to go to the University of Michigan, but
gave in to his demands, sent him money each month.

Paul Pew had a job already and was earning
enough to live on. But Winfield must find something
to do. He had told his parents he would find work. The
Detroit Post needed an assistant correspondent and
tried to get Paul away from his paper by offering him
more money. His own paper then gave him a raise in
salary. He told the Post correspondent about Winfield.

—You ought to look up young Payne, he's from
Michigan, worked a long time on the Benton paper
and used to write Sunday feature stuff for your own
sheet. He's a good man. Got a good nose for news too.
You might get him for a little less than fortyfive a week.
He isn't doing anything now. Going to school in the
morning, but he has the whole afternoon off. I'll send
him around if you want me to.

The Post representative said, all right, I'll look him
over. Send him around tomorrow morning. You should
come over with us, though, Paul. It means more you
know. Better chance for you than the Record Herald,
any day.

Winfield went to the offices of the Post at ten next
morning. Let his classes go, school wasn't very interesting
then.

It's a little early I guess, just ten o'clock.

Ought to wait a few minutes.

He stepped into the elevator and went to the fifth floor of the Metropolitan building, saw the door marked Detroit Post, quickly arranged his necktie, brushed back his hair, and walked in. Legs feeling a bit weak. It was no fun interviewing a man like Hamilton. Would he be hired or passed up?

—Mr Hamilton?

—Yes, are you the young fellow Paul Pew told me about? Good morning.

—Yes.

—Do you know the work? Yes, he said you did. Well I'll try you out. Thirtyfive a week. Is that all right?

—Yes, starting, I guess I can do it all right.

—Your name is?

—Payne.

—Oh, yes, Payne. Well Payne, just stay around here until twelve. I'll be back. You can get anything that comes over the phone and if anybody drops in, tell them I'll be back. You better look over the papers. A newspaper man has got to read the papers every day. I'll take you to the capitol this afternoon. Meet me here at two. Just go out to lunch at twelve if I'm not back then. Well, good luck to you, boy. Good luck. There's lots of work.

—Good bye, Mr Hamilton. At two o'clock.

Winfield was uneasy sitting around this office. Hamilton wasn't a man to put one at ease. Suspicious of everybody, Hamilton. He surely went after Wilson. Dug up facts about his private life that no one ever imagined were true. Newberry. It was Hamilton that spoiled his political career, not Ford. I don't like that fellow. Too damned uncanny. What am I going to do sitting around here?

Winfield didn't read the papers, just sat there thinking, waiting until twelve o'clock. He had worked on a newspaper, true enough, but a small paper, sports writing, highschool correspondent. The only real work he had done was writing Sunday feature stories for this same paper, stories that he took bodily from old state reports and historical publications. This was different. Here he was assistant correspondent to one of the biggest dailies in America and sitting around waiting until twelve o'clock.

Could he do the work, he wondered. Suppose he fires me tomorrow? No nose for news after all. I know. I hope it works out all right though.

He wrote a letter home, on newspaper copy paper. Told his parents about the new job, the wages, and the splendor of being one of the Washington representatives of the press. Plenty of confidence in the letter, a bit forced though. If he only believed what he wrote. The trouble was that he felt sure he wasn't the man for the job.

I won't last.

Hamilton didn't return at twelve, so Winfield left the office and went to find Paul. They ate lunch together at the Press Club. Paul was an active member. He pointed out national figures, famous characters, newspapermen, congressmen, and told anecdotes of the Press Club. Wanted Winfield to join, now that he was also a newspaperman. But Winfield wanted to talk, wanted to tell Paul about the new job.

—Say Paul, that Hamilton isn't so much. I don't like him. Told me to stay around the office all morning, nothing to do at all.

—Well, it takes a little time. He'll show you the works this afternoon I guess.

—I know. I ought to get along fine with that job, Paul. We've got good offices. I've got my own desk and typewriter. You saw it didn't you?

—We're going to have new offices pretty soon too.

Paul was a little jealous now that Winfield no longer needed his help, now that Winfield had a job and was independent.

—Hamilton is a bum, I hope you get along with him all right.

—But he's a good newspaperman, though I don't care for him personally either, but he's a good man, I guess. I'll see you this afternoon at the Press Gallery won't I, Paul?

At two o'clock Hamilton and Winfield went to the Senate Press Gallery. Winfield was registered as a member and given a card.

—Well, Payne, you might walk around the office building and speak to the Michigan delegates. No, come along with me. I'll introduce you to some of them. You'll have to step into their offices every day and find out what's happening.

Winfield met five of the Michigan representatives and one senator from the state. The other senator was an enemy of the paper and not on speaking terms with Hamilton. Hamilton didn't get any news items this afternoon, but nevertheless felt that he had done his work. Most of his articles were taken from the

Congressional Record anyway, or from the local papers.
He left Winfield. Told him to look around and be back
at the office at five or fivethirty. Next morning he could
go to school, to his classes.

Not knowing what to do, he went to the press
gallery again and found Paul there writing something
for his paper.

—Have you got some dope Paul?

—Yes, a little. Not much account though. How
are you coming?

—Pretty good. I haven't done much yet though.
What have you got?

—Oh, nothing much. Just a stick. Paul wasn't
going to show any more stories to Winfield. Feeling their
rivalry Winfield walked away from him, sat at a writing
desk, and wrote a short letter home on the stationery
of the Senate Press Gallery. Official looking. Now his
parents would see what kind of a job he had. Looked
like a senator's mail.

At fivethirty he again saw Hamilton at the offices
in the Metropolitan building.

—Did you dig up anything Payne?

—No, couldn't find a thing. Looks pretty slow
today.

—It is slow. Will you copy this story off? I wrote it
today. Want to get it out tonight. Copy it off and take
it over to the Western Union. I'm going home now. Oh,
say. Never mind being here in the morning. Go over to
the capitol after your lunch tomorrow and be back here
at five. Show me what you write.

—All right. I didn't find anything today. Good
night, Mr Hamilton.

Then Winfield copied the story, five typewritten pages, and took it to the telegraph company to be sent to Detroit. He went home tired and unhappy. No stories. He may can me. He will can me if I don't get busy.

Paul was already at the fraternity house, lazily briefing some cases, working at the study of law.

—Now let's make carbons of those cases. You do half of them and I'll do the rest. There's no use in both of us wasting all that time.

It was agreed to study in this fashion from then on, Winfield doing the work one day and Paul the next. They worked at it for a few days but both tired, the law was too uninteresting.

Occasionally Winfield picked up the book on criminal law, it was better than torts and contracts, and read cases in it. This wasn't part of his work in the law school though, the study of criminal law wasn't to begin until the next semester. They both let their studies drop, copied the briefs from fraternity brothers and answered questions put to them by professors when they were able to. The law school had attracted them because they could have gotten degrees in three years. Then nothing would be needed but to pass the bar examinations, and they could practice. It was enticing, the study of law, but they now knew that it wouldn't be so easy. They both lost heart and overslept oftener than was good. The boys in the fraternity house told them again and again to work harder, the first year men like Winfield should work harder. Paul had flunked out the year before, he was really still a first year man himself. Both of the fellows should study

harder. But they went on studying less and less, and
the weeks went by. Both were too much interested in
newspapers.

The second day of the new job, after classes
were over, Paul and Winfield went to the capitol, ate
luncheon in the house restaurant. Winfield tried to
kid the good looking mulatto waitress, seeing it was
the expected thing. The other pressmen did it and
so did a congressman, a fat one from the west, who
sat at the same big table as Winfield, Paul, and a few
correspondents. Winfield was a little unsure of himself
as yet though. He still felt as if he had no right to
be eating in this place with older men, writers and
congressmen. Only Paul being there made it easier.
Milk toast and eggs and potatoes au gratin, or graham
crackers in milk, for lunch.

Paul left him after eating and he wandered slowly
to the House office building and called in on the
congressmen he had met the day before.

—Anything doing today?

—No, things are going along pretty slow. But
I might give you a story for Detroit on the new
Charlotte post office. I put it across. Got all the money
we needed.

Things really were slow. And Winfield didn't see
how he was going to get news in this way. He must find
out the trick. No nose for news, none at all.

He went back to the Press Gallery, talked with
some of the men he had met, read a few short items
in the day's papers, found something about Michigan,
wrote a few paragraphs. Then he saw Paul, asked
him what he had been doing. Paul was a little freer

today and told him about two stories which Winfield decided were good. He went back to the House Office Building, interviewed one representative and wrote another story, a longer one, not bad either, though hard to write. Newspaper stories were devilish hard to write. He hoped this one was good. He saw that part of the trick was to find a clue and follow it up. Find out about some bill before Congress that dealt with his state and then interview some of the state's law makers and write a story with plenty of quotation marks. It was going to be easier from now on. But he knew it would never be really easy, he simply couldn't get the clue, he had no nose for news. If Paul told him what to write he could do it, or if some congressman suggested a good story he could write it, or if Hamilton told him to look up something special he could write it, but to go out on your own that way was too hard, he didn't know how to begin, where to start.

Hamilton liked his story. Said he had thought of writing it himself but had too little time. This new appropriation bill was taking all his time. Foolish waste of money, he said.

Winfield knew the two little stories he had written were not enough to assure him of his job, he must do more, do something big. But he just went along day after day doing little things, now and then a fairly interesting bit of news, but mainly unimportant things. But Hamilton didn't say anything to him, didn't warn him of losing the job, so he began to feel more secure. Thought one or two stories a day were all that was expected of him. And then too, he had to copy some of Hamilton's stuff and send it out, and go dig up old

copies of the Congressional Record and do odd jobs
for Hamilton. He began to feel that he was earning his
money, that he was doing all that was expected of him.
But he wasn't sure, he couldn't be sure. Hamilton never
talked to him, never gave him advice, just let things
slide along. It would have been better if Hamilton had
scolded him or warned him, but to go along and not
say anything, good or bad. It made Winfield nervous.

He went to school right along, though he did
miss a number of classes, and he had stopped studying
entirely, just copied the briefs from other students, read
them carefully and tried to recite when he was called
on. He was initiated into the fraternity and enjoyed
the pleasure of wearing his jewelled pin and shaking
hands with a mystic grip when he met brothers. He
felt grown up and a little above it all, but he enjoyed
himself in his fraternity life and in his daily canvass of
the congressmen from his state. Life in Washington was
good.

He met an old member of the fraternity, a
Harvard graduate, queer, eccentric fellow, who worked
in the Department of Agriculture. A scientist, specialist
in plant pathology. This man, Raymond Harrison
Lankin, wrote free verse, collected Japanese prints
and kept an apartment of two rooms where Winfield
was always welcome. Lankin liked the social life
and was accepted into many of the best Washington
homes. He introduced Winfield to friends and then
Winfield began his social career. Sunday afternoon teas,
debutante parties, dances, etc.

Paul Pew and Winfield were separating though
they remained roommates. Paul was not taken up by

Lankin and Winfield was willing to be shown this
other new life. So they grew apart, both working on
opposition papers and neither studying as they had
at first, and now Winfield gadding about to teas and
parties.

Schoolwork went completely to the dogs, no time
to study and most of the days too little time for classes
even. Winfield went on with his life in society, met
more people, and in three months wore out a dress suit
and a dinner jacket.

The Moore family, with their three daughters, kept
him busy. On Sunday nights he went to their home for
dinner and after dinner sat and talked politics with the
father. They thought Winfield was an interesting young
man, he could talk so well and he knew people in the
government, at least he knew enough of them to talk.

He was quite fond of the younger daughter,
Georgina, and used to take her to the movies once in a
while or to a musical comedy and he would cautiously
try to make love to her. But she wasn't going to have
anybody making love to her until she was engaged. She
might let him hold her hand for a while, but no kissing
or arms around the waist business for her. But she liked
him and thought of him at night and hoped with a
little hope that he might someday be her husband. The
wedding spread itself out before her in imagination.
She wanted a nice big wedding, and she thought how
nice Winfield would look walking down the aisle. She
really loved him in a schoolgirl, romantic sort of way.
Winfield gave the Moore family one night a week, but

he saw Georgina oftener, perhaps twice or three times a
week. Not oftener than that though.

Hamilton said nothing to him about the
newspaper work and Winfield went ahead as he had
started. One or two stories a day, waiting for the knife
to fall. This couldn't last for ever, he thought.

He got a letter from home one day, from his
father, telling him that Austin Thompson was in
Washington. Winfield should call on him. Old friend
of his father. The Marine City Thompson. Your mother
told you. Thompson had something to do with the
Senate. Secretary, clerk, or something.

He went to call on Mr Thompson.

—Good morning, Mr Thompson, my father
wrote that you were here. I didn't know it before. I'd
have called if I'd known.

—Well, it's Winfield Payne. How's your father?
Sorry didn't know you were here. You've grown since I
saw you last. Little fellow then. Must be well over six
feet now.

—Six two. Father's well. He sent his regards to
you. How is Mrs Thompson?

—She's well. Christabel is at Wellesley, now.
Coming down for Thanksgiving though. You'll have to
come over. She'll like to see you. You ought to write to
her. You didn't know her. Both too young then.

They chatted a little more and then Winfield
left the Senate corridor. Thompson was a secretary of
the Senate. He got the job through working on the
Republican Committee.

Mr Thompson called Winfield on the telephone and asked him to come to their home and meet Christabel and Mrs Thompson. Christabel was in Washington for the Thanksgiving vacation. She might be quite a girl, Winfield thought.

—Yes, I'd like to come over Mr Thompson. I'll be there in a few minutes.

After dinner he dressed in his blue cheviot suit. Blue looks well on me, he thought. Makes my face distinguished. What tie shall I wear? He debated a moment and then put on the knitted silk one, his favorite. She hasn't seen it yet.

Then he remembered that the Moores expected him this evening.

—Hey, Paul, call up Georgina for me and tell her I'm sick. Will you?

—I'm not doing all your dirty work, Winnie. Call her yourself.

—All right. I'll do something for you sometime. Like hell I will.

Winfield telephoned the Moores and told the maid to kindly tell Miss Georgina that Mr Payne was not feeling well and couldn't be around this evening. The maid wouldn't know who called anyway.

Then he left the house excited and expectant. He hoped Christabel would like him and he would like her. He wanted to fall in love with her.

He rang their doorbell, removed his hat, pushed his necktie a little to the left, wanted it straight. Mr Thompson ushered him into the house. He met Christabel and fell for her right away. They talked for a long time about Benton and Winfield's parents and

Christabel asked Winfield questions about himself.
They were getting on famously.

She suggested a walk, it was warm and the moon
was shining.

—Yes, why don't you children walk around a little?
But come back early, and don't go too far away, Mrs
Thompson said.

It had been easy to talk there in the house with
the people around, but out on the street alone with
Christabel, all Winfield could say now was, isn't the
moon nice? It's a great night. Wonderful night.

Christabel talked about Wellesley, told about a girl
there, a funny girl. Must be something wrong with her.
Had a funny room, all decorated exotic like. Winfield
didn't understand and Christabel only knew the girl
was funny.

She asked Winfield what he did all the time in
Washington and he told her about school and his work
and a little, very little, about his social life. About the
school, he let her think he really worked at it and really
went to classes. He wanted to take her hand in his, but
couldn't get up the courage. She rather wanted this too.
They walked a long way and then went back to her
home, said good night, squeezed hands together, more
than a cordial, good-night handshake. Winfield felt as
if he had kissed her.

Gee, what a girl she is. Better than anything I've
had to date, I'll tell you. Gee.

Winfield was in love.

He went home and to bed. Thought of her in bed.
Wished he could kiss her lips, put his arms around her.

He thought of her and satisfied his desire thinking of her. Then he slept.

He saw her next afternoon. They went to a tea dance at the Washington hotel. This was good, dancing with her and holding her tight. He wouldn't forget this afternoon very soon.

She left the next day and wrote to him immediately from Wellesley. He answered it and signed his letter. With love, yours, Winnie. It thrilled him to write that. With love, yours. She was more reserved, but now she started the letter with a, Winnie dear, instead of, Dear Winnie. That was just as good as saying she loved him.

He didn't tell the Moores anything about this. Didn't let Georgina know she had a rival. But he went back to them again and in a few days Christabel was tucked away in a corner of his brain. Not forgotten, but shelved in his brain. His life resumed its former course. Dancing, teas, work, classes. They exchanged letters, one every two weeks, and at the time Winfield was writing to her he felt that warmness for her that he had felt the first night when they walked on the moon lighted streets together, when he had tried so hard to find words, a way to make love to her. He hadn't dared begin. In his letters he was freer and told her how he missed her, little lies, and how he looked forward to seeing her again. It was too bad he would be going home for the Christmas vacation, but he would see her when he came back. He might even return to Washington a day or two earlier than he had planned.

Now Christmas was two weeks away, so he went to Hamilton. Say Hamilton, do you think I could get

off a couple of weeks at Christmas time? I haven't seen
my folks for over six months. He was afraid of the
answer but had decided he was going home even if he
got fired for it.

—Sure you can get off for that time. There's not
much doing then anyway. Of course.

—Thanks a lot, Mr Hamilton.

—And when you go, drop in the office in Detroit
and introduce yourself to Mr Lindsay. He's managing
editor now. Tell him who you are. I wrote him about
you. He'll show you around.

—I will. I'll be in Detroit on the way home. Have
to stop off there anyway, I guess.

A few days before Christmas, Winfield left
Washington, travelled all night and reached Detroit in
the morning. He checked his luggage in the station and
went to the Detroit Post building, asked for Lindsay,
met him, and told him he was Hamilton's assistant.

Lindsay looked up at the beardless face. Winfield
was over six feet tall. Oh, so you're the young fellow?
You'll be a great help to your folks when you grow up,
won't you?

What's this? thought Winfield, supersensitive,
misinterpreting. When I grow up? And he was
frightened. Thought he wasn't doing his work right
and therefore was no good now. Have to grow up. He
colored a little. Wished he hadn't stopped in Detroit
after all. Just to be insulted. As if he wasn't already
grownup. I guess they're going to fire me all right.

Lindsay told him to look around the building.
Directed a guide to take him through the marvelous,
new, up-to-date newspaper building. The finest

newspaper home in the world, they advertised it. He
went around as fast as the guide would let him and
went back to Lindsay. Said, Good bye. Heard a few
words about working hard and putting all he could
into the job, and then he left and took the first train to
Benton.

I guess they just got me in Detroit to put a scare
in me. I can't do any more though. I'm doing my best.
I can't write that stuff. I guess I'm no good. They'll fire
me sure. Probably as soon as I get back.

He was glad he hadn't stayed longer in the office in
Detroit. It was uncomfortable there, he didn't feel safe
around that place and the reporters, all good reporters,
safe in their jobs, what would they have thought if
they knew how near he was to being fired? But didn't
matter. Any of them would have been glad to be in
Washington. That was better than working at a desk,
any day. The train went through Williamson. Almost
home now. How was it going to be at home? His folks
treated him better than he had thought they would,
after that running away from home business. They
would be glad to see him. Since then, they had been
good to him. Why, a year ago they wouldn't even have
let me stay in Washington. It was a good thing I went
to Cleveland. Only they did think I was crazy.

He arrived in Benton in the evening and was
welcomed home by his mother with a reserved kiss on
the cheek. His father shook his hand, man fashion. The
two brothers, who were still young enough to look up
to Winfield especially since he was now a Washington
newspaper man and college student, shook his hand
lustily and said, Well the hero's back again. Did you get

all the girls in Washington? Some boy hey? Quite the fellow.

The family sat around a while, talking local gossip, just as if he had been there forever. It didn't please Winfield either, he wanted to be made more of. Here he'd been away from home a long time too, and then just this greeting, and he was back into the swing of family life. It should have upset them more, he thought. They ought to ask more questions. The brothers wanted to, but they were waiting for a better time, for a time when Winfield could divulge a few intimate experiences, the sort of thing that interested these young highschool boys. What did the newspaper business amount to beside a love affair? Some necking in the moonlight? Winfield decided to tell them some good tales about life in Washington. But they had a tale to tell him also. After carelessly reading the newspaper and banking the furnace with coal for his father, Winfield went up to bed.

Upstairs, one brother said, Say, you goose, don't you know what mother asked you all about Paul Pew for? You acted silly. Paul's sister has been hitting it up some. I wouldn't tell anybody I knew her if I were you.

—Say, what are you talking about George? Helen is a decent little kid.

—Hey, wait till I tell you. She's been taking on everybody in highschool and the whole town knows it except her folks. They don't know.

—Well I'll be damned. Is that true? Helen? Why she was a nice quiet kid.

—All the boys go out with her, I tell you. Doesn't Paul know?

—Of course he doesn't. If he knew, he'd raise a
little hell I tell you. Say, who's been with her? What
fellows?

—Jay Barbor, Ralph Brunner, the whole bunch, I
tell you.

Winfield was sorry, Paul's young sister gone wild
like that. If Paul knew, it would kill him. He'd be
madder than hell. And her parents, Paul's parents, were
good Methodist people, religious Church people. Mr
Pew worked in the state capitol, clerk, and led a quiet
respectable life. Why, if they had even known how Paul
chased around on occasions it would have driven them
mad. And then to have this young Helen doing this
sort of thing. She's a regular skunk, Winfield thought,
treating her people that way. And Paul, good God, here
I am his roommate. People won't think much of that,
I guess. I hope he doesn't find out. If our fraternity
brothers knew about that? That would hurt Paul in the
house. I hope she braces up.

After hearing about Helen, Winfield couldn't even
call on the Pews. He did telephone and tell Mrs Pew
that Paul was well and sorry not to get home. Too little
money, but he would be back in the summer surely. He
was making out fine in Washington, working hard, had
lots of influential friends. Some day Paul would be a
great man.

Come over and see us Winfield, she asked.

—I'll try and get over Mrs Pew, thanks awfully.

Whew, but he was glad that was over. He couldn't
stand it to see that little Helen, living as she was, and
her parents not knowing. He didn't call on the Pews
before going back to Washington.

Two days after Christmas he met Helen Pew on
the streets.

—Hello Helen, how are you? Paul sent his best to
you.

—Oh fine, how are you Winnie? You look well.
She shook his hand. Helen was olive skinned, black
haired, with a body full of curves. Delicious body,
rounded and graceful. Winfield looked at her carefully.
Huh, bobbed hair, he thought Looks keen though, the
kid. Sixteen. Too young. It's too bad.

She was beautiful. It was easy to see that she was
also passionate, probably make a good party. Animal
like, vigorous creature.

They talked a while about Paul and Washington.
She said she wanted to leave town. Not much of a
place. Highschool was a bore. But she was careful in
what she said. She knew Winfield was Paul's best friend
and Paul must never have an inkling of what she was
doing. It wouldn't do to let Winfield even guess it.
She hoped he hadn't heard anything. People had been
talking about her, she knew. Probably telling more than
was true too, they always did.

Winfield was nervous, talking to her on the streets
where people might see them. Think he was playing
around with her. Paul's best friend afraid to talk to
Paul's sister on the street. Ashamed to be seen. Winfield
was sorry he felt that way, but he did close their talk as
soon as he could.

—I got to be getting along, Helen. I'll see you
again. Good bye.

After the vacation, the highschool society dances,
Christmas celebrations and calls on old friends were

over, Winfield went back to Washington. Christabel
Thompson would be gone, but the Moores would like
to have him call, and it would be fun to see all the
fellows at the fraternity house again too. But he hated
to see Paul, knowing all he did. Knowing about Helen
and what she was up to there in Benton. He couldn't
possibly tell Paul, he would just have to keep quiet
about it all.

When he entered into the routine of life in
Washington again he gave Paul more of his time, talked
with him evenings, asked him to go to movies and they
became friends as they had been when Winfield first
went to Washington. Paul poopoohed the society life
Winfield had been leading. He was a little jealous. He
began to suggest newspaper stories to help Winfield in
his work. He knew the job was too much. And besides
that, he wanted Winfield to be his friend, he needed
him now.

One night, late, they were talking together in
their little room before turning in. Say Winnie, I got
something I want to ask you. Don't get sore now.

—Well go ahead, why should I get sore? Winfield
knew what it was going to be, something about Helen.
He could tell the way Paul looked. Serious, quiet,
brooding. Something on his mind, no doubt about
that.

—Well, read this letter, Winnie. I got it yesterday.

Paul handed Winfield a letter from a highschool
friend, a fellow named Hazelton. Both of them had
known him well. A snoopy sort of fellow, one of those
boys who know it all. He told Paul, in the letter, that
Helen had gone on the loose. Paul ought to help her

get straight. People even thought that Winfield Payne
had been with her. Paul could set her right if he tried.
Nobody else could make the girl do as much as Paul
could. Knowing it was my duty to let you know about
this, I wrote this letter, the fellow said.

As Winfield was reading, Paul said, now I know
you haven't been with her Winnie. But you must have
known about this. Why didn't you tell me? Did you
know?

—Well I'll tell you, Paul. I just thought it was
a wild rumor. You know that kind of thing. I didn't
believe it. My brother George told me. I told him he
was a damned liar. Do you believe it Paul? Course I've
never been with her, Paul. You know that well enough.
I wouldn't do that. That's a plain damned lie, all the
way through. It's a lie.

—God, that makes me feel awful though. Helen is
just a little girl. What he says there, it's as if the whole
town went with her, it's awful. Winnie. I could cry
about it. That's what I get for running around myself.

—But this skunk, Hazelton. Imagine any fellow
writing that letter. He's a nosey guy. I think it's mostly
lies, don't you?

—I've got to find out more of this. Do you know
anything? Tell me if you do, I've got to know. I'll go
right back and beat her up, I will. I wish I was home, I
could fix her. She's scared of me, I tell you. Who would
have thought, my sister? By God, I wonder what fellow
started her? I'll get him. God damn him, Winnie, I'll
get him. Sure as you live. Damned skunk. Dirty devil. I
wanted to talk to you before. I couldn't. Couldn't even
start. I'm going to write home and get the truth of this.

A few days went by and Paul still planned to
write. If he could find out who the first fellow was he'd
get him. But he didn't write, he wasn't sure how to
go about it, what to say. If his folks knew it would be
worse. This was a matter just between Helen and Paul,
their parents must not know. It would kill them, Paul
said that. They would never live through it.

Both boys worked and went to their classes again
with more regularity. Winfield went less to dances and
teas and spent more time with Paul. The days passed
quickly.

In Benton Mr and Mrs Pew heard a rumor that
their daughter had become a bad girl. They didn't
believe this, but still they were not sure. And they
didn't dare ask her outright, they didn't even dare
make enquiries and find out. It might be true. And yet
she was their own flesh and blood. No, she had been
such a nice little girl, never gave much trouble, a little
headstrong perhaps. No, it wasn't really true. But Mrs
Pew saw to it that Helen was home after school every
afternoon and that she remained at home during the
evenings. If this thing was even partly true, there was to
be no more chance of rumors getting out. She almost
seemed to believe the rumor, all the time denying it
to herself and her husband. They heard about it in
December and had been strict with their daughter since
that time, watching, playing cat and mouse with her,
haggling her too, making her hate her life. But they
told no one, never even spoke about it to each other.
Just went along, building a wall around the girl. She
knew that they suspected her, but she also knew they

had no proof. And she felt guilty, she had sinned and felt it to be sin. So she let them wall her in.

Mrs Pew didn't see that her daughter's giving in to her was a direct confession of guilt. She thought that Helen was too good a girl for that. But she wouldn't let her into the way of temptation, I should say not. If only Helen had not felt that it was sin, this thing, she would have been more healthy, but the feeling that she had sinned made her feel sneaky, mean. She would always have to be a sneak to do this. And she needed it, her whole body cried for passion and now that she had tasted of it she must have more. But she was walled in by her mother, and she allowed her mother to wall her in that way. No more dances, no automobile rides with the highschool boys, she must stay at home.

—Where are all your girl friends? her mother asked her.

—Girls don't like me. I'm not in any sorority and they all are, so they don't like me. I haven't any girl friends.

The truth was, the moral middleclass girls in school were afraid to be seen with her and snubbed her on that account. Of course she had no friends among them. But with the boys it was different. Only now her mother wouldn't let her go out with the boys. Her mother kept her shut in until the middle of January.

On a day at this time of the month Winfield and Paul were in the Senate Press Gallery together when the man Paul worked under, the chief correspondent for the Record Herald, came in and gave Paul a telegram from home that had been delivered to the office when Paul was not there.

Helen kidnapped by two men in auto. Cannot locate her. Father.

—By God, Winnie. What will I do? Look at this. She got into it, I've got to go home now. Look after my stuff here.

Paul's eyes were hard, murderous. He was going to protect his little sister, going to get those men, he'd show them.

The two boys took a taxi back to the fraternity house. Paul packed his suitcase and dressed for the journey mumbling to himself, I'll show them. I'll get them. The devils. I'll get them, Winnie.

He left the room after shaving and rummaged around the house, still mumbling, threatening, murderous, half mad. Came back into the room. Held up a heavy hardwood cane, about two inches thick.

—That'll do the business. I'll get those fellows. Come on, let's go down to the train. Wait till I catch them, I tell you.

After Paul left, Winfield spent an anxious ten days waiting for his return, broken once by a long letter from Paul.

Dear Winnie, the day I got home they had found Helen out at Williamson with that Redmond girl and had detained her until we should call. I went out there with the sheriff in a car and we brought them both home. Helen acted awfully sheepish and wouldn't say a word to any one. They tried hard to make her talk. The other girl didn't talk either at first. When we got home I took her into her room and threatened to beat her to death if she didn't tell the whole story, so she told me. She and that Redmond girl went from school and were picked up by two fellows in a car. Somebody saw them going down Washington Avenue. The fellows took them to a hotel for the night where they worked. Next day they took them out to Williamson, put them in a house one of the fellows had rented and planned to go out there nights and stay with the girls. My folks missed her that night and told the police, so a search was started and three days later, when I got home, they were caught on the streets and held by the Williamson police until we got them. She gave me a list of the fellows she had been with, that damned Fitch fellow got her the first time. I'll make him pay. The police have got the two men in jail here in Benton and we are going to make them suffer. My mother is sick in bed, she had a nervous breakdown, and my father is so upset he can't talk to anyone. Helen sits at home quiet too, and she is afraid of me. This other girl was at fault for it all. She got Helen to go away like that. She never was any good. I can't stay long after the trial, because I have got to be back at work. I will be back in a few days when my mother is better. Tell my boss I'll be back about next Tuesday. I'll tell you the whole story then. I can't write it all now. It's made an awful howl here in town. I tried to get the paper to keep quiet but they printed an awful yellow article, made it out twice as bad as it is, and it's bad enough. I think those fellows must have given the girls some kind of dope. Helen says they did. She is scared and has told the truth. The Redmond girl blabbed the whole story as soon as she got home that night, or it wouldn't have gotten out so easily. Paul.

Paul returned to Washington bringing with him clippings from the Benton papers telling the story of the girl's abduction, the search, and the trial of the two men. One of the men made a statement trying to explain the whole thing. The fellows were clerks in a Benton hotel. One had an automobile. That afternoon they picked up the girls they were driving around waiting to go to work. Both of them had night jobs and started work late in the afternoon. They recognized the Redmond girl, everybody knew about her anyway and they naturally thought that Helen Pew was also a loose one, since she was walking arm in arm with Nellie Redmond. They asked the girls to get into their car and the invitation was accepted. A drive into the country, a few drinks from a bottle of bootleg Scotch, and the girls decided to spend a night with the men in the hotel. They could have a room and the men would go up and see them when things were quiet down in the office. And besides, the two fellows told them about a house in Williamson one of them had rented. They would keep both of the girls there. They could do their own cooking. The men would drive out every day and see them. The idea appealed to the girls.

The story the girls told was a little different. The liquor must have been doped. They wouldn't normally have done such a thing. They didn't remember going into the hotel, and went to the country next day only because they felt the terrible disgrace of having been in the hotel all night with the men.

Both men were sentenced to prison for two years. The girls were let free, their parents cautioned to keep close watch over them.

Paul believed the girl's story. Winfield felt a little
sorry for the men. Why any fellow might have done
the same thing. Girls always get off easy anyway. But he
didn't tell Paul what he thought, just tried to console
Paul.

—Well, the fellows got what they deserved. That
was better than beating them up. It's a good thing you
didn't use that club of yours. Say, what happened to
that Fitch fellow? Did you see him?

—No, I decided there was no use raising any
more trouble. I guess he feels pretty cheap anyway. The
dirty skunk. If it wasn't for him that never would have
happened.

Winfield and Paul went on with their work and
school. Hamilton spoke to Winfield once in a while
now, asking him if he had anything special. One day
he asked what was doing on the new Michigan St
Lawrence river waterway project. Winfield hadn't heard
anything about developments in this thing.

—Well Payne, that's a pretty important thing for
Michigan. They've got it in committee now. Didn't you
know that? You've got to keep your eyes open. That's
the way to get news, you know. You better look into
that tomorrow.

Gee, I missed that all right. Didn't have any idea
it was up already either. Wonder what Hamilton will
do about it? He was not going to have to wait long
to find out. About a week after this conversation,
Hamilton asked Winfield to sit down, he wanted a
little talk with him. It's coming now, he thought. I'll
get it now.

—Well Payne, I'm sorry to have to tell you what
I've got to. You're a good boy. But you ought to do
something besides newspaper work. You will never
make a newspaper man. I've tried you, but you aren't
a newspaperman. Now that's nothing against you, you
know. You ought to finish your school anyway. This is
no place to go to school. You can't work and study at
the same time anyway.

—Yes, I'm sorry. I thought I was getting along.
But I guess, maybe, you're right. I kinda thought, all
the time.

—Well don't take it hard, Payne. I'll give you a
month's pay and you can get something else. But take
my advice, stay out of the newspaper game. You can't
write the stuff.

Winfield was all in after this. He just choked,
couldn't answer Hamilton at all. Felt helpless, bloodless.
Christ Almighty, no good. Never be any good. Now
what'll people be thinking about me? I've got to tell
them I was fired. Couldn't do the work. That's Hell. Oh,
Jesus, it's Hell.

Hamilton was writing a check for a month's salary,
which he handed to Winfield.

—I ought not take this, Mr Hamilton, but I've got
to have a little to get started on.

—Why, sure, take it. Don't be silly. That's what
our paper always does when they fire a man. You ought
to get in the bond business. Young fellows make lots
of money in it. This is no game for you though. Finish
your college first. That's the best thing.

—Well, good bye, Hamilton. I'm sorry I wasn't
any good.

—Now don't feel that way. Buck up, it'll be all right.

Winfield did buck up for a little while. Hamilton wasn't going to see how he felt. He left the office with head held high. Called out, So long, and went down the elevator.

God damn it, why do people look that way at me?

He walked out on the street with his head down, eyes on the pavement. Walked along slowly, thought all his life was spoiled, nothing to look forward to now. God what will I do? I hate to go back to the fraternity house. He felt all in, tired and weary, and he was only nineteen. He had parents with money enough to send him through college. He didn't have to work at all, and yet he was spent by this defeat, a defeat he had expected to come even sooner.

God damn that Hamilton. I'd like to show him something. I'll bet I could he a newspaperman. He didn't even give me a chance. Here I told my folks I was getting on so well. What will I write to them? Can't tell them I was fired like that.

He told Paul the whole story, he would have known it later anyhow. But neither of them told any of the fraternity brothers, they would have kidded him about it, perhaps.

The first semester of college ended ten days later. Winfield failed in three subjects, passed two. Just barely passed, through some sort of fluke. He couldn't go on with the law, just passing two subjects. He thought of New York. Ought to go there and get a job. He was tired of Washington now, no job, a failure at school too. I guess I'll go to New York. He had about fifty dollars left. He wrote to his parents telling them he had lost the job. Favoritism. Son of the managing editor got the place. He was going to New York and work. Would be living at the National Club of his fraternity. Send mail there. Better send me fifty dollars. I'm not working now.

V

Winfield went to New York, lived at the club and waited for money. He thought it would be a good idea to take a few courses in Columbia University in the extension department nights. He signed up for a few courses, sociology, psychology, English literature. Wrote home that he was going to Columbia. Why didn't they send him money? He got a letter a few days later with a check for one hundred dollars.

He paid back a few dollars he had borrowed to keep him over the last few days. His father had sent another fifty dollars to a wrong address. Winfield found the letter at this address and now had one hundred and fifty dollars. With all that money there was no need looking for a job right away. He decided to see a little of the city and went to a few cabarets with fraternity brothers, bought bootleg liquor, had a few dates with girls, and found at the end of two weeks that he had very little money left.

He thought of going to sea. A cattle boat job, or something like that. Might even be a steward on some ship. He tried for jobs at various steamship companies, but couldn't find anything. They asked him to sign his name, they would let him know if they could ever use him.

Not much use trying, he thought.

Guess I'll try for a salesman's job. I can do that. Sold garden seeds all right. Winfield had also worked in a jewelry store during Christmas vacation one year.

That would be a good business. Wholesale jewelry
or perhaps in a New York shop. Wholesale sounded
better than retail though. He looked through the
papers, called at a few large wholesale jewelers, but
a week went by before he found work. Then he saw
an advertisement, salesmen wanted in old established
novelty jewelry firm. Commission and salary. Only
experienced salesmen in this line need apply.

He went immediately to this firm, located on John
street. It was ten o'clock in the morning. He went into
the offices, talked with the manager a few minutes, told
him about the retail jewelry experience he had had.
Said he had worked a year at it. He was twentythree
years old, he said. Had also worked four summers
selling garden seeds for the biggest producers in the
world. He knew the road and could sell. It was scary
telling them all that stuff, they might find him out, but
he had to do it, that was the only way to get the job
after all.

The firm of Finkel and Blum had been importing
and selling Swiss wrist watches for about six years and
had built up a good business during the war, when the
demand for wrist watches for men had been big and
when the fad for wrist watches for women had been at
its height, and now they were going to sell imitation
pearl necklaces. These things were now in vogue. They
would also handle their regular line of watches. Finkel
had charge of the pearl department and was running it
as a separate branch of the firm, only his name would
let the customers know that the watch company had
anything to do with the pearl company. The firm
could buy these strings of pearls for a small amount in

France, import them and sell them at five to ten times their cost. If the fad for pearls lasted long enough the business would be a good one.

Finkel told Winfield that they had a factory in France making these imitations for them, the same factory that supplied the famous Thelma Pearl company with their product.

—Now you know what they get for their pearls. From fifty to three hundred dollars a string. We can sell them for ten dollars to one hundred, depending on their beauty and degree of perfection. There is no reason why we shouldn't do a wonderful business.

It sounded good to Winfield. He knew those other pearls, they did cost a lot, he had wanted to buy a string for Georgina Moore, but they had cost too much. If they had cost only ten dollars though, why anybody would buy them. It sounded good, the proposition. Winfield thought it would be a fine job, he was enthusiastic from the start.

Finkel explained that the firm was just opening up this new line. They would have to get samples ready, do a little advertising. Not much though, it would make the product too expensive, you know.

—It's a good thing for us, your being a Christian too, especially out in the middle west. That's where we'll send you. In a month we ought to be ready. I'll let you know when we need you.

Winfield was planning on going to work immediately. He was low on money, couldn't possibly wait a month.

—Can't you start in sooner than that? I'm not working now. Would like to be doing something.

There's no good being idle. Besides, I am a little low on money just now.

—Certainly, you can help fix out the sample lines for the men and sort the stock here in the office. It'll be a help too. Get you used to the stock. You'll learn the various grades, BB, AB, and so forth. How much do you want a week while you're here in the office? We're not selling anything yet you know. You'll make more on the road of course, ten percent. Ought to make a lot. How much will you take working here?

Winfield didn't dare ask too much, but he had to work, had to earn money. If he didn't work there was only one thing to do and that was go home and do what his parents really wanted him to do, go to the University of Michigan, and stay around home. They wouldn't pay his way to Columbia. They wanted him nearer home.

—Well for a few weeks, until I go on the road, I'll do it for thirtyfive a week.

Finkel's expression lighted up a little, and Winfield knew he should have asked for seventy at least.

The little pearl merchant was quick to come back. Yes, that's only while you're in the office of course. Of course when you're on the road you'll make real money. But we're just starting. All the money is going out now. Thirtyfive. That's all right. We can give you that much all right.

Finkel was happy. This young fellow was pretty green, he thought. But he's a live wire. Talks well too. Make a good salesman. Glad he's a Christian, may have him write some letters for us. Always sounds good to have a Christian sign the letters. Finkel was a Jew who

would have liked to be Christian. Nevertheless, a real
Jew.

Winfield went to work at ten o'clock in the
morning, sorted out samples of the pearls, packed them
in cases, beautiful plush velvet cases, worth twice as
much as the pearls themselves. He placed price tags
on each string, and also little bronze medallions, to
give that highclass air desired. Bronze tags with the
words, Sunbeam Pearls, in big letters. Under them,
Bring Pleasure, in smaller type. In still smaller type the
words, Guaranteed Indestructible. The little bronze
tags did give the product an air, no doubt of that. And
the pearls themselves were beautiful, a little irregular
though.

He learned they were mostly seconds, that was
why they were cheaper than the others. But Finkel
explained that that was a very good thing, really. Now
as you know, he said, if a real genuine oriental pearl was
perfect, it would be worth a tremendous sum of money.
Real pearls are all more or less irregular in contour.

Finkel was talking big now, he had rehearsed this
talk.

—We make these pearls in this way to give the
illusion of the genuine article. If they were all perfect,
people would know they were imitations. Do you see?
That's what you've got to tell the customers. It's rational
too.

Winfield began to think they were not seconds
after all. Maybe they were made that way. The
argument was good. And the fact that they were made
by the same firm that made the famous Thelma pearls,
that fact, well, it made Winfield want to sell them. He

could sell them to a blind lobster, even. It's the best
job I ever had. He enjoyed working in the office and
he learned the business in a very short time. Finkel's
enthusiasm made Winfield enthusiastic, he was anxious
to get out on the road. Besides, thirtyfive dollars a
week was too little in New York. He felt that he had
cheapened himself in asking so little, and so he had, in
Finkel's mind at least.

One day Finkel took him to Brooklyn to call
on a few customers and sell some of the pearls. He
wanted to see how they would be received. Finkel did
all the talking. Winfield listened. He heard the sales
talk and remembered every word. Easier than learning
Kipling's poetry, which he could reel off by the hour.
He remembered every word Finkel and the customer
exchanged, storing the talk in his mind, ready to spring
it on his first customer.

Finkel cautiously told the jeweler, these pearls of
ours, now, we make them for the Thelma firm too.
That is, our French factory produces the pearls for
Thelma also. Show me a string of them. Have you got
some in stock?

The jeweler suspected trickery, but brought out a
string of Thelma pearls. Finkel looked at it carefully,
then took a string from his sample case.

—There's the same product, identical same thing.
The bronze pearl, we call it, grade AA, indestructible,
warranted. That pearl is a fine one. How much did you
pay for it?

The jeweler said he didn't know.

—Well, it cost you twentysix dollars. Didn't it?
Here is the same thing for twelve. What do you think
about that?

The merchant saw he had been beaten by the
Thelma firm. I won't buy anything more of that
damned Grossman. Bring out your line Finkel. I'll take
some of your stuff.

Finkel sold several hundred dollars worth of
pearls to the man. Winfield was anxious to get out
and begin selling. It was a fine business, all right.
Ten percent commission on all sales too. And he was
learning the lingo. Something like the seed business.
Lots of superlatives. Our stuff is the world's best, and
the cheapest prices too. Most beautiful pearls on the
market at rock bottom prices. He could sell those
pearls.

At the end of three weeks the sample cases were
ready for six salesmen. Finkel had decided to send that
number of men out on the road. Winfield now knew
the various qualities of pearl strings, he knew a lot of
the lingo, and was ready to start work selling. Finkel
gave him a list of New York stores to call on and show
the line to, this would be good training before going
into the hinterland. He worked a week in New York
City, called on various merchants, had a reasonable
success selling the goods. He made in all, for the week,
about one hundred dollars in commissions, these
commissions to be paid him when the goods were
delivered and paid for. He had a drawing account of
one hundred dollars a week for expenses and found it
quite easy to use the whole amount. Being a salesman,
it was necessary to buy a certain amount of bootleg

booze and to take a girl out once in a while at least.
One hundred dollars a week was not too much,
counting everything.

While he worked in New York he used the sales
talks Finkel had taught him and played especially
on the one about the Thelma pearls being made
by his own firm's factory in France. It was a good
argument and made many sales. A jeweler could tell
a customer that these pearls were exactly the same
as the famous, much advertised, Thelma brand, at
half the price, and the customer, if he ever read the
Saturday Evening Post or other national periodicals,
would see immediately the distinction in having such
really elegant pearls. Winfield liked the business but
was anxious to get out of New York. The City was
hostile to him. He would feel more at home in smaller
provincial cities, where the people were more like his
own Michigan people.

One day the great Grossman, owner of the
Thelma company, walked into the offices of Finkel and
Blum, asked for Finkel, walked into his private office
for a consultation. A buzz started around the offices.
Everybody there knew Grossman. Grossman had made
Thelma pearls as well known as Wrigley's chewing
gum, he was a blustering big fellow, neatly dressed, but
decorated with as many diamonds as a French general
with war medals.

What was this fellow doing up in the offices of
Finkel and Blum?

Winfield was there at that moment, just getting
ready to start out calling on the New York trade.
He decided to wait and see what was up. Grossman

wouldn't be up there for nothing and Winfield felt that
he might be partly at fault. All that stuff he had said
about Thelma pearls, high prices, inferior goods, taken
from the same barrel as their own, and so on. Perhaps
he had said too much. He waited.

In a few minutes Finkel came out of the office,
closed the door and walked to Winfield.

—Say Payne, come in the stock room a minute.
That's Grossman.

—I knew it was. I heard one of the stock boys say
it. What's he want?

—Well, of course, we said too much about our
pearls being made by the people that make his. Now do
me a favor, Payne. Don't think about it. It's business. I
told him that one of our men must have told that story.
It would hurt the firm if he knew I'd said anything.
Besides I only told that one merchant, didn't I? Have
you been telling that?

—Sure, I told them all. You did too. Isn't it true? I
didn't know.

—Well, of course it's true, but you've got to be
careful. Business ethics. Now listen here Payne, you
tell him you did it. Will you? It won't hurt you. You've
got a good job. He can't do anything that way. But he
might raise hell about the firm you know. It'll be all
right.

Winfield thought it over quickly and said, sure,
I'd just as soon take the blame. He was a little afraid
though. Grossman might get at him personally. The law,
and all that.

Finkel and Winfield walked into the office.

—Oh, so this is the young fellow? Do you know what you've done? That isn't business. There are rules to be followed. The ethics of business.

Business ethics, bunk, thought Winfield.

—Now I know Mr Finkel is a straightforward honest man, with good instincts for right, but it's you young fellows. Say what is your name?

—Payne.

—Payne, hey? Well Mr Payne, you're a young man. I'll tell you this much. You've got to learn what business means in all its phases. That backbiting don't go.

—I'm sorry Mr Grossman. I didn't think what I was doing. I only told a couple people that anyhow. I'm sorry about it.

—That doesn't do any good. You'll never make any success my young man, that way. I could raise a lot of trouble. Do you know that was slander? Deliberate, malicious slander? I hope there won't be any more of that sort of thing. That's why I came here. I told Mr Finkel about it and he agrees with me. And Mr Finkel, I can tell you now, that young men like that will never do you any good. You say his name is Payne? Well he isn't the kind of man to build up a real business. As for that, go ahead. You can't even take a bite out of our business. Thelma pearls will be staple article when your Sunbeams are forgotten. You flybynight fellows never last. I warn you.

Finkel puckered his lips into a slight smile. Well perhaps, but I'm sure Payne will be careful. I'll tell our other men to be careful also. Wherever they got that idea. I'm sorry, Mr Grossman.

When Grossman had gone Finkel was very angry. Flybynight. We'll show him. Why the firm of Finkel and Blum is known all over America. We were the biggest producers of wrist watches in the country. Flybynight? That's a direct insult. I'm glad you used that argument, Payne. Only be careful, he might cause trouble, that fellow. Thinks he's a big man, I guess. We've got everything on him, Payne. Prices, quality, everything. All you fellows need is the pep and push. We'll show him. It all lies in our selling department now. You've got the goods, go to it.

Winfield was a little uneasy. One of his best selling talks was spoiled, the talk he had been using to clinch every sale. He would have to think out something else, or possibly make a variation on the old story. That was what he finally did, varied the story a little, merely suggesting that this was so, showing the merchant, pearl for pearl, that the two brands were alike, not directly telling him this. The argument was almost as good as the old one, after all.

A few days later, Finkel told Winfield he was ready to send him out. Be down at the office tomorrow at ten o'clock, have your personal baggage with you. I'm going to send you into New England first. Try you out there. It's a hard place, lots of competition, but it'll be good for you. I'll give you final instructions in the morning, and I want Mr Blum to give you a little talk too. He knows the game, been on the road himself. Knows all the ins and outs.

Next morning Winfield was there, dressed in a tweed suit. Just the thing for the road, looked like a salesman. Trains won't make it dusty, either.

—Well Payne, are you all ready? You're going
out now to sell the Sunbeams. I hope you have great
success. Every penny made for the firm means money
in your pocket. With pearls selling like they are, why,
there isn't anything in it but money now, I tell you. Mr
Blum wants a few words with you before you go. He's
an old salesman himself. Been in the game for a long
time. He can give you some good pointers. Hey, Blum.

Blum came out of his office. This was the first time
he had spoken to Winfield. He attended the watch end
of the business and had very little interest in Finkel's
end. A short man, like Finkel, they might have been
related. Hook nose fellow, but sharp eyes.

His eyes made Winfield a little uneasy. What
would he have to say? Probably thinks I'm no good, the
way he looks at me.

Finkel told them to go into his office.

—Sit down Payne. You're a young man. I always
like to speak to the men before they start out.

He was serious, rather quiet talking, not blustering,
like Finkel. It made Winfield a little nervous. He wasn't
used to it. And then, what the devil? This young man
stuff again. Everybody telling him, Hello young man.
You're a young man. It wasn't pleasant, not at all.
Winfield sat silent, waiting. There was nothing to say.

—Now Payne, you've got as good a pearl as
there is on the market. Indestructible, waterproof,
sweatproof, and the price is low. You know that, the
price is low. It's lower than any others, isn't it?

—Yes.

—Well Finkel said it was. Now if you were selling
watches it would be different. But you're selling these

pearls. I told Finkel we shouldn't monkey with pearls.
But that's neither here nor there. We've got them, and
got to sell. Got a lot of money tied up in them already.
Now the thing for you to do is sell them. That's what
we want. Meet your customer man to man. Tell him
all the points about these pearls, he'll know you. And
mention my name to them, Blum. They all know
Blum. Watches. My father was in the business too. He
lost out. Don't tell them that, say the firm is under the
firm of Finkel and Blum. Put my name first, they know
me better than Finkel. This is his game though. Well
Payne, go out and sell the stuff, that's all we want. I'll
let Finkel talk to you, he's been doing the pearl stuff. I
take care of the watch end. Good luck, Payne, sell the
stuff, that's all we want.

He opened the door and called to Finkel. Finkel
came in beaming from ear to ear, took the seat Blum
had vacated. Winfield thought this was all rather the
bunk, like the seed people had done, this final sendoff
advice. Didn't mean much. He knew what to do
already, and besides, what had Blum said? Just sat there
mumbling that was all.

—Well Winfield. Finkel had decided this was the
moment to be personal, his men should all be brothers,
even if they didn't drink a Bruderschaft together, as the
Germans did. I guess Blum gave you a good talk. He's
a fine man, Blum. Knows the business, was a salesman
himself. I hope he told you all about it. He's got money,
helped me out. My wife's his sister. Did I tell you that?
Well it doesn't matter. I let him talk to you. You know
the line as well as a man could. We want results. Of
course, as you know, it's money in your pocket. The

more you sell the more you make. You're a good man.
You saw me calling on those people in Brooklyn. Well
that's the way. Sell the goods. Remember for every
penny they give, they get a nickel back. If you can
put that in their heads you've made a fortune, I tell
you. Sunbeam pearls will be known wherever the sun
shines. That's a damned good slogan. I hadn't thought
of it. Sunbeam pearls, known wherever the sun shines.
I'm going to put it in the jeweler's weekly. Have to tell
Blum about that. Sunbeam pearls, sunshine. Very good.

—You're a younger man than I am, but I know
you are going to go out and get 'em. I told Blum when
I hired you. But it means work. I almost forgot. You've
got to work. That's what we demand. I remember when
Blum told me that same thing. I was starting. It's true
though. If you think of that you'll succeed. Nothing
like success for succeeding. It's an old quotation from
somewhere, but it's true, I tell you. Now I won't talk
to you any more. Service to the trade, that should be
our motto. And say Payne, Winfield, I meant to ask
you. You'll get ahead better than some of the others.
You're a steady sort. Drinking never made a salesman.
Women either. Some of the men don't return what they
get from us. Work is the thing, from Monday until
Saturday. Most fellows don't work Saturdays, it's too
busy, but I always said, Try it. If the stores are too busy,
all right. But that might be the very day you got that
big order. I didn't do it myself, but it's the best way.
That's right, Winfield. We expect great things from
you.

It was the same old bunk. Just mixed him up, that
was all. Winfield was all muddled, he hadn't learned a

thing from all that talk, and here it was noontime. He'd
have to be going, get a train for Bridgeport, his first
stop.

—Don't worry Finkel. I'm in the game now. Out
to make good, don't worry. I'll sell the stuff. Why if I
don't sell it I don't make anything. Sure, you needn't
worry, I know the stuff, Finkel.

—That's right, Winfield, go to it. Write in every
day or two and let us know how things are going.
Send your orders in regularly too. We want to see what
things are going best. May cut down the line to a few
best sellers. It's the best way. Good bye. Good luck.

Winfield worked in the New England territory
for about two months. It was true, there was plenty of
competition. Providence, Rhode Island, is the jewelry
center of America and also the center of this New
England territory. He met jewelry salesmen in every
town and more than once found a rival pearl salesman
ahead of him, in some store. In that event there was
nothing to do but quietly leave the shop and go to the
next one. He only called on the dealers who had a good
rating in the jeweler's rating book, the Bradstreet of this
business. They were the only ones Finkel dared trust,
those that were rated, quick pay. On this account he
could call upon only two or three stores in a town, and
then must move to the next place. Business was not
good in New England. It would be better to get out in
the middle west, business would surely be better there.

In this New England territory his commissions
amounted to very little more than the amount of his

drawing account. He needed the whole hundred for expenses. Trains, hotels, liquor, dances. He stopped at only the best hotels. This gave him the air of a highclass salesman, which he needed to sell highclass goods to highclass customers.

In the seed business he had been lower down in the social scale of travelling men, now he was nearer the top. At the bottom of the scale were the specialty salesmen, with cocked derby hats, horseshoe tie pins, who sold, say, five dollar adding machines to country merchants, or some other similar product. Then came the tobacco salesmen, with their little Ford trucks to carry the stuff directly to the dealer. His seed job had been better than this. Then the men who sold roofing materials, paints, etc. At the top of the scale were the bond salesmen and the fine jewelry men from recognized important wholesale jewelry firms. He wanted to be one of these though he knew he belonged in the strata below.

He couldn't work Saturdays, found the stores were always too busy, and besides, no other salesmen did this. Why should he? He even found it a little hard to work Mondays, the buyer would generally be late to work on Monday, or not in a mood to buy. But he tried to put in a little time on this day, enough time to ease his conscience.

Now Winfield thought he must write and tell his parents he was on the road and not in college. He hated to do it. The lectures he had heard, the few, had not been especially interesting and he was sorry he ever started going to them.

He wrote home.

A few days later his father wrote him and said he was glad Winfield had gone to work again. He might as well waste a whole year as two thirds of a year. They wished he would settle down to something. Even work in a factory was better than this constant changing of schools and jobs. Next year your mother wants you to go to school at Michigan. They considered at home that he had completely wasted a year, in being so self willed. It had been a bad thing to let him have so much leeway. Ever since you went away from highschool you have been different. Mother is worried about it. You should think of her feelings.

The letter made Winfield feel bad. They could have cut him off without money and forced him to go home, but had always given in and sent him what he asked for. Now they wanted him to go to Michigan.

Never go to that damned place, he thought. After being in the east, none of this fresh water stuff. Sooner die than go to Michigan. Besides, what about that drinking episode at Ward Howe's fraternity house. They've got my name on the college books already. Probably kick me out in no time, if I ever went there. No, any place but Michigan. I'll stay in the jewelry business. When I get in the middle west making money it'll be fine. Maybe start something myself. I could run a pearl firm myself, or rings. Novelty men's rings, with big stones, semiprecious stones in them. Get in business for myself and make a cleaning.

When I'm thirtyfive I ought to have a half million, if I really work. If a man worked like I could, he could have that much easy. Just set your mind on it and say, I'm going out and get it. The people always waiting to be fooled, want to spend their money, just have to get the right article and you can sell it to anybody. What good do colleges ever do anybody? Those fellows in Washington will never be anything but clerks. I'm doing a damned sight better than they ever will, right now. A hundred a week isn't so little. How many people make that? And I can make more than that. Just wait until I get into the middle west.

Winfield wanted to tell somebody all about it and couldn't very well write to his father or mother, they would just smile. Young kid with such big ideas. He'd have to live a while first.

He thought of Christabel Thompson. He hadn't written to her for two months and she didn't know what he was doing. He wrote to her.

She answered with a warm, friendly letter, which made him love her as he had before. He answered, writing a love letter, telling her how he longed for her out here in a strange hotel, nights, with nobody to talk to. He had been loving her ever since that night they walked in the moonlight, only he hadn't dared to tell. She answered his letter, ending hers with the words, with love. Oh, what a difference that made. He knew she loved him. No girl would write that if it wasn't true, they were all afraid to give themselves away like that if it wasn't true.

He wanted to see her.

In May Finkel and Blum called Winfield back to New York. His sample line was renewed, clean boxes for the Sunbeam Pearls, and a few new grades of pearl strings were added to the line. Fancy gold and platinum clasps to fasten the strings together around the neck. His samples had that distinguished, highclass look. Much better now than when he started into New England. They sent him to the middle west. He was to call in all the cities over thirty thousand population in five states. Ohio, Indiana, Michigan, Kentucky, and Illinois. He listened to another final service talk by Finkel. Practically the same thing he had heard before. Then he left New York.

Business was better here but he worked less and made very little above the hundred dollars of his drawing account. In Cincinnati he was sick for four days, all the money going out and no business. Once in a while he sold a large order and then didn't work for a day.

If I made fifty dollars yesterday, why should I work today? And he also felt that a bottle of booze would not be too much of a luxury after a good day's work. The expenses stayed about equal to the income. And once in a while he went to dances, picked up girls, bought them drinks. Once he gave a cheap pearl string from his sample line to a girl for favors from her.

In Evansville, Indiana, he met a young Jewish salesman of women's underclothing, a young gogetter, working for a Chicago ladies outfitting firm. He called his line Jewish hardware, so many of his coreligionists were in the business.

Winfield and this fellow went to a dance near Evansville in a public park, a miniature Coney Island, and they picked up two girls, took them back to the city and walked the streets with them, kissing now and then and passing dirty stories back and forth. They told the girls about their work and the cities they had been in. The Jewish boy promised his girl a silk chemise for her favors. He told the girl to go next day to a big department store in the city and ask for Mr Hastings, the store manager.

Tell him that Mr Gerson, of Simons Company Incorporated, sent you there to get a package he left. A silk chemise. Mr Hastings will give it to you. I told him a girl would be in.

Winfield didn't know whether the girl was foolish enough to go, but he did think it a dirty trick on Gerson's part. What would the girl feel like in that store? Gerson didn't even sell them anything and besides, his firm wasn't Simons Company Incorporated. There wasn't any such firm. Winfield and his girl said good night to the other couple and walked toward the outskirts of the city. The girl expected something to happen, but Winfield didn't want anything. He just wanted a kiss or two, that was all he wanted. They stopped in a dark place under some thick leafy trees. He kissed her a few times on the lips. She seemed dirty to him. He didn't even enjoy kissing her.

—I guess I got to be getting home. I got to go to Louisville, tomorrow morning early. My hotel is a long way from here too.

—I'm tired myself.

She knew he didn't want her.

—I got to be home. My mother will wonder where I am. She makes us girls get in pretty early and it's late now. I'll get a calling down I guess.

Next day in Louisville he got two letters from Christabel. She was going home for the summer vacation. Would he be able to come and visit them?

They would be in Marine City all summer. Swimming,
boating, and a good time. He could stay with a boy
friend who lived there, Raymond Brown. She knew he
had an extra bed and would be glad to put Winfield up
for a few days. And she was so anxious to see Winfield.
The letters were signed, with love, again.

He was going to Indianapolis next week. Might
run up to Marine City from there. He wrote that she
might expect him within two weeks, or three at the
latest....

He decided he must see her and kiss her. Make
love to her. Now he could do it. She had just as much
as said she loved him. He was sorry he had kissed that
girl in Evansville the day before. She wasn't worth it.
That would make Christabel pretty sore, he thought.

Business was good in Louisville. He planned to
stay there at least a week. He met some travelling men,
good fellows, who always had their hooch and knew
how to get it. Good stuff too. Two of these fellows
asked him to their room. The three drank together and
then somebody suggested shooting craps. Winfield
thought he suggested it himself first, but changed his
mind later. They got the dice out of a travelling bag.
Each man looked at them carefully. Winfield faced
the fives and turned them slowly, this was the way to
tell if they were a genuine pair. He picked them up
and turned them slowly with one eye partly closed,
professional like, to see if the dots matched all around.
Made him feel like a real crap shooter. He had seen
the niggers in Washington doing this. Rather silly,

but makes you look as if you knew the game. In a half
hour he lost sixty dollars. They seemed to know how to
make the things talk. Could make them turn any way
they wanted to.

None of this stuff for me, he thought.

—Well fellows, you got me all right. I'm cleaned.

—Got you? Hell. You don't think anything's
wrong with them dice do you?

—No. Who said anything about the dice? I said
you beat me. I'm done, that's all I said. You fellows
know the game. I got to quit. Thanks for the liquor,
you can pay for it now. So long.

And he went away sheepish, beaten. They had the
things loaded all right. Sixty dollars isn't any small sum.
Jesus, I got to sell six hundred dollars to make that up.
Good God, I ought to know better. Damned crooks.

He wished he might get revenge, beat them in
some other thing. But what the hell could I do? Beat
them in a swimming contest, that's all I could beat
anybody at. Dirty bums. Jesus, that's Hell. No more
craps for me.

He went to his own room, wrote in a note
book, If I ever play craps again twenty dollars goes to
Christabel. Signed, Winfield Payne.

I guess I ought to run around with somebody like
that Bloomer fellow. He's a good chap. These damned
drummer cheap tobacco men, they're no damned good.
That Bloomer was a fine fellow.

Bloomer was the son of a jeweler to whom
Winfield had sold a big order of goods. The young man
would have liked to be on the road himself and talked to
Winfield for a long time, asked him to go to a baseball

game, wanted to have a longer talk with him. Next day Winfield called on him in the store and they went that afternoon to a ballgame. In the evening they decided to go to a public dance.

At the dance they met three sisters from a bourgeois Louisville family. They were at the dance alone, waiting for men to ask them for dances. One of the sisters was tall and liked Winfield because he was so tall himself.

—You're the first man I've danced with tonight that was taller than I am. You're a good dancer, she said.

Bloomer danced with the other smaller sisters, and so did Winfield, once or twice. The next day was Sunday. The girls asked them to call in the afternoon, they would go for a ride in the girls' car, out into the country.

After leaving, Bloomer and Winfield talked them over. Pretty good stuff. Ought to be able to get them all right. That tall one likes you, Payne. She told me she did. She's pretty good stuff. You're sitting pretty.

Winfield was too much in love with Christabel to care a great deal about these girls. He did like to dance with them, but beyond that he didn't want to go.

—Yes, they're good stuff all right. The little ones are the best though. The big one is too damned big. I always liked them smaller. Pick them up and throw them into the air, you know. Put them on your lap too. The little ones are fun to play with. Take a big thing like that, she's too big, heavy. Can't do anything much with her. A long board makes a good teeter though. I never thought that, much, though. I like them small.

—Well, we'll see what happens tomorrow. I'll be at the hotel about three o'clock and then we'll go to their place.

The girls lived in a small yellow frame house on the outskirts of the city. A few flowers, weedy, uncared for, grew around the front porch. A cane porch swing, a table and a couple of chairs were scattered, careless, on the porch. The Sunday paper was strewn around.

Winfield and Bloomer walked onto the porch, rang the doorbell and waited until the oldest of the three, the big girl, opened the screendoor, greeted them, asked them sit down.

—The girls will be right down. Powdering their noses. Hee, hee, she giggled.

No sign of parents around.

—Where are your folks? Got the place all to yourselves? Winfield asked the question and gave a meaning look to Bloomer. The prospect was pretty good. Wouldn't need the automobile.

What kind of a car you got? asked Bloomer.

—Oh, we got an old Peerless. The old man won't buy a new tub. Can't get him to. The old thing puffs along though. It's too heavy. Regular tub, really. I drive it. We'll take a ride when the girls get down. They'll be here in a minute.

—Peerless is a good car. Those old cars are better than the new ones. Better stuff in them. Why I've seen some of those old cars that would outdo anything. Now a friend of mine, for instance, he's got an old Cadillac, four cylinders. But say, it sure does go. Goes all the time. Those old cars. Well I'll bet that thing of yours is all right. This from Bloomer.

—Oh, yes, it's a good one. You'll see. Kinda shot now though. Told the old gent he'd have to buy a new one.

Winfield wondered what the old gent did for a living. Looked respectable this house, the auto and all that. The girls though, they weren't exactly what you would call bluebloods. Had good clothes, looked pretty good too, but rather wild, impulsive girls. Probably always had their own way. No brothers and three girls. Probably the folks weren't very strict, probably never had been very strict, else these girls wouldn't have been at that dance alone that way.

It looked funny to Winfield. In Benton girls like that acted more respectable. Might be the effect of the whiskey business down here. Used to be a lot of it made here. Perhaps it's the horse races. The girls talked about the races. Made the people a bit loose, racing, whiskey, and all.

Another boy appeared on the scene. The girls had invited him to go along that afternoon. He met Winfield and Bloomer with a glad to meet you, good day ain't it. Then turned to the girl. Spoke to her friendly, Hello Grace, what you been up to? Got a swell dress on. Where did you get that?

He wanted the new boys to see that he was an old established friend of the family. Belonged, whereas they were new, not yet tested. He asked personal questions about the other girls. Show them fellows I know them all. When he thought he had convinced them he turned to them.

—Good weather. Good day for a drive. You a salesman?

—Yes, I sell Sunbeam pearls, on the road.

—I guessed it. You don't look like most of them though. Grace kinda goes in for that, don't you Grace? He was a little too fresh.

Don't be a smarty, she answered.

Winfield sat in the front seat with Grace. She was driving. The other four were in the back, arms twined around each other. The car was old, heavy, bulky, clumsy old thing, but it seemed to go along as well as any.

They drove far out into the Kentucky hills, stopped at a roadside hotel, drank some nearbeer and turned back. The brakes were faulty and Winfield had to pull back the emergency brake handle when they went down hills. The foot brake barely had any effect.

Darkness was coming on. They stopped, lit the old fashioned gas lamps and went on. Coming to the top of a long hill the girl driving let the engine slow down and stop, when she was changing into a lower gear. The car started backward. Winfield grabbed the steering wheel. Twisted it around. The car backed into the ditch beside the road and stopped. Everybody was frightened. The two girls in the back seat screamed, short, stifled screams.

God damn those brakes. I couldn't see anything, Grace said.

—Say that's kinda dangerous, let me tell you. We might have gone down that damned hill on our heads. I don't like this at all. No brakes. This from Winfield.

Another car came up to them. Four sailors in it. One of them, an officious, help every body, goodnatured sort of fellow, jumped out of the car.

—What's the matter? Your lights are going out.
What you lying there in the ditch for.

The lights going out? Oh, Jesus, said Grace. Now
the damned lights are out. What are we going to do?
The old man will be as sore as hell. Told me to be home
before dark too. Might have known there wasn't any
gas in that tank. Ought to have electric lights anyhow.
Say, I'm not going to drive this thing. I'm scared of it.
Getting loose that way.

What's the matter? the sailor asked again.

Well look and see, she said. The brakes are no
good. We can't go down that next hill like this.

—Oh, that's easy. I'll take her down for you. I
know those cars. Used to be a mechanic. Can't fool me
when it comes to an old Peerless. They'll go any place.

Winfield, Grace, and one of her sisters sat in the
back seat. The other sister sat in front beside the sailor.
Bloomer and the boy friend of the three sisters stood
on the running boards to see that the car didn't get too
near the ditches on either side. It was a long hill, no
fun going down it.

I'd rather walk, thought Winfield. No use being
foolish. Still I guess that guy can drive. The emergency
brake is still good. No danger.

The sailor started, the car went over the top of
the hill and carefully started down the other side. The
three fellows he had been with were already nearly
at the bottom of the hill, nearly to the place where
the road was fenced by white picket fences, fences to
keep the cars from going over down the twenty feet of
embankment on either side. They were going slowly,

waiting for their friend to pilot the clumsy car down the hill. After that the girl could drive herself. No more hills going into Louisville.

I've driven a car since I was twelve, but I'm scared of this thing, Winfield said. Grace nodded her head, assenting. She was frightened herself. That fellow can do it if he wants to, not for me. Jesus, it's going too fast. Tell him to slow her down. No use hurrying down hill.

The sailor couldn't slow the car. It was too heavy, the brakes were too weak, he just had to let it go. He was more frightened now than anyone in the party. Tried to throw the gear into low, that would slow it some. Going too fast, gears just rasped and shrieked, grinding.

Jesus, what did I drive this thing for? Tub. God damn it. Hurry up you bastards up ahead. I'll lam into you. Hurry, for Christ sakes. We're going to die. Jesus, you fellows, Hurry up ahead. Got to hit you or the fence, can't get between. God, what did I do it for. We'll get it. We'll get it. Going too damned fast. Can't stop her. Can't stop her. Look out you fellows on the side. Look out. You'll get it.

Bang, crash, rip, thump. The car ran into the fence. Knocked down five fence posts. Broke the windshield into bits. Threw glass. Stopped dead.

—Where's Bloomer, Where's Bloomer?

It was Winfield calling. His friend had been thrown clear of the car, over the fence, into the ditch below.

Dead silence. Then a groan from below, I'm dying. God. Bleeding to death.

Both girls in the back seat with Winfield fainted. The girl in front jumped out of the car, screamed, Help, murder, dying, oh, help.

The boy who had been on the left side standing on the running board groaned, Oh, God, he's got it. Shook his hands and stood still.

Winfield retched, God, I know his father. He's my friend. My friend. Not yours, you whores. My friend, customer. God Almighty.

He ran from the car down the embankment, saw Bloomer lying there. Struck a match. Legs cut almost off, just below the hips. God Almighty.

Bloomer spoke, God, Winfield I'm bleeding to death.

The fact that he could talk steadied Winfield. He tore the arms from his shirt and tried to bandage the legs, tried to remember what the Boy Scouts did. Tourniquet. Something with a stick. No sticks around here. He simply tied the bandages as tight as he could. Then called out, Come here and help, you sonsofbitches. Help get him. There isn't any time for monkeywork. Hurry up. Can't you see? For God's sake.

A Ford had stopped by the wreck. The man rushed down, helped Winfield carry the wounded boy up the embankment, put him in the back seat of the Ford.

Winfield told the man, Get to a doctor, he's dying. Legs cut damned near off.

Winfield was half insane, hardly knew what he was doing. He got in the back seat, forgot the girls, the car. That sailor? He's gone, run away. Sneak. Scared. Dirty louse.

The sailor fearing Bloomer was killed had run away. Didn't want to get in any mixups while he was on a furlough. Told the fellows, get out quick. He felt exactly like a murderer running away. Thought he had killed the boy. Jesus, got to get out quick.

Poor simp, dirty bum, should have stuck around.

They hurried to a hospital. Doctors came out, carried Bloomer into the operating room. Winfield went along and stood there. Then sat down, waiting. Would get over it? They stitched the boy's legs. Ought to cut them off though. Way down to the bone. Cut on a barbed wire fence, he had been thrown against a fence.

Didn't see any fence around, said Winfield.

Winfield sat a while, then walked up and down the room. There were the bloody clothes.

—I could puke, Jesus.

The doctor walked up to him. We got him fixed now, you better get to sleep. Look white as the devil.

—Fixed up, got him fixed? Winfield fainted.

They called a taxi, took him to his hotel, put him to bed. All next day he was in bed. Nightmares, automobiles running down hills, wild rides, down hills. Crashes. Night sweats, nervous sweats, he had had them before. Too highstrung.

Poor Bloomer, thought Winfield. What will his father say? Lay it to me if he dies. Lay it to me. Those girls. If they were only decent girls. I can't see the old man, he'd kill me. God he'd think I did it.

The very thought of seeing the father of Bloomer frightened him. I can't do it, he said. And then he thought of going down a hill. It made him sick, sick to his stomach. And the blood. If he dies? God.

The following morning he went to the hospital. Saw Bloomer. He was pale, bloodless, but looked cheerful.

Don't worry Payne, I'll come through. My father just left. He's all right. Say, I told him the girls were decent. Don't let him know. They weren't bad girls, were they Payne? Winfield, were they? I told him, good family, you know. Tell him, will you? Doctor said I'd get out. Be lame though. It's hell, be lame. But not awful lame. Will be able to walk all right. Walk around lame. Thought I would die sure. The girls been damned nice. Came over. Flowers there from the girls. Nice to me. Come again Payne. I like you. You're white. Say, the sailor came over. He was nice. Flowers there from the sailor, those, there. He was sorry. Wasn't his fault. I felt sorry for him. Took it hard, he did. Came yesterday afternoon. Nice fellow, the sailor.

Winfield was sorry he had forgotten flowers. I'll send them this afternoon.

—I'm glad you're better. I'll see you day after tomorrow. Got to go to work Lexington tomorrow. Be back day after tomorrow. Got to hurry my work. Didn't work yesterday. See you then. Get better. Glad it's no worse. You look better than I thought you would. Glad it's all right.

But Winfield felt that it wasn't all right. He was too pale, Bloomer. Too white in the lips. No blood. That was awful.

Leaving the hospital, a doctor told him they feared only gangrene. Possibly it might set in. Deep wound.

Not much time to clean it right. Had to go right to work on him. Too bad for the boy. Be lame.

Winfield ordered some flowers to be sent to the Hospital, Catholic Hospital. Sacred Heart, Harry Bloomer.

He went back to the hotel, upset, shaky, packed and took the first train to Lexington. Next day he did a little business and went back to Louisville that night. Called the hospital. Bloomer was dead. Gangrene.

God, I knew it, Jesus. Got to see his father. What'll he say? I can't go.

But he did go, went to the father's house.

Bloomer's sister, nice girl, fourteen, highschool girl Winfield could have loved a girl like that. He felt sorry for her. She came to the door.

—I'm Winfield Payne. I'm the boy that was with your brother. Went to the hospital with Harry. I'm awful sorry about it all. It's too bad, cut off that way.

Tears formed in her eyes. I'll call father. He would like to talk to you. Poor man, he's all broken up about it. Mother died last year. Harry was going into the business. Father's a wreck. Were they good girls? I couldn't stand it. You're the boy? Father would like to see you.

Father, she called into the house.

Mr Bloomer came out on the porch. You the boy? He shook hands very weakly with Winfield.

I'm sorry Mr Bloomer. It was too bad. I liked him better than any of my friends too. Was a fine man. Would have been a fine man. He and I were friends. I'm sorry. Did all they could, I guess.

He was a good boy, said Bloomer. Fine boy. You're
the fellow? You an actor? Said in the paper, actor. No
actors.

—No, I'm a salesman. I sold some pearls to your
store. Don't you remember when I came in? Sunbeam
pearls.

—Oh yes, I'm glad. Pearls. Yes, I do remember.
How did I get the idea? An actor. All I wonder, were
those girls good girls? They sent him flowers. Were
pleasant girls. I thought they were good. Hope so. It's
too bad. If they're not good girls. He was a good boy.
Would have taken his second degree in a week. Studying
hard. Always worked hard, the boy. Going to be a
Mason. Was studying hard for it. The Masons will bury
him anyway. He started in six months ago. Working
hard. Second degree. Only next week. Ought to be in
the paper. Catholics all right. Treated him good. Never
liked the Catholics before. Sisters very good though.
Catholics good people.

I'll write a story Mr Bloomer. I used to be a
newspaperman.

Winfield felt easier. The talk with Mr Bloomer was
not so difficult as he had thought it would be. But he
had heard all he could bear. Too hard on the nerves, all
that about young Bloomer.

He asked for facts of his life, and bid the father
and sister good bye. He couldn't be there for the
funeral, must go. Work and all. Was awfully sorry.

He went from their home to the newspaper
office, introduced himself as a former Washington
correspondent, wrote the story himself. A story to please
the father and sister. Left the office, went to the hotel

and tried to sleep. Thought the whole thing over. His stomach felt weak. Going down hill like that. He never wanted to see an automobile again.

Next day he ordered a large, expensive bunch of flowers to be sent for the funeral. Then he left Louisville and went to Indianapolis. Louisville looked too much like death now. Everything there reminded him of death. I've got to forget it, it makes me crazy. Young fellow dying that way. Awful thing.

Winfield went to Indianapolis. Business was not as good here as it had been in Louisville. He couldn't seem to keep his enthusiasm up to its old pitch. His sales talk sounded hollow. He kept thinking of running wild down hill, and of blood. There was a stain of it left on his wrist watch. He couldn't get it off. He removed the wrist watch, put it away in his travelling bag.

He called on store after store with very little success. In one very fine shop he told a man all about the pearls, how they were made, what made one more beautiful than another, how these pearls were better than any others because they were made by a special painstaking process. It was old stuff, this talk. He used it every place, buyers swallowed it whole too. At least they let on that they did.

This time though, the fellow said, my boy, you've got a good line of talk. But I know that stuff. All comes out of the same barrel. One is just like the other. You can't pull that stuff on me. Ha, ha, thought you had me hey? I know pearls. Seen them made. In France once. You got a good line of talk though, go to it. I can't use your stuff.

And after he had let Winfield talk for a full fifteen minutes. It was a little too much, this assurance, this insult.

Calling me a liar huh? Hell, he could have said something before.

Go to hell, said Winfield, and walked out of the store. He didn't feel like selling pearls anyway, and after this he couldn't call on another store. He went back to the hotel room, smoked a cigarette, thought of Louisville, Bloomer. Had to go down in the lobby, couldn't stand it in that room alone.

He bought some corn whiskey from a bellboy, went back to the room, ordered grapejuice, mixed the two liquids and drank deeply. He felt better. Thought he would loaf around town that day. Still very depressed though. Even worse someways. It was awful, alone this way. Thinking always, today Bloomer will be buried. I couldn't have stuck it out there. Good thing I left Louisville. If there was only somebody to talk to. This being alone was the worst part of it. If he had a friend in Indianapolis. He walked to the hotel bar where James Whitcomb Riley used to hang out. He had heard that the old bartender was there, some dirty poetry by Riley was supposed to be down in the bar. He might get a chance to talk with the bartender. It was a soft drink and icecream place now. Girl waitresses too. No sign of any dirty poetry around the walls.

Must have been mistaken. Guess I'll write to Christabel. She owes me a letter though. No, I'll write to her, like to see her, wish she were here. I ought to go and see her, she wants me to.

Back in his room he took another drink and wrote
a long love letter to Christabel. I'm so lonely. Had an
awful experience in Louisville. Feel terrible after it. Like
to see you. I may be up there before long. I think I'll
take a few days off come up and see you. As he wrote
the letter the determination to go to Marine City and
see Christabel grew. I'll be there day after tomorrow,
day after you get this letter. Meet me at the train with a
kiss. I'll expect it. He sent the letter special delivery.

Then he wrote to Finkel, told him he was feeling
on the rocks. Going to take three or four days off.
He sent the orders he had taken in Louisville and in
Indianapolis to the firm.

The next day he went to Detroit, telegraphed to
Christabel that he would arrive in Marine City next
morning at eleven, interurban electric cars. Meet me.

It was only five in the afternoon. He wished he
had gone straight to Marine City. Here I got to stick
around this place all night now. He knew some people
there but didn't want to see them. They would tell his
folks he was seen in Detroit and they would wonder
why he didn't come home and see them, so near home
there in Detroit. He didn't want to see his folks.

He walked up and down Woodward avenue. Saw a
copy of the complete verse of Kipling.

Ought to buy that book, he thought. Some good
stuff to learn. I'd like to know that one about learning
about women from her. Great stuff to recite to the
boys. He bought the book and went back to the hotel.
Learned the verse by heart. Might recite it in Marine
City at a party or something. People like to hear good

stuff like that. It makes a hit. He learned several others
also. Boots, Danny Dever and such.

Good stuff, Kipling and Service. Nobody likes to
hear that stuff we read in highschool anyway. No use
learning it. Good poetry though, I guess. Like the stuff
Raymond Lankin wrote. Didn't sound like much.

In bed with the lights out he thought of
Christabel. He should have gone on. Stopping here
wasting time this way. He felt his heart beat faster
than it ought to. Jesus, she's probably thinking about
me too. Lying there in bed. I'd like to have her here.
Damned good girl, Christabel. Wonderful girl. Got lots
of brains. Reads good books. I ought to read more. I
guess those Wellesley girls learn a lot. Real people too.
I got all that newspaper experience back of me though.
Pretty good to be a newspaper man like that. Tomorrow
I'll kiss her when I get off the car. I'll bet she'll just turn
her head away. That would be awful though. Said she
loved me. Ought to kiss me, just coming in like that.
Haven't seen her since last Thanksgiving. She's a pretty
girl all right.

Winfield slept lightly that night, anxious for the
morning, anxious to get to Marine City and get that
kiss. Glad I wrote her to kiss me that way. Hope she
does it. Ought to.

He had forgotten Bloomer.

Next day on the interurban electric train he was
even more excited. Wish we would get there. He read
some of the poems in his new book, but read them
without interest. The whole scene of the accident went
through his mind again. He shuddered. God, I got to
forget that.

He thought of Christabel. Soon be there. He got up, took his luggage in his hands, walked to the end of the car. Coming into Marine City now. The salt factory, main street, then the station.

There was Christabel. Looked as she had in Washington. Same damned dress. Can you beat it?

—Hello Chris.

He was beaming, excited. Will she kiss me?

—Oh, Winnie.

She threw her arms around his neck, up around his neck, on her tiptoes. Kissed him on the lips unembarrassed. Winfield was embarrassed, shy. First kiss. Damned good sport, Christabel. I like her a lot.

Walking to her house she told him people probably saw them do that. Small town like this. But I don't care. I guess I've got a right to do that. How have you been Winfield? Tell me all about yourself.

Winfield stammered a little talking. Exciting this thing. Meeting your sweetheart like that. He felt selfconscious walking up the hill to her home.

—It's good to see you Chris. How are your folks?

He met the Thompsons. They talked for a few minutes and then had lunch together. Rather embarrassing all this. Winfield was careful to be a gentleman all the time, here in their house. It was new for him. If he had known the people better. Why he didn't even know Christabel very well. Not as he knew girls in Benton. This was different, and her parents too, seemed different people. They made him feel selfconscious sitting there at table. Hard to talk to them all. Christabel seemed miles away, even after that kiss. It hadn't broken down any barriers between them. Left

them as they had been before, at least as far as Winfield
was concerned. He would never have the nerve to kiss
her again that way, unless maybe when he left. Then
he'd make her kiss him.

After the meal, Christabel and Winfield walked to
the boy friend's house. Winfield left his baggage there
after he had met the fellow. They were going to the
country club, the golf club, to dance that night. That
would be fine. Winfield liked to dance with Christabel,
hold her tight, dancing with her.

Christabel and Winfield talked all afternoon, sat
in an icecream parlor for a short time, walked up the
river, back to the house, went to meet a girl friend of
Christabel. Nice girl, Winfield thought. He felt more at
ease with this girl around, talked freer. It made lots of
difference. But Christabel didn't like it as well as being
alone with him. Thought he was paying more attention
to that other girl, Mildred Jenkins, than he should.
She was a little jealous. She told Winfield that Mildred
was engaged to the boy he was to stay with, the fellow
he had met just after lunch. Christabel wanted more
attention, but Winfield was just too afraid to give it.
He couldn't talk to her as well as he could write. It was
like in Washington. He was just sort of tonguetied
around her, that was it.

They danced at the country club. Winfield felt
better here. More people around. He felt easier with
Christabel too. Dancing with her. He told her he loved
her.

—I love you Chris. Honest to God I do. I knew it
all the time. You know that stuff I wrote you in those
letters. Well, it's true.

She held him a little closer dancing. Said nothing
though. She loved him too, or thought she did. Liked
him a lot anyway. Between dances he talked glibly with
the fellows he had met there. One of them offered him
a drink. They walked around behind the club house.
He drank deeply, coughed, gagged on the raw whiskey.
Raw Canadian Whiskey, smuggled across the river.

Back on the dance floor he did a shimmy dance
for them, a short dance. He recited some Uncle
Wiggley stories. He was feeling good now, only still shy
of Christabel.

I must love her to beat hell, the way she makes me
feel. I choke when I try to talk to her. Can't talk at all.
Why, if I didn't love her I'd be spreading an awful line.

She was dancing with another fellow. He asked the
Jenkins girl to dance. Felt at ease with her.

—Say, you know, I love Chris. She's the finest girl
I ever knew. I hope she knows it. You tell her will you?
She'll believe it if you tell her.

Mildred Jenkins said she would whisper it to
Chris. I guess she loves you too. All excited. Never
saw her this way before. Look how she's watching us.
Jealous I guess. That's silly.

But Winfield was watching her too, smiling at her
every chance he had. After the dance he went back to
her, talked, and then danced with her.

—Gee, but it's wonderful to be here Chris. What
I've been dreaming about.

After the dance they were going for a ride. Have
to go back to town and get the Jenkins car though.
One of the boys took Mildred Jenkins and her fiancé,
Raymond Brown, the fellow Winfield was staying with,

into his car, then called to Christabel. Told her to come out. You too, Payne. Hurry up.

The two couples sat in the rear seat of the car. Winfield and Christabel were last to get in. Christabel had to sit on his lap. Her face was level with his and her lips near his lips. It was easy. He just moved his face towards hers, kissed her. She parted her lips a little, the embrace lasted long. Winfield was left shaky, it was too much. He expected it to be a little, sisterly kiss, not a real, deep, long kiss like that one. And it had been so easy. He couldn't believe it. He had planned and planned. How can I kiss her? And here it was, just natural. He felt bound to her from that moment, loved her madly. He wanted her really, but wanted only her kisses consciously. She was too good a girl for more than that. He couldn't go all the way with her.

Wonderful loving though, nice girl like that. He thought, never in my whole life have I loved like this, Dorothy Jefferson not in it at all. It's too perfect. God, to think of it. How I've thought of this moment. After rehearsing, he told her that seriously, believing it. It was true too, it was the Gospel truth at that moment. He couldn't love more than he loved her without breaking. Impossible.

I love you Winnie, she said, and kissed him. That was all she said, I love you. But it was enough. Winfield couldn't stand any more. He was keyed up so high, had been for days. Accident and all. And now his emotions were at their highest point before breaking. He could go so far and no further up the emotional scale, then he would come to the breaking point. He thought he had reached the top, but he hadn't.

Riding toward town, toward the Jenkins' home, kissing, he cut her underlip with his teeth. A jolt of the car caused it.

Oh, she said. My lip's cut.

He was sorry, hurt, sorry. But he kissed the lip tenderly. Drank in the blood from her cut lips. Excited. Delicious blood. Oh God, how weak he felt, used up. She was too wonderful.

I never imagined anything, he talked on.

In the Jenkins car, they loved, legs tight against legs, arms wrapped convulsively about one another. And kisses. Long, drinking, awful, kisses. Maddening. He couldn't draw her close enough to him, loving her this way. It wasn't enough. But the thought of going with her, of taking her to himself, never entered his mind. At least he didn't consider it, if the thought did enter his mind.

She was too nice. Couldn't do that with a nice girl. He wouldn't have done it had she asked him to, and she would never ask him to do it. Nice girls. That would be impossible. But not so impossible morally for her. More impossible on account of children. Might have children. That was it with Christabel more than the morals. With Winfield though, it was the other way. A fellow couldn't take a nice girl that way, cheapen her that way. But he didn't think so very much about it, too enveloped in her arms, kisses, legs, to think about it. She satisfied him just loving him this way. She was so wild, natural, insatiable. Warm early summer evening, perspiration, faces slippery with sweat, sliding one on the other. Lips, slippery, wet, against one another. Hard, cruel kisses. Warm.

Christabel tried to talk, tell him how she loved
him. Never knew what love was.

—Oh, I'm crazy Winfield. You're killing me
Winfield. It's too wonderful.

And her voice was only a whisper, harsh whisper.
Her voice lost in passion, she whispered harsh to him.

—I can't talk.

And she kissed him again and again. There in the
rear seat of the Jenkins car.

Raymond Brown told Winfield he would wait
for him. Leave a light so he could find the room when
he came home. Christabel and Winfield tiptoed into
the living room of the Thompson home. Sat on the
davenport. More loving. More intense than in the car,
undisturbed. Only they must be quiet. He kissed her
breasts. She cried, passionate. He felt of her legs around
the knees. He didn't dare feel more of her. Both were
lost in passion. Hot, sweaty, weakening. Time went
rapidly by. He must go. Father and mother would
wonder why they were up so late. On the front porch
more kisses. He held her body tight to his. Felt all of
her against him, warm. And kissed her, long kisses.

—Good night.

He started down the steps. She called him,
Winfield, Winfield.

He went back, embraced, kissed, broke away again.
Three times. She was weeping, couldn't talk above a
harsh whisper, voice lost. Winfield. Oh, Winfield.

He left the house. She stayed on the porch, head
in her hands, till he was out of sight in the night, the
darkness. Then she went into the house, quietly to her

room, quietly to bed, thought of Winfield, what love, what it is. And then slept. Tired sleep. Heavy sleep.

Winfield walked to Brown's house. No lights. Two o'clock. Surely ought to be home. Said he would leave a light. God, I'm weak. Dead. What a girl. Brown must be doing what Christabel and I were. Jenkins girl, nice kid. Jesus, I love Christabel. She didn't want me to go. That was wonderful. Loves me, can see that. Never had anything like that before. I didn't either. Awful. God, we were hot.

He sat on the porch, rain started falling. He waited for Brown to come home. Streets dead silent. Only the rain, sleepy rain, sleepy Winfield. Green leaves under electric street lamps. Rain. Sitting on the small front porch waiting anxious to get in bed, sleep. Three o'clock.

Brown must be home. Too late now.

He tried the door. Unlocked. Groped his way to the staircase, walked up, stumbled. Awful noise, still house. Found Brown's room, his room. Struck a match. There was Brown asleep in bed.

—Hello Brown. I waited on the porch an hour. Thought you were still out. No light.

—Thought you would come up. Sorry Payne. Bed's all ready. Got pajamas?

—Yes, turn in now. Christabel is a wonder Brown. Never loved a girl so much. Wouldn't have thought it four years ago.

—She loves you, I guess. Never saw her carry on that way before. Fred Zeller went around with her. Never had the necking you got tonight. Don't go all the way Payne. Good girl. She's impulsive. Would do it.

God, you two were wrapped in a ball back there. Don't go too far. Got to be careful. Glad you love her. Be awful. Mildred said so. Be careful.

—Don't worry, I know how to treat a girl. I like her too much.

He thought of Kipling. Couldn't do such, loved her too much. It's true, love them too much. Kipling's right.

He went to bed and to sleep, still aching. Love. Couldn't get enough of it. Wonderful girl, fine family, fine girl. Best I ever had. Think of it, all that we did. Could have done anything. She'd let me. Never saw a girl like that before.

Next morning he had breakfast with Brown, met his mother. They talked.

After breakfast, in the room he and Raymond had slept in, he decided he would give Christabel a string of pearls. Couple extra strings in his samples, good ones too. Good present. He thought they were extras. Finkel would never notice it. I'll not say anything to him. Almost time to go to her house. She'll be waiting.

He hated to go. Felt funny after last night. How was she going to greet him? Maybe he shouldn't have gone so far. A little too far, perhaps.

If her father and mother knew about it, they would kick me out quick.

He packed a string of his best grade pearls in a velvet case and went to her home.

She met him at the door. Tired looking. Black hair rather straight this morning. No time to curl it yet. She drew him into the living room. Kissed him hard on the lips.

—Winfield, oh, Winfield. I love you.

He smiled, man fashion, happy. She loved him. Was his now. He patted her gently on the shoulder, drew her close. Kissed her quickly.

—Did your folks hear anything?

—No, didn't say a word. It's all right. We were a bit noisy though.

—I got something for you.

He put the string of pearls around her neck. Thought, hope Finkel doesn't find it out. Guess he doesn't know it was in there. Extra string.

Do you like them Christabel? he asked.

—Oh, Winfield, I love you. Here, let me kiss you. They are wonderful. I love them. From you too. Oh, you're too good. I love you, Winfield.

She took him in another room where her mother was sitting, reading the morning paper. They exchanged greetings.

—Look mother, from Winnie.

—Oh, my, isn't that nice? Too nice for my little girl.

She got up from the chair, rested the pearls carefully under the fingers of her left hand. Her right arm went around Christabel, she kissed her daughter. Then she smiled at Winfield.

It looked strange to Winfield. Funny, a mother acting that way. Might have thought that was an engagement ring, the way she acted. Mothers taking things for granted that way. He didn't like it. Looked too thick for him. Mrs Thompson must have known more than the young people thought she knew.

—Gee, Christabel. I'd like that picture of you there. He pointed to a large portrait photograph on top of a bookshelf.

—That's mother's. Could he have it mother?

—Well, that's the only picture I've got of my girl. You'll have to have some more made, Christabel.

She whispered in his ear, I'll get it for you Winnie. Get it tonight or tomorrow, before you go.

In the afternoon Raymond Brown and Mildred Jenkins came to the Thompson's home, asked Winfield and Christabel to go up the river in Brown's canoe. Big safe sailing canoe. Go up to the island. Good day.

They went to the island, were caught in a rain, sat under the canoe. Brown and Winfield built a fire, dried the clothes. Both girls sat in their underclothing. Winfield and Christabel talked only of impersonal things. Not of their love. Talked about their mutual acquaintances. It was as if they had never kissed. Both felt apart. Winfield felt that even more than Christabel. As if he had never kissed her. Wondered if he would even dare start it again. Maybe she hadn't liked it at all. Had to kiss him in the morning, he thought. Might never want to again. Maybe she feels sorry, ashamed of what she did. Wouldn't wonder.

He told them he would surely have to go tomorrow, back to work.

She urged him to stay longer, but he said, no, I've got to work.

That night if Mildred could get her car they would go down to the Flats, a summer resort, and dance. Good music, lots of people. When they were back in Marine City from the canoe trip they had to change their clothes. Winfield shaved and put on dry clothing. After dinner they drove away to the dance.

Winfield wanted to make love to Christabel. He couldn't start though. Didn't know how she might feel.

She wanted to make love herself. Only the powder. Hair all done up nice too. She thought it better not to start anything. Plenty of time coming home. Want to look nice at the dance. Lots of people there, people I know. All the resorters will be there. Detroit people too. Better not kiss till after.

After fifteen minutes Winfield could not hold back longer. Slipped his arm around her waist. She drew away a little. It hurt Winfield.

Doesn't want me to touch her, I guess.

—What's the matter, Christabel?

—Oh, nothing. Winfield give me a kiss. Only easy. Lips, rouge.

Winfield laughed, understood. Vanity, he thought. Kissed her.

Oh, I can fix it when we get there, she said, and kissed him hard. They made love, as they had the night before, but not quite so passionately. Both more careful. Winfield didn't want to muss his suit as he had the night before. They were more reserved, passionate though, just the same.

Outside the dance hall Winfield combed his hair. Christabel went into the ladies room, combed hers. More rouge, powder.

They danced a few times. Anxious to get back in the car. One dance, a fellow Winfield didn't know asked for Christabel, wanted to dance with her. She danced. Winfield was sore. Stood pouting like, at the outside of the ring of onlookers, waiting. He didn't want her dancing with other fellows that way.

Going home they were carefree again, as they had been the night before. The same scene in the living room at her home later. The same good night, her voice lost in whispers. Couldn't talk out loud. But through it all Winfield felt a certain disgust, not much, just a little disgust, at the thing. All this wet kissing, sweat. It was a little disgusting. It had limits too. Strict bounds. Could go only so far with a decent girl. He wanted everything, but wouldn't have even suggested it. She wanted it all even more than he did, but she wouldn't have suggested it.

In his bed that night he thought it was pretty thick, the whole thing. Nothing more left to do, but go all the way. Have to marry for that though.

Next morning he left Marine City. She kissed him good bye, gave him the photograph. They would see each other in two or three weeks. He had to work the state of Michigan and would be through in Ohio and Indiana in two or three weeks.

It was pretty thick. If it ever got out, all they had done, her mother would make them marry.

I don't want to marry. Rather marry her though than most of them. Wouldn't marry anybody now though. Just love them, that's enough. Hope she's that way too. Guess she is. Never said anything about marrying. Have to write her a letter, write her mother too. Thank her for the meals. Bread and butter letter. Got to do it. Never know what to say in those darn letters. Have to write them though. Easier to write

to her, thank both of them. Easier. Have to write her
mother though, it's the way.

He wrote from Indianapolis when he was back
there. A love letter, a rather reserved one, to Christabel,
a note of thanks to Mrs Thompson. Christabel had
already written to him, the letter was there at the hotel.

I love you madly. No one ever made love to me the
way you did. I want only you. Can't sleep any more.
I've got to have you. You're mine, all mine. Without
you life is nothing for me.

Gee, that's a hot letter. Got to be careful, got
to be careful. No telling what a girl, crazy like that,
might do. Can't let things go too far. Makes me kind
of cold, letter like that. Too much. Ought to hold
herself in a little. Scares me. Might have to marry her.
We did make love hot. Too much. I'll have the girl
plumb crazy. Better tame down a little. Hell to have
to marry. Get engaged and all that. Maybe she thinks
I'm engaged to her. Can't let her think that. Tame her
down. Write a letter to her cooler. Let her know I don't
want this thing going too far, like that.

He did write to her. I love you Christabel, but
we have got to be careful. I am not through with my
school yet. I expect to go back again. I can't get in too
deep, it would spoil my whole career. However I love
you.

Something to that effect, the letter.

Christabel was stunned by the letter. She hadn't
asked him to marry her, hadn't thought of it even, just
loved him madly. And then for him to write that way.
It stunned her, chilled her. Her heart seemed broken.
Twisted cruelly. She didn't deserve such a letter. Never

even tried to make him become engaged to her. It was awful, that letter. She had been just made impulsive. Loved him freely, openly. Let her passion loosen itself with him. She loved him. And he thought she was trying to make him marry her.

She wrote to him, a cooler letter. I didn't expect you to marry me, Winfield. How could you say those things to me? I loved you. I never in my life let a man kiss me the way you kissed me.

This letter made Winfield angry. Boylike, he was angry because she made him out to be in the wrong. I in the wrong? he thought.

He wrote again. I guess it's better to forget and not be so crazy. I still love you, but we have got to be careful. You shouldn't have written me that way, it hurt me. The best thing for us is not to get in too deep.

She wrote him a beautiful answer. The answer of a brokenhearted girl, after her first love affair, when the world is darkest, when there seems to be no way out, and life seems worthless.

Thank you for all you have shown me of life. I shall never love again. I will never hate you. I have loved you too much. Whatever happens, let us be friends, you and I, Winfield, I am sorry but I shall never love again. You have destroyed something within me, my love for all men.

Winfield thought it a great letter. It made him so sorry, and yet so glad too. Broke her heart. Well, I guess it'll be all right. Better to have the thing end this way. Getting too deep for me. He saved the letter. Read it many times. Like to show that to Paul Pew. He felt sorry for himself now. If he had shown the letter he would have shed tears doing it. It made him really sorry, deeply sorry, but happy too. Think of it, a letter like that. Not many men got letters like that one.

But he was a little afraid it might be true. She might never marry. Her parents might get after him for hurting their girl's heart. I hope she gets over it, finds some fellow she loves.

But the letter killed the little love that was left. Put pride in its place. Pride instead of love. Fear too, no little amount of fear. He did hope she would get over it. Hate to see her again, now after this thing. He wouldn't know what to say.

Finkel had added a few new grades of pearl beads to the line. He sent samples to Winfield, enclosed an invoice of the goods in samples which Winfield already had. He compared the invoice with the samples, and found that there were still three more strings in his samples than were listed. He took them out.

I guess I'll just keep these. Do a little business on the side. Make good presents. Fine quality too. They were some of the best grade strings in the line.

He sent one to his mother.

Make them see that I'm making money.

On the next Sunday he used the hotel adding machine, added up the amount of his sales, figured his commissions, and saw that he was just about keeping even with the amount of his drawing account. Averaging one hundred dollars a week. Sickness, vacation, took all the profits away. He would have to work harder to make any money at the game.

In August several banks in the middle west failed. The merchants began to buy with more caution. Thought they would put off buying until things were more stable. No use stocking up when hard times are on the way. Banks failing might mean a reaction from wartime prosperity. Better be careful. He found it difficult to sell enough to cover even the amount of his drawing account.

Rather discouraging, the business, he thought.

He finished his Indiana and Ohio territory and went into Michigan. Went to Benton. Saw his father there. Sold some goods to two local merchants. They could not easily refuse to buy from Winfield Payne. His family bought enough jewelry from each of these places in a year to make them feel obligated to the young man. His father told him he should go up north, to their summer cottage. Mother and the brothers were up there. He would have to go to school in two months. Might as well stop working now, while business was slack. He was fed up with selling anyway, besides, it would be nice to get up in northern Michigan. Sailboating, swimming, one thing and another. Working was not much fun. All this bunk about pearls. Fine grades, nature's one complete jewel, complete without the hand of man. Better than diamonds, finer, more reserved. Diamonds had to be cut to be beautiful. Pearls were God's gift to adorn womankind, the American woman. He was sick of it. Quite ready to quit work.

He wrote to Finkel. I have got to go to school. Probably be out east somewhere. I will finish in a few

years and work for you again then. I'll send my samples
back by express. See you in New York later.

His father still talked of sending him to the
University of Michigan. Winfield thought of some
eastern college.

He went to northern Michigan, to his parents'
cottage in the woods, on a beautiful springwater lake.

One day a letter came from Christabel. Dear
Winfield, my parents want me to go to the University
of Michigan this year. They think it would be better
for me to go to a coeducational school to finish. I have
been at Wellesley long enough and would like to go to
a university. I thought I would write you, because if
you thought of going there, it might make a difference
to you. However, you can be sure if you do go there
I will never do anything to make your life unhappy. I
have to go there myself though. I thought I had better
tell you. I hope you are well and making good with
your work.

Of course I'm not going there. They would kick
me out anyway. After that drinking fuss down there.
Ward getting kicked out and all that. Never go there.
Folks want me to though. Wouldn't go now. Jesus, she
must be trying to follow me. Hope I don't run into her.
He had two good reasons for not going to school in
Ann Arbor, both of which he could not explain to his
parents.

He didn't answer the letter.

His mother talked naturally of Michigan, as if it
were an accepted fact that he would go there. He would
have to hurry and arrange something else. He wrote
letters to Brown, Colgate, Dartmouth, and Cornell.

Asked for catalogues. It was too late now to enter any
of these schools, but he thought he might get in one of
them. He should have written last spring.

That's what the other fellows do. Write the year
before. I hope it works though. I can't go to Michigan
now.

His mother walked into the cottage one morning.
Winfield, she called. He noticed the tone of her voice.
Strange. What's up now?

—Winfield I want you to tell me the truth. Have
you always been honest in your dealings? Tell me the
truth.

Honest, dealings. What the devil did she mean?
Honest. Pearls. Maybe Christabel.

—What did I ever do? Why of course I'm honest.
I guess I'm your son. What are you talking about?
Coming up to me this way.

—Now tell me the truth. I know more about this
thing than you think I do. Your mother knows you
better than you think. Don't lie to me. What about
those pearls? Did you pay for them?

—Why mother I, why I. Now mother see here.
That's no way to come up to a fellow. I been on the
road. What are you talking about? Pearls. Why there
aren't any pearls. Don't you see how that was? What do
you know about anything? That's what I want to know.
I got a right to know, haven't I?

—Winfield, tell me the whole truth. The truth is
the best. A registered letter. I opened it. Had to sign
for it. From your firm. A hundred and twenty dollars,
Winfield. Is it true? The best thing is to tell me all

about it. Everything. That's the only way. Did you take them?

—Let me see that letter. That damned Jew, Finkel. Just like a fellow like that. Let me see that letter. I got a right to haven't I? He's a liar. Said I stole something? That's a lie. Trying to cheat me out of something, hey? Please let me see it. What did he say? Dirty Jew trick, that. Why mother, you know me.

She gave him the letter.

We have written you three times. No answer. There are three pearl strings missing in the samples you returned. You do not answer our letters. If we do not hear from you there is nothing left for us to do but turn the matter into hands of our agents who will deal with you directly. Why do you fail to answer our letters? Of course, we trust there is some mistake. The matter will have to be attended to. Send us the one hundred and twenty dollars or the pearl beads if you still have them. They were the following: One twentyfour inch string, grade BB. One sixteen inch string, grade AA. One grade AAA length twentyfour inches. The matter must be attended to by return mail or it will be out of our hands.

Threatening me hey? Well, I'll see. Say those three strings. Hell, they weren't listed. How did that damned Finkel know? Might arrest me. Take the matter out of his hands. Probably means give it to some shyster lawyer. Jesus, might get arrested. Dirty skunk. Could get me, all right. But I never got those letters. Must be down in Indiana some place. Never got a one of them. What is he talking about?

—Mother, now listen here. Those pearls I gave you
were not those grades. You can tell if you look at them.
He knew she wouldn't know one grade from another.

—Now see here. Finkel put that up. I must have
lost them. Say, I'll bet that's it. I probably lost them
and didn't know anything about it. You can lose a thing
easy, mother. For instance. You know how you lost that
diamond ring of yours. It's easy. You wouldn't have lost
that if you could help it, would you? Well, that's the
way it is with me. I probably lost those things. Thought
they were all there when I sent them back.

—Well Winfield, the matter must be straightened
out. You'll have to take it up with your father. I can't
take it on myself. You had better go right back home
and tell the whole thing to your father. It's very funny.
People don't lose things like that. And what about
those letters? Why didn't you tell your mother? Your
mother is the person to tell those things to. I told your
father he shouldn't have allowed you to go out. Be a
salesman. You just wasted your time in Washington.
I've got letters from you. All the things you were going
to do. Business. All you do is write home for money.
It's terrible. I hope it isn't true. I wouldn't have let you
go to Washington like that. Your father though. We've
been too good to you. Let you loose. I'm afraid. Tell me
the truth, Winfield. It's best to tell it all.

—Why mother. Now about Washington. You
know that things were, well, they weren't good. I
couldn't help it. Thought I would make money. Paul
too. We both thought so. It was a good thing for me.
Experience. But say, this damned Finkel.

—Now you don't have to talk that way. There's no use swearing. Winfield you go right home and tell your father. Straighten out this thing. They would put you in prison for that. That's a very serious thing. It hurts me. I hope you tell me the truth.

Winfield's mother felt that he had stolen the things. Knew it in fact. But she didn't want to admit it to herself. She wanted him to deny it. Motherlike. Didn't want her boy to be in the wrong.

Winfield went back to Benton. He still had two strings of pearls at home of the number he had taken from the samples. He had given four strings away, and had two left. Finkel had missed three. He found the two. Told his father they were accidentally laid away, not returned. That left one to settle for. One string, the very best grade. Eighty dollars.

His father gave him the money, cautioned him about fair dealing.

—Be careful. Must always be careful in a position where you handle money or valuables. Look at that bank cashier here who killed himself. He just borrowed the money from the bank. Couldn't pay it back when the inspector came, so he shot himself dead. Must be very careful.

His father gave him the eighty dollars. The deal with Finkel was closed. Only Winfield wanted to keep himself in the right. Wanted to whitewash himself. He wrote to Finkel.

The two strings were accidentally mislaid and I found them at home in Benton. The others I know nothing about. I guess I'll just have to lose the money. I am sorry you thought I was dishonest, for I wouldn't have taken the things for the world. Hope now that every thing will be all right and that we will meet again in New York, friends. It was all quite accidental.

Finkel wrote a pleasant answer. He hoped Winfield would work for them again when he got out of college. Sorry about the misunderstanding.

But Winfield had a heavy conscience. Now when Michigan was suggested he couldn't say no. His father had helped him straighten out that mess about the pearls. He would have to do what they wanted now. Go to Michigan. Mother knew very well. He could tell she did. About those pearls. Father perhaps didn't. But anyway, under the circumstances, he would have to be quiet. Do what they wanted him to.

No other way out. Go to Michigan that fall. Might get in a mess there, but I'll try it. Guess they have forgotten down there that drinking trouble anyhow. Christabel won't bother me. Fellows don't fuss there anyway. I'll have to leave the girls alone to keep in good with the fellows.

Yes, he would go to Michigan.

VI

At the University of Michigan Winfield should have been classified as a freshman. His two law credits from George Washington University were worth no thing to him here. He was entered in the literature, science and arts department of the university. Even with two credits he would still have been a freshman. However, he managed to sign up as a sophomore, and told the boys at the fraternity house in Ann Arbor that he was a sophomore. It would sound better.

For a fellow who has been out in the world as I've been, there's no use lining up with the freshmen. It would have been much more humiliating than his last extra year in highschool had been.

The knowledge that he was really a first year student posing as a second year man made him feel outside of either class. He remained more or less by himself. His business experience gave him a superior feeling. He felt that he was far above the rest of the boys in his fraternity, and even his professors were marks of scorn for him.

He never met Christabel on the campus. He was relieved. He didn't know what he would say to her if they should meet.

Weekends he went into Detroit, bought booze, bootleg stuff, and went out with friends there. When he didn't go into Detroit he got drunk in Ann Arbor and amused his fraternity brothers with the Uncle Wiggley stories and verses of a more or less crude and rough sort. He studied a little, but felt that he was above it all. He felt that he knew more about business, and the newspaper game, than any of the teachers there, let alone the students. None of the boys in the fraternity house were atheists, so he had little respect for their opinions.

It was his atheism that brought him into contact with an intelligent young student with a literary bent. The young man lived in Detroit and invited Winfield to stay at his home weekends. They drank together in Detroit and through this boy Winfield met some interesting people in the city. The young man knew that Winfield was not literary, that he was without appreciation of art and music, but his atheism and his dislike of college and fraternity life, as well as a skepticism regarding women made them friends. Winfield's newspaper experience gained him a certain respect too.

Winfield listened to his talks about literature and art and was frankly interested.

It would be foolish to get too much tied up in such things, he thought, but they are all right. He was at least tolerant, and felt proud to be a friend of a young man who knew as much as his new friend did.

The friend, Richard Patton, wrote criticism of books for the college paper and planned to devote his life to writing books. That was all right, Winfield thought. I hope he makes good at it. These highbrows never make much. It's a fine thing though. I would like to take him home and let the people there see him. He's got lots of brains. Can talk about anything.

Winfield read books the young man gave him.
The ones which were more or less pornographic pleased
him and he began buying a few books of this kind. Not
seriously interested in their literary value, just reading
them because they were a bit questionable.

Through Richard Patton he met Alice Wright, a
Detroit girl who had been one of the most popular in
her highschool. Her father had been a well known and
respected business man of the city. In Alice's last year of
highschool he had died, heavily in debt through losses
in speculation, and Mrs Wright and Alice were left
with practically nothing except the hollow good wishes
of their friends in Detroit. Alice was a young girl who
wanted to be modern, that is, she wanted to believe in
free love, equality of women, and the other panaceas
of the downtrodden sex. She read books without
understanding them. It was only that her father's death,
and disgraceful death at that, had left her with few
friends. She was alone and wanted to have friends.
Boys liked her. Girls she had known in school left her
alone. The Wrights were no longer proper people for
young girls to associate with. And the girls noticed that
since her father died Alice was being talked about as
easy loving. She did let the boys kiss her and make love
to her. She didn't like being alone. The girls snubbed
her, but the boys would go with her if she gave them
kisses.

She liked Winfield. Thought he was very
intellectual. Any boy that could talk that way about
God, as if there were no God, and quote poetry from
Kipling as Winfield could, must be very intellectual.
She liked him.

They went up the Detroit river on a moonlight pleasure excursion one night. This was the first night he was alone with her. On the top deck, sitting in a corner under the shadow of a lifeboat, he made love to her and kissed her many times.

—Why Winfield. This is the first time a boy ever kissed me, the first time I went out with him. You're awfully nice, Winfield.

He told her he loved her, and he did. Regularly weekends after this first time he went into Detroit and had dates with Alice. And made love to her too. They talked of free love and of philosophy and religion. Both were equally versed in the things they talked about. They agreed that free love was the proper thing, but they didn't have one another. They just went on loving, kissing and talking.

She wrote to him on perfumed stationery during the week. He answered her letters, wrote love letters to her.

You are the first real girl I have ever known. It's wonderful to love a real girl. College gets on my nerves. If it wasn't for our few hours together each week, I never could stand it. You are all that is desirable in woman.

Several times they talked of taking each other but both were afraid. They just went on making love.

His fraternity had a house party late in October, the fall house party. He invited Alice.

Warm fall evening. Winfield was standing in one corner of the room talking with the chaperones, telling them his favorite polite stories. Watching himself, that he didn't say something too shocking.

A tall girl from Rochester, New York came up to
him. Why don't you ever ask me for a dance Mr Payne?
I think you're horrid.

—Why you're always busy. I haven't had a chance.
You've got about fifty fellows chasing you all the time.
Let's dance now. Will you?

They danced, bellies rubbing against one another,
shimmying. It was warm. The perspiration rolled down
under Winfield's collar. Gee, that girl is mean, he
thought. He held her tightly. She drew him to herself.
They danced speechless, both passionate. Masturbation
on the dance floor. After the dance.

—Let's go outside, Winfield said.

Vacant house next door. They walked into a dark
corner. Skirts raised, sweat, indecency. Winfield was
shaking, nerves. The tall girl and Winfield were there a
long time together.

Guess it's the liquor, he thought. I wouldn't have
done it. What will Bill Fallows say? If he knew. His girl
too. God, I never thought she would do it. Looks like a
decent girl. What a girl.

They walked back to the fraternity house. The
orchestra had played two dances while they were gone.
Two men waited for her on the steps. Winfield and
the girl came hack, feeling ashamed of themselves.
Vulgar, the whole thing. Winfield felt a little sick to his
stomach.

I could never speak to her again, he thought.

He saw Mary Whitman standing in the hallway
alone. Jesus, that was my dance. I was supposed to have
that last dance with her.

He went up to her. Why Mary, where have you been? He was more cool, collected now, his senses. I walked a little too long that last time. Forgot. I'm sorry.

They danced together. A quiet dance. Winfield was tired now.

He left her with her partner. Thank you, Miss Whitman. You are the best dancer in the place.

Oh, you know better than that, she said. But she believed him. Any girl would.

He looked around for Alice. She was talking with one of the boys. Winfield was jealous. Hope she didn't hand out any loving tonight. Make me feel bad with the boys.

He went up to her. They danced together.

—I see you were out quite a while with that tall girl. She uses too much rouge. Do you like her?

—Oh, she's nothing, bores me. We walked out a little way from the house.

—I saw you walk.

Winfield hoped she hadn't seen anything else.

The following weekend he went to Benton. It was his first visit to his home since school had started. Friday evening shortly after he came into Benton he was in an icecream parlor, drinking a coca-cola. A slender blondhaired girl walked up to him.

—Hello Winfield. I didn't know you lived here. Thought you lived in Detroit. It was Mary Whitman.

—No, Benton's my home town. I've been in Detroit a lot though. I didn't know you were here. Do

you go to B. C.? I didn't know it. Nobody said anything
about that down there.

At the house party Winfield had paid little
attention to Mary Whitman. He had danced with her
two or three times, that was all. But here in Benton,
in the icecream parlor, she looked wonderful to him.
Lips a little bit thin. Hips too large, maybe. But nice.
Goodlooking, just the same. Baby face.

—Say Mary, why don't you come out to the
country club with me tomorrow? Dance.

—Oh, I'd love to.

She forgot her other engagement. It would be so
much nicer to go to the country club with a Benton
boy. These fellows at Benton College weren't so much.
Payne there is a Michigan man. Michigan much better
than old B. C.

They went to the dance the next night. Winfield
thought Mary was a whole lot better than she had
seemed at the house party. He was glad she was going
to school there. He might see her every time he came
home. He told her he thought she was a lovely girl.

—I didn't know what a wonder you were. Say, you
dance better. Oh, I told you that once.

He told all the girls that. He must have told Mary
that too.

—But say this is fine. I'd like to have a girl like
you. I like you, do you know it?

She liked him and besides, it was nice to go to the
country club this way. She had never been asked before.
She held him close to her when they danced.

On the way home, driving in the Payne's new
automobile, Winfield tried to make love to her. That

was really all he wanted from her then. Just a little loving.

She knew it. She refused to kiss him. Thought she would try and hang on to this young fellow. Make a good dancing partner. Nice to have a town boy when I'm here at school. He might take me to another house party. I'll have to play him right. Ought to be able to get him.

—No, you can't kiss me Winfield. You wouldn't like me if I let you do that. I know how boys are. Think less of a girl for it. I would kiss you if I thought you really cared for me. But why, this is the first time. No, Winfield. Don't make me angry. I tell you, no. Please don't Winfield. You just are awful Winfield. Don't do that. Please don't.

And all Winfield wanted was a little loving. He had a good girl in Detroit, Alice Wright. Thought it would be nice to have somebody to make love to in Benton. And here this Whitman girl was holding out on him. He thought she must be a funny one.

I know damned well she hands it out to other fellows, why don't I get mine?

Mary wanted to keep him and she knew how. She acted tenderly and told him she just couldn't yet. If she had known him two or three weeks it would be different. But the very first night they went any place together she couldn't do such a thing. It was quite impossible.

Winfield was disgruntled. He left her determined to have another try.

He wrote to her from Ann Arbor. Told her he loved her. One kiss from her and he could die happy.

Mary Whitman had an aunt in Benton. The aunt told her to hang on to that Payne boy. He was one of the best boys in the town. His parents had money too. Were one of the most highly respected families in Benton. The aunt urged Mary to get Winfield.

She wrote to him that she longed to see him, she loved him. Next weekend he came to Benton again. His parents wondered why he came home that way, just having been back at school one week. Alice Wright wondered why he didn't come to Detroit, he hadn't even written for over a week.

I thought you came home to see your parents, his mother told him.

—Well I did, but I might as well. You know. There is a girl out at the college. The girl I took to the dance last week. I thought I'd like to see her. Might as well. I'm home this way.

His mother was a little jealous. Wanted to know more about this girl. She didn't like to see Winfield falling in love with so many girls. He had gone around with too many in highschool. There was no need for a young boy in college to be always going with girls. But she had to let him have his way.

—Well mother, she's a nice girl. Lives in Grand Rapids. I met her at the house party. Nice girl. Good girl too. Not the kind the fellows kiss. I know that. She wouldn't kiss me. Not that I tried, but I know. She's fine type of a girl. One of the best mother. I know too. I just wanted to come home, that's all. I like to get back and see the folks. Kinda like to see her too. Don't blame me for that do you? She's nice, really.

They went to a dance together again. Winfield was determined that this weekend would not be wasted. He would kiss her at least once.

He told her he loved her. He did. He told her he had always been looking for just her kind of girl. I'd marry you tomorrow, he told her.

She liked him. Thought it was fine to have a young fellow from a good family away from her home, in a place where he could be of use, making love to her that way. She encouraged him. I like you, love you too, maybe. I don't know how I feel. A man has got to prove to me that he loves me though.

He danced with her, holding her close to hip, looking into her eyes.

The Benton girls looked at him. Noticed that he had fallen in love. There he goes again, they were thinking. Always making love to somebody. I wouldn't trust him two feet. He just talks and talks. All hot air. Tries to get a girl to love him. That Whitman girl must be dumb not to see through him. He couldn't fool me. She just drinks it all in. He's got the worst line of bunk in the world.

Winfield had brought with him a small bottle of whiskey which he had stolen from his father's small stock. He had been drinking it out at the dance. Felt amorous as a result.

Going home he insisted on kissing her. You are the only girl I ever really loved. Now I can show you. There was that Jefferson girl in West Virginia. I never told you anything about her, but she was a wonder. Christabel Thompson too. Fine girl. But you, why it's only you I think about. All night long I'm awake thinking about

you. See here Mary, you've got to kiss me. Do you want
me to go crazy? I can't stand it thinking about you. I'd
do anything for you.

She kissed him. He slowed the car down and
stopped. He put his arms around her and held her tight.
He did love her, he did really. He had never wanted
a kiss as he wanted that one. And it did something
strange to him. Made him something that he had never
been before, another new person. Tingling, excited.
Mad with love. And all on account of this one kiss. He
kissed her again and again. He did love her.

Something different, this. God, I wish I could
marry her. Settle down into anything, business. Marry
her.

—Oh, darling, I love you. Everything else, been
nothing. You make me crazy darling. I love you. Your
skin, dear. Kiss your skin. I feel weak. Oh, what love is?
Love. You must love me. I love you.

Winfield was suddenly really, deeply in love, the
first time he had ever felt the emotion so strongly. He
thought it must be the first time he had ever loved at
all. All the other just liking, this is love.

He drove the car further into the country, where
fewer people would be passing.

Mary told him she loved him. I loved you from
the first, Winfield.

He kissed her on the lips, the hair, the eyes,
around the neck and on the ears. She screamed a little,
short stifled passionate screams of pain and of terror,
quivered, and then crumpled in his arms. She couldn't
stand it, being loved this way. She was crying, low,

sadly. Pushed herself away from him. Huddled in the corner of the seat.

As if I had ruined her, looks like, Winfield thought. She's a passionate little devil. What's the matter with her?

—Say, Mary, what's the matter? What you crying like that for? I love you, don't cry. You shouldn't cry. We've been so happy. Come here. Kiss me. Don't cry like that.

She still trembled. Sobbing, wearylike.

—Don't touch me, please. Oh, please don't. Take me home. Please take me home. We shouldn't do this. We shouldn't. Please don't touch me, don't. Take me home, Winfield.

—Well you oughtn't feel bad. I love you. I never loved anybody like I love you. You make me feel bad, crying there. Get up, please, and look at me. Tell me what's the matter. Tell me. Look at me, please.

—Take me home. She said it firmly, almost angrily. Take me home.

Winfield started the car and drove slowly toward the girl's home at the college. She wiped away her tears, her face looked so frightened. She had been frightened, her body and all of her. She had lost control of herself for a moment, swept by passion, and it had frightened her. It had been pain to her. She was afraid of Winfield, but more afraid of herself. That such a thing could happen within herself.

I love you, Winfield said again.

Driving the car with his right hand, he unclasped his jewelled fraternity pin with the left, and then turned to her.

—Here this should make you know how I feel.
Take my pin. That means I love you. We never give this
pin to a girl unless we are engaged to her. I love you.
This pin is for you if you want it.

He would have given her more than a fraternity
pin. He loved her. So beautiful she seemed to him. Tear
stains still on her face. Sad face. He knew what had
happened to her, even if he didn't know how serious it
had been for her. How it had gripped and twisted her
soul and her body, and filled her brain with madness
and terrible fear. He would have done anything to
make her feel happy, to dry the tears in her eyes. He
thought of running away from school, working for her,
marrying her. He would have done it in a minute had
she assented.

—Why Mary. I'll go to work. Quit school. You
marry me. We'll get along all right. Even with little
money, we'll get along. I love you.

Every girl in his past life was forgotten. Mary was
the only girl he had ever loved, the girl he had been
waiting for. Christabel he had loved, but not with the
abandon with which he loved Mary. He was conscious
of what he did and what he said to Christabel. With
Mary though, he just talked on and on. There were no
limits to his love. He couldn't talk in superlatives. He
loved in that way.

Before they reached her home, Mary was calmer.
She regretted the thing that had happened. Wished she
had been stronger. She didn't love Winfield that much.
Not the way he talked of loving her. But she would
take the pin.

—I can't wear the pin, Winfield. My mother
would never allow me to be engaged now, this soon.
But I'll keep it. Wear it underneath. I can't announce
my engagement to you. We have got to go around
together longer. My parents would never allow it.

She was thinking of the boys she knew at college.
If she wore that pin they would no longer ask her to
dances. She wanted to go out as much as she could
too. No, it would be foolish to wear the pin, it would
spoil a lot of good times for her. But to have it,
that was different. She could keep it. Show it to her
roommate.

Nothing serious in the affair of course. I'll just
keep him thinking I love him. That way I can keep
him. The girls will think it's funny, having a fellow mad
in love with you, you not caring much for him. I'll
string him along.

She was entirely recovered, cold blooded now.
Little tigress ready for battle. She liked him well
enough, but she was not looking for love as much as
for conquest. She wanted to be loved more than to
love. Different than some women. And now she sat in
the car cool, thinking.

Winfield was not thinking. He was just warm,
hopeful. Hoping she would wear the pin, hoping she
would let the whole world know that she loved him
and that he loved her. He had never loved before, he
knew that. He was not thinking, just living in the
present, in the knowledge that he was close to her.
For Mary was there beside him, he could feel her
body and once in a while the softness of her leg, as it
brushed against his, with the jerk and jolt of the car. It

was maddening, this slight touch. He slipped an arm around her, pressed the pin to her and kissed her. Then they drove home.

Next morning, Sunday, he had to go back to Ann Arbor.

When the next weekend came he was uneasy. He wanted to go home, but knew that his mother would be very angry if he did. He didn't dare go back so often. So he went to Detroit with Richard Patton.

Alice Wright had written two letters to him since he started going with Mary. He had not answered them. Had forgotten Alice. Now he thought of her and hoped they wouldn't meet. He was afraid to tell her he had fallen in love. She knew it already.

No boy would stop writing, for no reason at all. Something like that must have happened.

When he arrived in Ann Arbor after the weekend in Detroit he found two telegrams and two letters, special delivery, from Mary. Also a letter from Alice Wright. He opened one telegram. Read.

Announced engagement. Thought I had better tell you before parents heard about it. Worlds of love, Mary.

The other telegram was from his mother. What is this about engagement? Why didn't you tell mother?

He was both happy and troubled. He wanted Mary for his wife and was glad now that she had announced their engagement. But then, not even giving him a chance to tell his parents. And here his mother was evidently very angry.

She should have let me know. But I'm happy, that means she's mine now. She loves me or she never would have done it. I wanted her to do it. Asked her to. How will I fix it up with the folks? She ought to have let me know.

He opened the letters, read the one with the earliest date. She told him that two of her friends had announced their engagement at a breakfast party in the dormitory and she wanted to also. They might as well be engaged. She didn't know what her folks would say. Maybe Winfield's parents wouldn't like it. They would know by this time because the Benton girls would tell it right away. She wanted to announce it though, and that was such a splendid time, just when these other two girls did the same thing. She said she had known that Winfield wanted that all the time and hoped he would be very happy. I loved you or I never would have done it.

The second letter was much like the first, except that it had a slight apologetic note in it. She was sorry she hadn't told him, but couldn't help it. You know how those things are, she said. You must come back as soon as you can and take your little girl in your arms. I am a little worried. You may not like it because I did that. But I loved you so much.

Winfield liked it and didn't. But he sent a telegram.

Glad you did it. Am very happy. Lots of love. Winfield.

He didn't know what he should tell his mother.

What if she did it just because she wanted to show she had a man? When those other girls got up and said they were engaged? There was a sting in Winfield's side.

She shouldn't have done it that way. It wasn't right. And yet, I'm happy. I love her. Everything will be all right.

He wrote a long letter to his mother explaining. Telling how Mary was the only girl he ever loved. That he was going to marry her when he got out of college. He was sorry he hadn't told the folks about it, but he was afraid they might try to stop him. He didn't know that Mary would announce it so soon anyway. He would be home next weekend and explain the whole thing to their satisfaction.

To Mary he wrote a love letter, telling her that he was happy and they would have such a wonderful life together, a nice little home and a wonderful quiet married life.

In the fraternity house that night he passed expensive cigarettes around the dining table and told them that he was engaged. There were many comments. The boys wondered why he had shown Mary so little attention at the house party. But they smoked his cigarettes and thanked him. Sang a little song,

For he's a jolly good fellow,
For he's a jolly good fellow,
Ein, zwei, drei, vier,
Payne's going to buy the beer,
Here's to Payne,
He's a damned fine man.

Winfield was very happy. Being engaged like this was all right. He wanted to go home and see Mary and make love to her and let her know how happy he was. He could hardly wait until the week went by.

The letter from Alice was in his pocket two days unopened. He had forgotten all about it. He opened it and read it. She told him there was no reason for him not writing. If he loved somebody else he could at least write to her. She had never done anything to make him dislike her. He ought to be decent enough to answer her letters.

He wrote and told her that he was engaged. Best girl in the world. Ruthless, his letter to Alice. He didn't think that she might be hurt. He was very thoughtless, had forgotten he had ever loved her. We'll call on you when we are married, he wrote.

His mother scolded him when he came home the next Friday. Why Winfield, however? Considering every thing you have had. How could you? Don't you realize how I must have felt? And that girl. Why they told me. Somebody called on the phone and said they were glad you were engaged. Engaged, I said. I couldn't help it. I had no idea. Why Winfield, I could cry. And that girl, Winfield. Are you sane? Well, your father and I have decided. We've decided. A young man. An engaged man has got to work. Earn money for his wife. Why, it's silly. Engaged. Winfield, and you didn't even tell your mother. I can't understand. I'm so hurt. If it had been another girl. But that Whitman girl. Why Winfield. When she called, Mrs Holcomb. Why Winfield. What could I say? Nothing. Nothing to say. I was so ashamed. Ashamed, I tell you. Any other girl. That Jewett girl, now, or if it was the James girl. But that little snip. That Whitman girl. It's unthinkable, Winfield. But your father and I, we've decided. Go to

work. Engaged men never stay in school. Got to work.
Earn money for your wife. Aren't you ashamed?

Winfield was hurt. He hadn't expected his mother
to take it so hard. She should have let me know
though, let me break it to the folks. But he didn't like
to have his mother saying mean things about the girl
he loved. He loved her more than he loved his jealous
angry mother.

—I will work. Let me know when. I'll leave
school, go to work. I'll do it. Glad to. She's a wonderful
girl. I know her better than you do.

His mother had never met the girl.

—I got to go out and see her. What will she think?
Me staying here all the time. She wants to see me too.

—Now Winfield, have some sense. Don't get so
excited. You can finish your year of school. Then go to
work.

His mother feared that he might run away again.
But she was so jealous that she couldn't help being
angry.

—We have never said a thing. You can go out and
see her. But do keep your senses. Be a good boy with
her Winfield. Remember. Later when you have a good
job. Enough money to keep a wife. Then. You can go
Winfield. Don't be so angry with your mother.

Winfield drove out to East Benton in the
automobile. Mary kissed him right in the reception
room of her dormitory. This was some new thing. But
being engaged, of course, that was all right. It didn't
matter who saw them kiss now. They were engaged.
She wanted to know what his mother thought of it all.
The news of his engagement had gone over Benton in

two hours, and every one had known it long before Winfield did himself. He resented this, but still was happy. Friends of his mother had called her on the telephone and told her they thought it was awfully nice. Most of them knew that she hadn't an inkling of the fact and were just rubbing it in. Catty old women.

Mary was afraid she had acted too quickly. She wasn't even sure she wanted to be engaged. But when two girls get up and announce to the world that they have found their men, that they at least have found their mates, another girl like Mary just wouldn't be able to keep from doing the same thing. That is, if she had the right to do it. And Mary knew that she had that right.

Winfield told her he was happy. Now he felt more secure. They were in love with one another. They would be married as soon as possible. She said she would have to wait until she was through with school. He would have married sooner. Told her his mother had said he must go to work after the year was over. She didn't know what to say, but she thought it was a very good idea. If he goes to work and earns money, then we will have more when we marry. Besides there was no use making the Paynes angry. They might be expected to give their son money. There was no doubt that they had the money to give.

Winfield and Mary walked through the woods together, made love and talked of the future. Mary was always uneasy. She thought she had been rather silly to get up that way and announce the engagement. Her own parents might take it all right, but it would be bad on account of Winfield's folks.

Winfield told her, I guess we ought to go and get a ring tomorrow. I haven't got the money myself now. I can get a ring from Morgan's jewelry store. I know Morgan. He'll give me credit. I'll just go to him. You've got to have a ring.

She was delighted with this. It would he nice to have a diamond ring. A fraternity pin wasn't so much, anyway. It wasn't like having a ring.

—I won't tell the folks anything about it, we'll just go get it.

He told her she would have to eat dinner at the Payne's on Sunday noon and meet his mother and father. That's got to be done, sooner or later.

Next day they went to Morgan's jewelry store and bought an engagement ring, a diamond set in a platinum, filigree setting. Winfield made arrangements to pay on the installment plan. Morgans knew his father and were willing to do it and keep quiet. If Winfield didn't pay they could get Mr Payne anytime. There was no need for them to worry.

Now Winfield was happy and proud. He was engaged. Mary had a ring and everything was settled. He would have to go to work next summer after school was over, but that didn't matter. School was a bore anyway. He learned a great deal more in other ways than he learned in school.

The professors were all dumbbells, he thought. I know more than most of them do. He would be glad to get out of school. It was a waste of time. He didn't belong. Even his fraternity brothers seemed stupid to him. He would be glad to get out of it all. He decided to start looking for a job at once, as soon as he got back to Ann Arbor he would begin to look for work.

Why, I can get a job and settle down. A little apartment, Mary. That's the thing for me. Just make enough to get along on, that's all I want. Hell with big business. It's all the bunk anyway.

On Sunday Mary and Winfield ate dinner at the Paynes home. Dinner at midday. Winfield would have to leave Benton and go back to Ann Arbor at four o'clock in the afternoon. Mary hadn't worn her new ring yet. She was going to wait until Christmas time and then tell everybody it was a Christmas present from Winfield. Winfield thought it was a good idea to wait a while, until his mother was used to the idea of the engagement. No use antagonizing her.

Mary was frightened when she walked into the house. Mrs Payne stood in the doorway. Gave a sharp look up and down, smiled a smile that bordered, almost bordered, on a sneer. Mary knew that Winfield's mother didn't like her, probably never would like her. She was ready for battle though, and quite willing to draw swords with Mrs Payne. But this time, on the enemy's territory, she was afraid, bashful. She hung back a little. Then reached out her hand carefully to shake hands with Mrs Payne.

Winfield's mother knew the girl was afraid of her. With a slight smile, triumphant, she walked up to Mary and kissed her, pecked at her, on the check. I'm so glad to see you Mary. That was all she could say just then. She didn't intend to admit even that the two people were engaged.

Mary said, How do you do?

Then Winfield thought he had better cut up a hit.
The air was pretty thick there. He started talking at a
great rate. Took Mary's coat and hat, hung them up,
tried to make a joke with his mother. The joke failed,
but he went on talking.

—Come on, let's go in the other room. No use
standing in the hall. Come on, by the fireplace. Got
a fire in it. Mrs Payne was out of the room, in the
kitchen, helping the maid prepare the dinner. Mr
Payne walked into the room.

—Oh, say father. Here's Mary. This is my father,
Mary.

—How do you do Miss Whitman? Nice day.
Getting cooler. Funny, no snow yet.

Mr Payne wasn't sure whether he could call the girl
Mary or Miss Whitman, so he decided on the Miss.
Mary felt bad about it, she liked Winfield's father much
better than she liked the mother. She wished he had
kissed her and liked her. Mr Payne was so quiet and
pleasant and kindly. But he was so reserved too. She
was afraid she never could break through his reserve,
never make friends with him. She and Winfield would
simply have to live somewhere else. Not in Benton.
Parents hating her.

When she was alone with Winfield she told him,
Your parents hate me. Your mother hates me awful. I
can see. She hates me. I don't like her either.

—That's all right. You're not marrying the folks.
Never mind, Mary. We'll get out of this dump. Go to
New York or someplace.

Winfield's brothers liked Mary and talked with
her. She was glad somebody in the family, besides

Winfield, showed a little liking for her. The dinner was
an unpleasant affair for everyone. Even the brothers
failed to liven things up. The whole thing was flat. Very
little talk. Mrs Payne took every opportunity to look at
Mary. Watching her, trying to pick out her flaws. She
was going to stop this thing between her son and this
young snip of a girl. She was going to find out as much
as she could about Mary Whitman and then start
working on Winfield, to make him dislike the girl. She
would let them go at it for a while, thinking they were
engaged, but sooner or later she would start her work.
Winfield would never marry that Whitman girl. That
was all there was to it.

Mary and Winfield decided they would write
fewer letters back and forth, every day was too often,
every third day would he better and both of them
would have more time for their school work.

The first madness of the love affair was dying
down, and now he thought of the way she had
announced their engagement.

It was a funny thing to do. She was carried away,
that's all.

But he was glad they were engaged. Only he did
wish it had come about in some other way.

She complained that his letters were getting
shorter. He had less to tell her now. But he still loved
her as much as he ever had, he was just becoming more
sensible, that was all. But there was a slight noticeable
change in their relation. It worried Mary. She thought
he was getting further and further away from her.

They talked a little now and then of money, and of
their future. He knew she wanted him to make money.

He didn't want that kind of a life. But he tried to give
in to her, they weren't married yet. No use arguing
about such things now. She'll see my point when she
gets a little more of my attitude toward life. Plenty of
time he thought.

He went home one more time before the Christmas
holidays started. His mother was sick, nervous head
ache, and said that Mary could not come over for
dinner this time. She wasn't well enough for it. Winfield
spent most of his time at East Benton. They went to
one dance together. Went into the country in the car
together.

—We ought to have one another all the way Mary.
We're engaged. Why do we just have to make love this
way?

She was indignant. Why Winfield, how could you
talk of such a thing? No never. Why, anything might
happen. We couldn't do that. No, not until we are
married. I wouldn't do that. My mother and father.
What would they think of such a thing?

He tried to argue with her and convince her that
there was no harm in doing the thing. There was no use
trying.

She knew what she knew and there was to be
nothing of that kind until they were married. No, that
was the thing that would keep Winfield to her. If she
gave it away she might lose all her value. She would
guard it till the end.

But they might better have had one another than
make love the way they did. Both of them wet, hot
and perspiring. Making love in the car. Masturbation.
It was much more indecent than the other thing.

Winfield knew that. But that was all she would give him. He began to think, maybe she isn't as passionate as she seemed that first night. Maybe she wouldn't be all that he wanted. But he loved her as much as ever, he was sure he did. When he went with her once she would be different.

That often makes the difference with women. You go with them once, they don't like it, but after that, they are all right. He believed that after the first time, women were generally different than before. Mary would be much more passionate, loving too, after he had once taken her.

Winfield wanted to know when they would be married.

—I'll have to finish school first, she told him. Mother and father will insist on that. Then we can be married. Besides, you'll have time to get a good job by that time. Have some money.

—We can't wait all that time. Almost four years. I got to quit school in the spring because we're engaged. Going to work then. Why can't you quit too? We're old enough to be married I guess.

—No, I couldn't do it. But as soon as I get out of school, then we will be married. Right away.

She wasn't anxious to be married so soon. It was all right being engaged, having a ring and a man. But marriage. No. She wanted Winfield to have money too.

—But you'll have to have money. We can't be silly about that.

—Now see here Mary. That kind of talk about money shouldn't enter into the thing at all. All we want

is a quiet little home, and happiness. Don't even want
kids.

—We must have money. I could marry a man in
Chicago. Money, cars, everything. We've got to have it.
That's what I want.

Winfield noticed the scolding tone in her voice.
He was hurt. Maybe he was losing her this way. He
might lose her love. She might leave him, give back the
ring.

—I'll get money then Mary. I'll get it. I'll get the
money. Get a job, earn it. We can marry when you
want to. I love you. Come here. Kiss me Mary.

She had won. Felt happy. Wonderful, Winfield
giving in this way. She knew how to handle him. She
was very happy: Loved him because he gave in to her
that way. She kissed him, held him close to her. Told
him she loved him more than any one in the world.

—More than my mother and father. I wouldn't
marry that fellow in Chicago. I don't love him. Never
marry him. It's you I love. We can have everything,
Winfield, nice clothes, everything. With money. I do
love you. You're so nice. You're the nicest boy I ever
knew.

He was a little boy to her. She had had her way
with him.

—Come, we must go home now. It's late. She was
going to run things now. She knew she could.

Winfield resented it though. That about the money.
He had thought so long of other things. It hurt him that
she couldn't understand and appreciate what he wanted.
And then the, come now, we must go home. The way

she said it. Bossing. He didn't want any woman bossing
him that way. Telling him, come now. It wasn't right.

—Suppose we just stay right here? he answered.

—All right, she said. We'll stay here. I'll sit right
back here.

He tried to kiss her.

—No, don't kiss me. We're going to stay here: Don't
kiss me. You'll have your way. We'll stay right here.

She had to get her hands on the reins once more,
had to gain control again. Winfield would never take it
from her in that way. It was a battle. Winfield wanted
to be the man. He didn't want Mary telling him Come
now. No indeed.

—All right then. We'll go home. He got in the
front seat and started the car. Drove toward the college.

—I guess you want your ring back, she said. Pin
too.

He thought, she must be joking. Couldn't be
serious about such a thing.

—Well, I guess it's high time. Don't get along
much, do we? Better give them back. Got the ring
there?

She had it tied around her neck. She handed both
the ring and the fraternity pin to him over the front
seat of the car.

—Take them, here they are. Take them, I say. Take
them. Here. You wanted them. Here they are.

He still thought she was joking. She couldn't be
serious. He decided to carry on the joke. He took the
jewelry.

Said to her, Well I'll send you a postcard once in a
while.

She was furious. That he would do all of those
things. He should have refused to take the ring, the
pin. And then to insult her. Postcard. Send me a
postcard. She was frightened now. Maybe she had gone
too far. But her pride was hurt. He had taken the ring
and the pin and said he would send her postcards. That
was too much. She was angry. Losing. She had been
winning. She would show him.

He didn't know that she really hated him that
moment, because he had taken the thing so lightly.

When she got out of the car in front of the
dormitory he thought the game had gone far enough.
Maybe I went too far. She had been silent in the back
seat alone for such a long time. He went to her, tried to
take her in his arms, to kiss her. She turned away and
started toward the dormitory.

—Come back here Mary. This is serious. Come
back here.

She turned. Stopped.

—Take this ring and pin Mary. Take them. Here.
Come here, please.

He was frightened. Maybe she was through with
him. And he loved her so much.

—I don't want them. You took them back. I'm
going in. Don't come up to me.

He had started.

—Go home Winfield. I don't want them. I'm
going in.

He turned back to the car. Legs weak and
trembling. Maybe this was the end. She meant it. I
thought it was only a joke. God, I've lost her. That's
awful.

He got in the car and started slowly toward his home in Benton. He wept, face covered with tears, and drove slowly toward his home. Drove slowly down Michigan Avenue. On the smooth street the electric generator was clicking away, click, click, click. He was driving so slowly that electricity was being used, not stored in the battery. And his electricity gone out of him. Dead he felt. As if everything in life had died and left him alone, the last survivor in a dead, cold world. Every thing that was worth while in the world had gone out of it. He was so alone, so helpless, and he felt that it was his fault. He tried to find a way to make it out to be her fault. He tried to blame Mary. She shouldn't have done that. She ought to have known it was a joke. She scolded me so much. I couldn't be a little ninny. It's her fault. And his mind was blank. Everything gone. That such a little thing could wreck a whole lifetime. It was awful. He cried in his bed at home that night. No girl ever had made him cry before Mary came into his life. But now he cried. He had lost everything that he wanted in life. He thought of calling her on the telephone. It was too late, they wouldn't answer calls at the dormitory this late. It's over, he thought. Mary had been so final. He had the pin and the ring in his vest pocket. They burned into him. Why couldn't she have kept them. Taken them back. She was cruel.

Mary suffered as much or more than Winfield did. He had left her so easily, she thought. If he had stayed a little longer I would have taken them back. But he left. I guess he's through. I acted too quickly. I should have known better. And he was so cruel in the car. The postcards.

He took them and said nothing. The ring and the pin. Maybe, maybe, Oh it was my fault, I guess. I should have been more careful. What will the girls here think? How will I tell people? I can't go out on the street without the pin. Most of them don't know something happened. I've got to find a way. I've got to get the pin back. The pin at least.

Opinion troubled her even more than the thought of losing Winfield. That thought was pain to her too though. She loved him. Loved him more now than she ever had before. She thought of the nights they had made love together in the car. They seemed like bridal nights. She had had pleasure in them, pleasure that she could remember with little thrills running up and down her spine. She thought of calling him that night but it was too late. She couldn't use the telephone in the dormitory. It was too late for that.

First thing in the morning. Got to call him. Fix up the thing some way. I was a little fool. I couldn't go out on the campus without it. And then he will never call on me any more. No more dances. It will be terrible. Maybe he won't speak to me on the telephone. Just refuse.

Next morning she called him at eight o'clock. He was awake when the telephone bell rang, wishing something like that would happen. Wondering if he should call her.

No never. He had decided during the night that if she could go back on him so easily he would never make a move. He steeled himself. And doing this

he almost killed his love of her. Almost ruined the
strongest love he had ever known. She must act. If she
doesn't call, I'll just have to let my heart break. I can't
stand it.

But down deep he knew he could stand it. Their
arguments about money, and marriage, the idea of
waiting four years to marry her, these things together
helped Winfield steel himself against her.

But he wasn't really cold or indifferent. It was
much less than this, that had killed his love for
Christabel, but he was older and he loved with more
tenacity. Still he could have let the whole thing peter
out. And his mother's dislike of Mary acted like poison,
slow poison, on him. Made him see that there were
flaws in his ideal love. He didn't know this, but his
mother's hatred of Mary had helped him steel himself
against her during the night.

She told him over the telephone that she was sorry.
It was her fault.

His heart beat faster talking to her. No, he said, it
was my fault. I tried to call you last night. Too late.

—Please come right out as soon as you can,
Winfield. Bring the ring and pin. I want them. I love
you.

He was very happy, willing to take the blame
himself, now that she had said it was her fault. He
loved her again madly. She was his. He would always
love her. He forgot all of the things he had thought
of the night before and during the morning. Thought
only of his strong love of her. But these thoughts
during the night and early morning had left a mark on
him. It would be easier after that last night to end the

love affair. Easier for Winfield. For Mary it would be harder, much more difficult.

He was smiling when he walked up to her and kissed her. Pressed her very tight to him. He wanted to have her back and he held her very tight, like a vise. She never would get out of his arms, never. He must hold her tight like that, always. He put the ring on her finger. They didn't care then if somebody did see it. And he pinned the pin on her blouse. They kissed again, a long kiss. They were alone in the reception room. It was still early morning.

She was happy. She had him back and she had the ring and pin. It had been easier than she had anticipated. She was glad things were easy.

It was a good thing, last night. We will love each other more now. Winfield kisses me so hard now, holds me so tight. Tested by fire. Love tested by fire. That's what it is with us. We've been tested. We came through, out of the test. We will just love stronger now. She looked at him lovingly. She loved him more now than she ever had before.

She asked him to come to Grand Rapids for a few days, during the Christmas holidays. There would be dances and they could have a nice time. Her parents wanted to meet him too. He said he would go. And then he asked her to spend a few days at his home after he had been in Grand Rapids. There were parties and dances in Benton too, and on New Year's Eve they would have a good time. Big party, New Year's Eve.

He went back to Ann Arbor, wrote to her every day. He couldn't lose her now. And he wouldn't see her

for a couple of weeks. Not until he went to her home
in Grand Rapids.

His mother had been angry because he had asked
Mary to stay at their home for those few days, but she
had to give in. It wouldn't look well to let the town
know she was opposed to Winfield's engagement, and
besides, he had already asked her to stay at their home.
It was too late to make other arrangements.

But Mrs Payne didn't like it. She didn't like the
idea of having that girl in her home for three or four
days. Winfield and she'll just be making love all the
time. I couldn't stand it. That going on right under my
roof. But she had to let Mary stay there, the matter was
all arranged.

At the railroad station in Grand Rapids Mary and
her father met Winfield. She ran up to him from her
father's automobile, spoke to him quickly, don't kiss
me, Winfield, don't. I'll tell you later.

He was taken aback. Expected a kiss from her.
Engaged to her. Why shouldn't he kiss her?

He colored quickly, What's the matter?

—Not in front of father. People see us on the
street. Mother said no. Wait until we get home.

The Whitmans didn't want people to see their
daughter kissing this young man. Besides they weren't
sure they would let her be engaged to him. She was
too young, they felt. They didn't know that she had a
diamond ring. And they thought that pin didn't mean
very much anyhow. They wanted to see Winfield and
talk to him and find out if he was really serious. No
getting their only daughter mixed up with a young

fellow who wasn't serious. They had heard about
Winfield Payne before.

When he went to highschool, he had spent a few
days of one Christmas vacation in Grand Rapids with
a young fellow he knew there, a member of the same
highschool fraternity. Winfield had been drunk at a
party and danced disgracefully, or at least the papers
had said that disgraceful things had gone on, and the
story went around Grand Rapids that the young man
from Benton had been leader of all the doings. He had
danced, drunken, at the party, shimmying and carrying
on, as they said, in front of young innocent highschool
girls. Most of the young innocent girls had been
drinking themselves. He got up in the middle of the
dance floor and recited some questionable poetry too.
The people of Grand Rapids, at least those with sons
and daughters of his own age, had heard of Winfield
Payne.

Mary had belonged with a quieter, more
conservative group of younger people, and didn't
know Winfield at that time. But her mother knew
who he was. She had heard of him at more than one
church club sewing circle meeting. Connected with
the Maitland girl and some other young ones of the
city who drank, and were considered a little bit loose
morally.

Winfield was handicapped when he came to
Grand Rapids by this highschool party at which he had
disgraced himself. He thought people had forgotten
that, but the elder women of the town had not
forgotten. Mrs Whitman had made inquiries when her
daughter wrote that she was going with the young man,

and had found out that he was the same fellow who had caused all that talk about four years before.

When he walked into the Whitman's home he didn't know that Mrs Whitman knew a thing about that affair. He was perfectly unaware.

He shook hands with her. Glad to meet you. It's nice to be in Grand Rapids.

They ate lunch together after he had made his toilet.

He felt very much at ease in their home.

Not quite as good a home as ours, he thought. Guess they haven't got so much money. Plain people. Mary got more class than either her father or mother.

He didn't think they were so much, but he did like them. Seemed to be genuine people. He felt that he could talk with them. He liked Mrs Whitman and talked to her. Kept up a fire of conversation with her.

She began to really like him. Thought he had gotten over his young foolishness. Wished he would marry her daughter. Make a good man for her daughter. Mary's aunt in Benton had written to her and told her all about the Payne family. Good family for her daughter, she thought. She was more than satisfied. She was extremely happy, and hoped that Mary would keep Winfield. When Mary gets out of college he'll be a fine husband for her.

Mr Whitman liked Winfield too. The whole family liked him. Much better than his family liked Mary. No comparison at all. The Whitmans really liked him right off the bat. And they let him know it.

Mr Whitman brought out a little bottle of Kummel. Have a little drink, Mr Payne? Good stuff.

—Now Harry Whitman, what are you giving that young man alcohol for? That isn't right, Harry. Mrs Whitman didn't like the cordiality of her husband. It might make a bad impression. If the Paynes knew that her husband had offered their son liquor.

—Oh, that's all right. I like a little bit once in a while. Now it's hard to get. Winfield wanted to put Mrs Whitman at ease. I just like a little dab now and then. My father's the same way. We have a little once in a while, father and I. It's good, a little. His father had never drunk anything stronger than beer with Winfield, but Winfield knew it would be better to put these people at ease.

—Of course, Mr Whitman said. It's good, a little. He poured out two liquor glasses full. His wife brought two more and told him to fill them. They would all drink. They raised their glasses, saluted and drank.

—That's good stuff. I get very little to drink as a rule. But I know good stuff. This from Winfield. It did taste good too. All liquor tasted good when the country was dry and stuff hard to get.

Winfield was very glad that the family liked him. Mary wasn't so glad. It detracted from her, having them like him that way. He paid so much attention to her mother and father. She thought it was nice, but she was a little jealous. She loved Winfield. And the thought that his parents didn't like her and that her parents liked Winfield, hurt her. She would like to pay him back for what she had suffered around his mother. But she was glad too, because they liked him. It showed that she had made a good choice. She had good taste. She was pleased too.

After the meal Mrs Whitman made her husband
go with her into another room and leave the young
people alone to talk. Mary kissed Winfield. She told
him that her folks didn't know about the ring. She
had already told him she couldn't tell them that. But
she had told her mother that she loved Winfield. Her
mother seemed to like him. She guessed everything
would be all right with them. Maybe her mother would
let her wear the ring.

—Why, you're not even wearing the pin? Winfield
said.

—Well you see, mother thought it was better.
You know. Not to. Now you see? People here in town.
Lots don't know. No use starting talk. See? Do you see?
That's it. You don't care? Do you? No, Winfield. Kiss
me. Here. I wear it at school. That's enough. Isn't it?

She was a little worried, but her mother had told
her not to wear the pin while she was home, and some
of her old boy friends had been to call on her, so she
thought it better not to. However, she decided, I'll wear
it now.

She put it on and wore it. He kissed her.

Mrs Payne in Benton was worried. She suspected
that that Whitman girl's mother would just try and get
her young son. Try to hook him. Scheming mothers
like that. You couldn't trust them. She wished Winfield
had stayed home during the vacation. It would be
safer having Mary in Benton than Winfield in Grand
Rapids. No telling what the young people might do.
Might get into all kinds of trouble. Young man and
girl like that. Girl none too good either. They might do

things they shouldn't. She was worried about her son, and jealous. Different woman than Mrs Whitman.

Going home on the train he was so lovesick he felt like crying. She hadn't kissed him at the train. Her father must not see her do that. She had kissed him good bye, before they left her home. He was hurt because she wouldn't kiss him at the train, but he loved her so much, he could forget his hurt. He thought he understood.

It was awful this going away from her. In three days she would be coming to Benton to stay at their home though. He hoped his mother would treat Mary a little better than she had before. He must try and make his mother understand. He was so much in love. If his mother only understood how wonderful Mary was. She was too mean to Mary.

Mrs Payne did try to be nice to Mary, but she just couldn't. Everybody could see that she didn't think much of the girl. But she did try to be nice. She was such a formal woman, even with her own children she acted distant. And with Mary she was much more distant than with her children. But Winfield and Mary, loving each other so much, had a good time. They went to dances every night and came home quietly and sat downstairs on a davenport making love.

—I like you to want me, Winfield. I like it when you want me. You must always want me. Sometimes you don't. I'm unhappy. You must always hold me close to you, tight.

The loving wore Winfield out. After an hour, or two hours of it, he was satisfied and didn't want her as he had before. Then she kissed him and tugged at him trying to arouse his passion again. She wanted him always to want her, always to be passionate with her.

At the New Year's Eve party at the Country Club Winfield spoke to one of his former highschool girl friends, Helen Thornton. She had just come down from the ladies dressing room and had heard Mary talking with a girl from Grand Rapids.

—Winfield, you're making an ass of yourself. I heard Mary up there tell a girl she wasn't really engaged to you at all. Said she was just kidding you. She doesn't know I heard it. Don't tell her. But you are a fool. Winfield.

—Well who asked you anything? Huh? That's not so. Lie.

—All right. Pardon me. You needn't be such a boor. When I tell you something confidential for your own good. I'm sorry I said anything. Good night Mr Winfield Payne. The joke's on you. Ha, ha.

Jesus, maybe Mary did say that. I don't believe it though. But she has acted funny all along. Maybe just kidding me. Maybe marry me for money. Hell, I get no money from my folks. I want to see her. Can't be true though. Not Mary.

Winfield was very worried. What if it was true? What if Mary felt that way? Only wanted him while she was in college to run around with her, show her a good time? It was impossible though. She couldn't be telling people such things without knowing he would hear about it. Maybe her folks feel the same way. He was worried.

Mary came down the stairway, smiling at Winfield. He scowled a little. Then decided he had better act as if nothing had happened. He smiled back at her, a sickly weak smile, forced.

—Mary do you really love me? Want to marry me? Tell me. I love you. Tell me, do you really love me?

She colored a little. She had been talking in a cold blooded way, about Winfield, but the girl upstairs knew a fellow Mary had formerly liked very well and Mary didn't want this young man to think she was engaged. He lived in Chicago and might ask her to a house party at the university there. She would like to go to it even if she did love Winfield. It was a harmless lie, she thought. I wonder if Winfield knows? It's uncanny, nobody heard us talking. But she colored. Afraid and sorry too. She had lied to the girl. It might have been partly true though. That was why she was afraid.

—Why Winfield, whatever can you be talking about? Of course I love you, dearest. You hurt me talking that way. I've got your pin. I couldn't wear the ring, it shows through my dress. That's why it isn't around my neck now. Of course I love you. Don't be silly.

She wanted him to love her, not to suspect her of being anything but madly in love with him. She really did love him more than she ever had before. But she wanted good times. Calculated for them, and didn't want her engagement to be in the way of having them.

Winfield believed what Mary told him. He was sure she hadn't said anything the Thornton girl had told him. The Thornton girl would lie anyway, he thought.

Try to spoil everybody's happiness that way. But he wasn't absolutely sure, and because he wasn't absolutely sure he was suspicious. He thought of other grievances. Of the night she had given the pin and ring back to him. He didn't love her as madly, as wholeheartedly, as he had before.

She knew it too, and from that time on she loved him more and more. From that night she never could tell a girl such a story as she had told in the ladies dressing room. She wouldn't have gone with that Chicago boy if he had invited her to ten house parties. She loved Winfield. Only Winfield. Because she knew that he didn't love her as he had loved her before.

That night, at home on the davenport, she told him how much she loved him. She cried, guilty tears, and told him she cried because she loved him so much. He was soft and loved her. He couldn't think of his doubts, making love to her. He only loved her. Didn't try to think.

When he went back to Ann Arbor he thought of her coolly. Of the wrongs she had done him. Of her holding out on the question of making money. He wouldn't make money. No. He would have a quiet job and a quiet life. Not make money.

She wasn't the girl for him. He knew that. He felt they would never be happy. They would argue and fight as they had the night when she gave back the pin. He never would be able to stand it. But still he wrote her love letters, and planned to go through with it all. He still thought that things would adjust themselves, that they might have a happy life of it.

And her letters were now so full of love. She
wanted him to love her. Womanlike, she knew the
moment his love began to die. She knew and wanted
to revive it. She told him of how she had made love to
him, so passionate.

It had made her sentimental, but Winfield had
tasted of greater sweets and wasn't touched. Just loving
her wasn't enough to make a bond between them.
Not enough for Winfield. He still loved her. But it
was different. He could look at it coldly in retrospect
now. He analyzed it and thought he knew just what it
was that made him love her, that made her love him.
He still had hopes that it would work out to a happy
climax. But it was breaking all the time. Breaking to
pieces in him. In Mary it was growing stronger. She
loving him more and more, he loving her less and less.

The first weekend after college started he went
back home. His mother met him, very angry. Started
scolding him. Talked of disowning him. Why Winfield.
I want to know about this. What about that ring?
What about that diamond ring? Are you a little fool?
Did you give her that ring? Tell me all about it. I want
to know.

Mary had worn the ring at college, she couldn't
help herself. She had to show the girls, who from the
first had said that Winfield was only kidding her, how
serious things were. She had worn the ring.

Mrs Payne heard about it the first day Mary wore
it. She waited, knowing Winfield would be home soon.
This thing could not go on.

—Now Winfield. It's perfectly absurd. This
cannot go on. You getting money from your father. No
engaged man can live on his father. You will have to get
that ring back. Say, I want to know where you got that.
Tell me.

—Now listen here, mother. Morgan's. Now there's
no use making all that fuss. We are engaged. That's all.
We are engaged. I'm going to work next summer. I can
get a job. One promised to me now. I can get it. Don't
make a fuss. You hurt me like that mother. Talking that
way.

—Now see here, Winfield. I am your mother.
I hope you realize that. Who are you speaking to in
that tone of voice? An engaged man cannot live on his
father. That's all. You get that ring and pin back or you
go to work. Leave the house. That's all. Engaged man.
Young fellow like you telling your mother. Aren't you
ashamed?

This talk of sending him from the house right
away frightened Winfield. Next summer would have
been all right, but now. Where could he go? He didn't
have a job in sight. That had been a bluff. He was
scared of his mother. And besides, he wasn't sure that
Mary was worth sacrificing so much for. Two or three
weeks earlier he would have left immediately. But now
he wasn't sure.

—Now mother. I'll tell you what I'll do. I'll get
the ring back and keep it till summer. Then give it to
her again. That all right?

—The pin too. There's not going to be any tom-
foolery.

His mother saw that her chance had come. She was going to do all she could while Winfield was in the right mood.

—You'll just have to cut out this foolishness. It's got to stop. If you could be sensible with girls it would be all right. But getting engaged without your mother knowing. It's that snip of a girl. She just wanted to show off. Show that she could get you. That's all. You ought to be ashamed letting a girl like that put it over on you. She only announced her engagement because the other girls did. She didn't care for you. I know all about it. Girls have told it all over. What a fool you made of yourself. Letting a little snip get you that way. You, a young boy. Talking of marriage. It's too absurd. No, you get that ring back, pin too. Have you paid for it? Where did you get the money?

—No. Installment plan. Morgan's. I'll pay it. Never mind.

—It's coming out of the money your father sends you for school. It's not your money. That ring is mine. Father's money. I want it. You get it back. She can't keep it. It's not yours, it's not hers.

Winfield was beaten, and the things his mother had said hurt him, they touched him on sore spots.

A lot of what she said is probably true. Probably Mary was kidding me. I'd just as soon get the ring back.

—I'll get it back mother. Till spring. Then. Different. But I'll get it.

Then he had to tell Mary all about his troubles at home. She cried. He felt sorry. He noticed that now that he was talking with her he felt as much in love as he ever had. It was only when he was away that he doubted whether he loved her.

—I'll have to take the ring hack. They're paying for it really. Money comes out of my school money. Else I'll have to quit school and go to work. I can't do that now. Not until summer. Besides, you said you wouldn't marry me until you got out of school. There's nothing else to do. She said I had to take the pin too. I hate to. I hate to. I love you so. But in the summer, then it'll be different. I can give them to you again and go to work and wait until you can marry me.

The very word wait, stuck in his throat. He didn't think he could wait that long. He would tire of waiting.

—Why don't you just run away with me now, Mary? He thought he would have to ask her that much. We could go away together and I'll get work.

—Oh, I couldn't. But your mother is mean. It's awful. What will people think of me Winfield? You only think of yourself and your mother. Do you love me Winfield? Really? Oh Winfield. You've got to love me.

—Why of course I love you. Sure. Why do you ask that? I love you.

He did love her. He felt so sorry for her. He loved her and he pitied her. Loved her because he pitied her, maybe.

—Take the ring, pin. She handed them to him reluctantly, almost with an air of finality.

Winfield was relieved. He had thought it would be more difficult, getting the pin and ring back. But

it had been easy. Only for Mary it had been hard.
But she knew she must do it. Either that or run away
and marry him, and she couldn't marry then. Too
much ahead of her in four years of school, and also,
her parents would be angry. She couldn't. She had to
think of herself. But it would be awful. She would just
have to tell the girls at college that it was Mrs Payne's
fault. That Winfield would give her the ring back again
anyway. But it would be awful to face them without
the pin too. She decided she just wouldn't say anything
to them, not even if they asked her. It was too much for
her. She was so hurt, so overwhelmed, that she could
hardly stand on her feet.

Oh, Winfield, she said. That you would let your
mother run you that way. It's too awful.

—But don't you see Mary? Don't you see? It's a
whole year. Next summer it'll be all right. You'll get
them back again. It's just so I can stay in school. Do
you want me to quit school? I will, if you say.

She didn't dare tell him yes, but she did want to.
She did wish he would do it without her telling him.
Her pride was so hurt. No one had ever hurt her pride
before, and she had never thought that Winfield Payne
would be able to do it. She had hurt boys, but no boy
had ever hurt her. She wasn't the kind of girl that boys
can hurt. But this time she was hurt. Hopeless, she felt.
As if there was no way for her to turn. No one for her
to turn to. She loved Winfield now, because he had
been firm and strong, because he had dared to hurt her.
Before she had only thought she loved him. She had
not known what it was to love a man. Now she knew.
And she gave the ring and the pin back to him.

—But Winfield, you must keep your promise. You must love me always. Next summer you must. Oh, you must. The ring Winfield. I would kill myself Winfield if you didn't. You don't know what it is, what a girl feels. What will I tell all the girls? My whole life. You must write to me every day Winfield. Promise.

—I will.

She was happier. The letters would show the girls. They would know by the letters. His name on the back of the envelopes. She would just leave the letters lying on the table in the dormitory hallway until the other girls had picked up their mail. Then they would all see that she had a letter, a letter from Winfield. The girls must never know. They must know that he loved her. She would read parts of the letters to some of them. Oh, there were ways. It wasn't so bad. But Mrs Payne was awfully mean, a mean awful woman, she thought.

Back at school Winfield was a little glad that he had the ring and pin back. Maybe they wouldn't be able to last it out together. In that case it was better to have those things. If she did too much to provoke him, he simply never would give her the ring again, and their engagement would be at an end. He was glad his mother insisted that he do it. Now Mary and he could try it out, loving one another, and if their love lasted until summer he would go to work and wait until she could marry him. He must find a job and decided to begin looking at once.

Leigh Mason, manager of the Rice and Belmont Silver Company, one of the oldest and best known wholesale jewelers in America had been a member of Winfield's fraternity when he went to college at Michigan. He was an old friend of both Winfield's father and his uncle. Winfield wrote to him and asked if he might get a permanent job with his firm. He must stop school in the summer and would be married in two years. He wanted a good job with an established firm and would work hard at it if he got it.

Mason wrote to Mr Payne. Asked him if Winfield was really going to stop school. Mr Payne, without consulting his wife, wrote back and said that Winfield was engaged and would be going to work. He had little respect for college education anyhow. He had been to college himself for two years and knew enough about it to think Winfield would be better off at work. He told Mason he would appreciate it if his firm would hire Winfield. The boy needed to be put to work at some stable, permanent job. He had gone to three colleges and had worked at several jobs, but didn't stick to anything. He hoped Mason would find a place for Winfield.

Mason was glad to hire Winfield. He knew him well from his boyhood and knew Mr Payne well too. He thought young Payne would be a good man for the firm. He wrote and told Winfield he could begin work for them after school ended for the year.

The job was a good one with an ample salary. Winfield would be put in the advertising and sales department of the firm and when he had gained experience they could use him to wait upon the buyers who came directly to New York, to Maiden Lane, to buy their jewelry. They needed a live young man with good personality to work into the business.

An old firm such as Rice and Belmont had too many older men in their employ and needed young blood. If Payne was like his father he would be just the young man for them. Because Mason was a fraternity brother of Winfield and an old friend of his father, Winfield got a very good job. He knew it was pull that got him the position, but he didn't care. He would be able to earn his money with them and he was almost positive of remaining on their payroll as long as he might care to.

At the end of the first semester he got low marks in all of his subjects. He hated his professors for giving him lower marks than they had given some students who didn't know as much as he did. It wasn't fair, the whole system. And he felt it was a waste of time too, going to college.

He would be glad to stop school.

He thought of the business he was going into. Business was a joke too, after his other jewelry experience, and the experience with L. M. Perry garden seed company. He had no respect for either college or business. But he would work, get his money, and have a comfortable place to live in. He was glad it was to be office work.

When he finished for the day he would be through and could go home to Mary. If Mary lasted that long. He was doubtful. She might kick about things again, and she was always acting so officious. Telling what to do and what not to do. He had liked that once, but he wouldn't stand it any longer. He loved her, but he was going to be boss of the family now, or he would be nothing. Wouldn't even belong to the family if he couldn't be wearing the pants.

He had the upper hand in the affair now. Could leave her when he wanted to and make her toe the mark too.

He wrote to Mary every day for about two weeks, then he said he couldn't keep it up longer. Had to spend more time for studying. So he wrote every three days from that time on. She continued to write to him every day, telling him each time that she loved him more and more. It irritated him to have her tell him this so much.

Now that he had the upper hand he wasn't exactly satisfied with it, he didn't want her hanging on to him like an old faithful dog. He began to lose respect for her, because she loved him too much. He was ready to end the whole affair at the slightest provocation. He would too, if she gave him a good reason.

There in Ann Arbor, when he was away from her, he just thought and thought and analyzed his love away. Entirely away. He didn't love her at all anymore. But he would go on with it, he had promised her he would. And because his mother was so opposed to the thing, he wanted to cling to it and make it last. When he knew he didn't love her any more he should have told her, but he couldn't. He would just hang on to the shreds of their love.

Mary knew he didn't love her, even if he said so in every letter. He scolded her so much, about little things. He had never done that before. And now he wrote that he had a good steady job, but it wasn't one of those jobs where you earn a million dollars in ten weeks. It was a steady, comfortable job, where you earned enough to live comfortably on. That was all he wanted. He told her she would have to agree on this, because he didn't intend to waste his life making money. He had decided that.

She gave in to him. Said she had been wrong. She really never had wanted money, only a quiet life and Winfield. It was Winfield she wanted. She loved him now, loved him more than she ever knew she could love. Now that she was losing him, she loved him. At night she would write him long letters, telling him how much she loved, how she must have him. If he failed her, she would just die. She couldn't live through it. She was afraid he might fail her. She knew their love was breaking and she was making a last terrible effort to hold on to it.

One day he walked right up to Christabel, on the campus at Ann Arbor. He had seen her three or four times during the year, but had avoided her, not daring to speak to her. He knew he had hurt her, and knew he had been a cad toward her. He felt guilty and so he had always deliberately avoided her. Now he met her face to face. And he was glad they had met. He wanted to speak to her and be friends with her. He hoped she wouldn't hate him, because he had been such a cad with her.

—Why, hello Christabel. He was uneasy. Didn't know what to say further. He knew his face was reddening. He hoped she would say something quickly.

—Hello Winfield. Shake hands. Shall we?

It was good for her to meet him. She wasn't afraid.
She wanted to meet him this way and liked to see that
he was uneasy. She was glad she had an effect upon
him. He might even come back to her.

—Why of course Christabel. I like you. You know
that. I've been engaged to a girl all winter. It's about
broken up now though. We don't get along. But that's
the reason I haven't called on you. I wanted to see you
though. He felt mean, a cad again. Disloyal to Mary.
Telling Christabel the engagement was broken.

—You could have called, Winfield. We're friends.
Come, let's walk along.

He couldn't ask her any questions about herself,
feeling so guilty. He just talked with her about school
and told her that his engagement was a failure. But he
was going to work anyway, after school was over. Live
his own life.

—Christabel, can I come over and call on you
sometime?

—Why yes, Winfield, whenever you want to. I'm
going to dinner tonight though. Tomorrow afternoon.
Good time.

She still liked Winfield and was enjoying seeing
him so in discomfort. It was fun for her. The pain of
their love affair had left her, but she did like to get a
little revenge, and she was happy to see that Winfield
was so disturbed at their meeting. She had known why
he hadn't called on her before. He had been afraid to.

At home Winfield thought, Gee, she would have
been the girl. Better girl than Mary. Make a better
wife. Aristocrat, she is. But I can't stand it around her.
I wish I wasn't going to call. I can't talk to her. Don't

know what to say. It's finished for us. No getting back now, after the way I acted. She was the best girl I ever had. Real genuine dyed in the wool girl. What'll I do tomorrow calling on her? Nothing to say. Rather not go.

But he did go to call. Walked slowly up to the house she lived in, dreading the meeting. She came to the door cheerfully. Shook his hand and greeted him merrily. In the back of her mind she thought she might make him love her again, he was so uneasy. He must still like her.

He did like her, even more than Mary. If Christabel had gone up to him and put her arms around his neck, he would have loved her and asked her to be his wife. He would have worked for her. He thought of this. If she wouldn't push me away. Said she would never love again. She wouldn't love me. She would laugh at me. Push me away from her, if I tried to kiss her. He really felt that he loved her.

They danced together to music of the phonograph. It was painful. He couldn't hold her to him. Didn't dare to that. Just had to dance along, stiff and formal. They talked of things at the college. If she would only start something about our love. If she just started something, then I could go on. I could kiss her. I'd like to. I guess I love her more than I ever loved Mary. But she would just laugh at me. She's through with me. Just friends now. The way I wanted to be. But I can't be just friends with her. It's too uncomfortable. I've got to have her, love her, or else it's nothing.

Christabel hoped he would start some talk. Tell her he was sorry for the way he had acted. No not that

exactly, for she didn't blame him really. She just wished
he would love her again. Not be sorry, just love her. If
he would only stop talking about school. Why can't he
be natural. Always trying to get away. He's so afraid of
me. He ought to be. But I do wish we could be friends,
as we were in Washington. That was best. We loved.
In Marine City, too much passion. In Washington we
loved. Wish we could be that way again.

They made another date, but Winfield wrote to
her and said he couldn't call. He guessed it was all over
between them. They were so stiff and uncomfortable
when they were together. It couldn't go on. He told
her he was going to go ahead with the girl he was
engaged to. He would marry. He had made a mess of
love once, with Christabel. He would not do it again
with Mary. No, he would see the thing through. It
would be better if he and Christabel didn't see one
another after this.

A few weeks after this, Christabel fell in love with
a young man at the university and they were engaged
to one another. Winfield was jealous when he heard
of her engagement, but he knew she would never care
for him. It's a good thing I didn't try to start anything
when I called on her. She would have had the laugh on
me. I'm glad. Glad she's engaged. Hope she'll be happy.

But he still loved Christabel and wished he had
not hurt her that last summer. He was sorry he hadn't
held to her when he had her. She would have been the
best wife for him. Everything that Mary had, she had,
and a great deal more. But he had lost her. There was
no use weeping now. It was his own fault. He must pay
the penalty.

But he disliked Mary now, more than ever. She wasn't the girl Christabel was. He should have a girl like Christabel. He compared Mary with Christabel and Mary lost by the comparison. He could never marry her. Love her perhaps, but never marry her. Be divorced in six months if he ever married her. She would just demand money, and gaiety. It would be a hell of a life.

He wished something would happen so he might break the engagement. He couldn't stop the thing right out of a clear sky. People would talk. Her mother and father would be angry. Her mother especially.

Mrs Whitman had told him never to do anything to hurt their little daughter. She had warned him, never to do anything to hurt the little girl. Or you watch out, she had said. He had laughed. Of course he never would hurt the little girl he loved so much. It was ridiculous talking that way. And now he was nervous, he was going to hurt her, going to have to hurt her. But he would wait for a good chance, when it might look as if she had done the hurting. If there were only a way to make Mary break the engagement. That would be all right. Then nobody could say anything. But if he broke it, then people would think ill of him. He wanted people to think well of him.

He went to Detroit again with Richard Patton and sat in a blind pig and drank red wine and talked.

He wondered how Alice Wright was coming on. He should call on her. She would be interesting to talk to. Perhaps she had come to believe more in free love.

Though that wasn't the important thing. Of course not.
But he thought he should call on her. It was only fair
to Alice, that he call on her. They had been such good
friends. She would understand. He could tell her all
about Mary too, and she might be able to help him out
of a difficulty.

Alice was very glad to see him. She said she was.
Why Winfield you are horrid, never calling on me. Do
you think that was nice of you?

—Well, I was in love. No more for me though.
Again he felt that queer sensation go through him, he
was untrue to Mary. It wasn't fair to tell people that he
didn't love her. He wasn't playing fair. He felt cheap.
As if he had played a dirty trick on Mary. But he went
on. We don't get along you see. She wants another kind
of life. Money. You know. Money and good times.
Theaters. Things like that. I want an easier life. That's
what I want. Mary's different. We're not a good couple.

—Well Winfield. You should never pick out such
a girl. Men will do the silliest things though. I suppose
you are like the rest. I don't know this Mary, but I
know she's not the kind of woman for you. You need a
woman to sympathize with you. I know you. But you
have been horrid. Not even to write to me. And when
you did write. I should never speak to you after that
letter.

—Why, I just told you I was engaged. That's all.

—Never mind, Winfield. We understand, don't
we? I understand you. You're not happy. You still like
me too, don't you? Kiss me.

He kissed her lightly first. Then he kissed again,
passionate. He found he liked Alice as well as he had

liked Mary. At least she made him passionate and that
to him was a sign of liking her.

—I guess it's you Alice. I guess I still love you. But
after this experience with Mary, I'll never get tied up
with a girl. I mean I won't marry a girl.

—Now, you silly. Who said anything about that. I
love you as much as I ever did. I knew you would be all
right. Mary was no girl for you. I can see that. It's too
bad. Your wasting yourself on such a girl. A man with
your temperament shouldn't get such girls.

Alice was glad Winfield had come back to her.
He was an intelligent young man. She thought she
was quite an intelligent young woman. They could
get along so well, Winfield and she. And Alice wanted
an experience with a man. She wanted more than just
loving, and had decided that Winfield would make a
good man for her. She wanted him all the way. Not to
marry him though. She didn't want that. At least she
wouldn't admit it. But she did want Winfield to have
her.

—Then you're not engaged any more, Winfield?

—Why yes, course. We haven't broken it. I want
to though. Don't want to hurt her feelings, that's all.
How am I going to do it? I thought you might tell
me. I don't want to hurt her. Make her folks sore, you
know. But it's all over. The love stuff.

—You ought to go right to her and tell her you
don't love her any more. That's always the best way. If it
was me, I'd want you to do that. She'd feel better too.

—Can't do that though. Impossible. Really. I'll fix
it up though. Never worry. I'll fix it. Mother's against
the thing too. Folks don't like the girl.

—Well Winfield, you are just like a little boy. You are. Really. Now if I were you. Well forget it, Winfield. She's not worth all that bother. Come here.

She had Winfield back again. That was the important thing to her. She didn't care about Mary really. Only at first she had felt that it was unfair, the way Winfield had treated his girl. She had been sorry. But now she didn't care. She could forget Mary, only she must be sure that Winfield didn't love her. She just wanted to know that he didn't love Mary at all. She wanted Winfield herself, and was glad that the other girl was out of the way. Only she wanted to know that the other girl was really out of the way.

They made love. She told him that some day she wanted to go away somewhere with him and have him. Not just loving, she wanted everything.

Winfield was excited at the prospect and determined that he would have Alice. She was short, blond. A pretty girl, beautiful. And she was an intelligent girl too. Passionate. She writhed when he made love to her. Couldn't be still. Her legs moved and her body too. She made him crazy, passionate. He wanted her. And she was so small that he could pick her up in his arms.

She would be wonderful, he thought.

Mrs Wright was upstairs. The young people were sitting down below, on a davenport, making love. Alice wanted him. They would have one another. Both were passionate, hot. Now was the time. He took her to him. Mrs Wright called down the stairs, Alice it's late. Come right up. This minute.

—My God, did she hear us?

—Oh, no, I hope not, Alice answered.

—Yes, mother. I'll be right up. Right away. In a moment.

They had been together. But were afraid that Mrs Wright had heard them. That she knew what had happened downstairs. It would be awful if she knew. Winfield was very frightened. Wished he was out of the house: Wished he hadn't done it. Mrs Wright would be so angry. He might have to marry Alice. He wouldn't though. Wouldn't marry any girl.

—You must go. Right away, Winfield. Mother will be angry. I'm afraid Winfield. What will I do, do you know? Quick, tell me. This is terrible. We should have gone away some place. That would have been best. What will I do. Maybe children. My sister. She had children. That same way. In the family, children. All had them. Easy too. Maybe I'll have a child.

Winfield gave her some advice to keep her from getting a baby. Do it at once, though, he told her. The quicker the better. Then let me know if everything is all right. I know other things. I'll see you tomorrow at Pages', have an icecream. I'll take you to that wine place I told you about. Quicker the better Alice. Oh, you're wonderful Alice. The most wonderful girl. I do love you, Alice. If Mary was half as good as you are I'd stay with her. But you are the best. You're wonderful.

—I'm afraid Winfield but I'll do as you said. I'll do it now. Go right away, please. Mother'll be very angry. I love you too. I do.

She went up to the bathroom thinking that it wasn't so much. She had read and heard so much about it. Liked the loving better, even. But she was glad she had done it. Now she was a woman. Stronger. She had needed that. And she did like Winfield better than she had before. He was very nice. He knew so much. Most of the young fellows don't know half what he does. I'm glad.

Winfield thought Alice was a wonderful girl, to give herself to him that way. Mary never would have done it. Wanted to he married first. Alice was a better girl. Christabel would have been the same way. I'll have to stick it out with Mary longer though. Have to. Maybe I shouldn't have told Alice so much. If Mary knew what I had said she would be angry. Not angry only, be sick too. If Mary knew what I had done. God, what would she do? That would be awful. Poor Mary. The end I guess. I hope she gets over it all right. I never can tell her. It would be better to take Alice to New York next summer when I go. Live together. No need to marry. She's intelligent. Be nice to have her there. Be wonderful. Have a lover. Better than being married. Better than Mary. Be nice, have Alice that way.

Winfield and Alice both knew a young fellow from Detroit who went to school at Michigan, Clarence Malcomb. He liked Alice and liked Winfield too. And the young man thought Winfield was very intellectual. Thought Alice intellectual too. When he went to Detroit to spend the weekends he took Alice to the theater or a dance. That is, if Winfield wasn't there. He had no idea of butting in on Winfield. But when Winfield was engaged he had taken Alice out oftener. He liked her. Thought she was the ideal girl for him. And because Winfield liked her he wanted her all the more for himself. He would marry her if he could. Anything to get her.

Winfield told Alice he would never marry. When he got free of that Whitman girl, that was the end. Never think of marrying even.

Alice was afraid she might have a child by Winfield. She thought she felt something inside her. It seemed so different now, since he had been with her. If I have a child, mother will kill me. I can't, I can't.

Clarence Malcomb called on her, made love to her. She married Malcomb three weeks after she had been with Winfield, there in Detroit. Malcomb was happy. Get a girl away from Payne, that's pretty good. And he loved Alice, even if she wasn't so fond of him. Malcomb knew that Winfield would be jealous and he married Alice. They ran away together, to Toledo, Ohio, and were married. That would show Winfield Payne who the right fellow was. I guess she loved me all the time.

Alice was glad to be married. She felt safe now. And she knew that Winfield would never have married her. All her arguments went under, her talk of free love, equality of the sexes, forgotten. She was married and glad. It was a good thing to marry right away. If she had a child her husband would never know that it might be Winfield's. Now she was married and thought that it was the best life after all. Winfield was all right, but marriage was better. Now she could do as she pleased anyway. She was safer married.

Winfield was jealous. That a fellow like Malcomb should get Alice. A dumbbell really. That was too much. He could imagine her marrying some intelligent fellow, but Malcomb, that was unthinkable.

Two weeks after their marriage he met Malcomb on the street in Detroit. The young man looked at Winfield with a triumphant look. Well I got her away from you. What do you think of that? He spoke to Winfield.

—Hello Payne. Well I'm tied now. Alice and I are living here with her mother. I'm working for my father. That was all he said.

Winfield congratulated him. Even though he was a little jealous and angry that Alice should have shown such bad taste, he was glad that she was married. It saved him the worry. He might have had to marry her. That, he never would have done. The knowledge that he was the first man she had been with, the knowledge that he had been with her before her husband was with her, made him glad. He had something on young Malcomb. Malcomb needn't be so cocky. If he knew that Winfield had been with Alice just a few weeks before the marriage, he wouldn't feel so cocky.

—You got a fine girl, Malcomb. One of the best. I always liked Alice. You know that. I hope you are happy together all the time. She's a peach. Got more brains in a minute than most of them have in their lifetime.

—Come out and see us Winfield. Come out anytime. Alice will be glad to see you.

Alice be glad to see him. That was too much. He just answered, Thank you. Walked away. I'll be out, as an afterthought.

Malcomb could see that Winfield was jealous. He was very happy. Hoped Winfield would come out. See their happiness. Be a good thing for Payne. He thinks he can get any girl he wants. I got Alice though. Show him that.

When Winfield went home from school, his mother would look at his vest and see that the fraternity pin was attached. She had the ring in her own possession. No need to worry about that. But she was going to make sure that Mary didn't have even the pin.

Winfield acted irritated the first couple times she did that. Then he didn't mind. Mother, you don't need to be always looking. You've got nothing to worry about. I'm through with Mary. You ought to be glad, you've done enough to stop it. We were happy. But now. Well, now it's all gone, about. She likes me, much as ever. I don't care for her so much. Don't want to marry. Glad I got the ring back.

Mrs Payne was glad that his foolishness was at an end. She had been waiting for him to tire of Mary and now she was glad. But of a sudden she felt a pang for Mary. She knew that Mary loved her son. And now that Winfield had said that he didn't love her. She thought of Mary, and of how it would hurt the girl. She was glad and sorry at the same time.

—Does Mary feel as you do, Winfield? You shouldn't have gotten her expectations all up like that. And then drop her. Is that right? I told you at first you shouldn't arouse a young girl. It's dangerous. Cause her lots of harm. I know, as a girl. You should not make that kind of love to young girls. It's bad for them. Might spoil their whole lives. I know. I hope you haven't got

her all expectant. I hope you don't hurt her, Winfield.
That would he awful.

—Now see here, mother. You can talk. You've
been trying all the time to get this thing to an end. I
know. Now you're blaming me, because I don't love
her any more. I'm going to go around with her. Act
as if nothing happened. I haven't even told her. But
I'll never marry her. I like her all right. As for hurting
her, I never hurt any girl. Nothing but harmless
lovemaking, that's all.

—Now don't get excited my boy. Just listen to
your mother. I know that it is a bad thing for young
girls to make violent love with boys. It's a bad thing.
Don't tell me. I was a girl myself. And now I don't
want you to do anything to Mary to hurt her feelings
either. You must let her down easy. It might make
a great difference to her. Let a girl down easy. You
are sometimes cruel with girls. I know some of your
highschool goings on. Let Mary down easy.

Mrs Payne was happy that her son had ceased to
love Mary. She was sorry for Mary too. She had just
the slightest suspicion that this talk of Winfield's about
not loving Mary was not all true. He might be bluffing.
Maybe he did still love her. She was not sure, and yet
she knew that he didn't love her as much as he had.

—You should ask Mary to come to dinner with us
Sunday.

He told Mary that his mother wanted her to come
to dinner Sunday noon. That she seemed to like Mary
more now than she had before. Seemed to be quite
satisfied with Mary now. He didn't tell Mary why his

mother liked her better now, but Mary suspected the reason.

It's about all over. She got the ring away, and now she just wants to patronize me. That's why she asked me to dinner.

Mary didn't want to be insulted. But she had to go, she couldn't very well refuse the invitation. She had to go to dinner at the Paynes'.

The family treated her much more cordially than they had the first time she came to dinner. Mrs Payne smiled upon her, beamed upon her, and patted her shoulders with mock affection. Called her, Mary my young girl, and stung Mary calling her that. As if she was too young for Winfield and too young to marry any man.

Mrs Payne was enjoying herself. She had beaten this little snip of a girl. Showed Mary that she couldn't get her son so easily. She was celebrating her victory. Mary felt humiliated, knew that the whole family were patronizing her. Even Winfield acted so patronizing.

He was glad his mother had changed toward Mary. They might be able to patch things up after all. But no. He never would marry her, even if he did feel then, that he loved her again. He knew that in time the love would wear out. She would say little mean things, or do something he didn't like, or ask him to make money. It would be a failure, their marriage. He would not do it. But he did half love Mary and he wanted to make love to her and kiss her. He wished he could be with her once. It would be wonderful. A wonderful way to end a love affair. Go with the girl once and then leave each other for good. He played with the idea, but dismissed it. Liable to make the girl love him too much. She would have a hold on him then. Or she might get pregnant. He couldn't do that. But it would be a fine way to end their love affair.

The night before they had danced together and later made love in the back seat of the car. She told him he was no longer as eager as he had formerly been. He answered that they were getting into a more sensible stage of love. He still loved her but it was a little different way now. Felt cooler, more sensible. Best way to love, he told her. He still held that they would marry. He told her four years would be all right to wait.

She was worried, he acted so willing to wait four years, and then he admitted that he felt cooler toward her.

It's your mother, she told him. She's been saying things to you and you just Kowtow to her. It's too bad you let your mother run you. I guess I ought to be enough for you. But you want your mother around too. Winfield you have got to love me. I'm afraid. If you should leave me I would just kill myself. You tell me you love me. But you act so different. I wish I knew.

—Now don't be silly, Mary. Of course I love you. That's all bunk about not loving you. As for my mother, you know damned well that she never puts anything over on me. That ring and pin deal, now. That was just so I could finish school this year. You wanted me to, didn't you? Well. There you are. I had to do it. Everything will be all right. We've got to wait four years anyhow. You said that yourself.

—I might get mother and father to let me marry
sooner. I'll try. I want to. If I lose you. If you don't. Oh,
I might kill you, the way I feel.

—Now, don't be silly. Everything will be all right.

—You don't seem very anxious anymore. When I
tell you I might marry you sooner.

—I am though. Really Mary.

They made passionate love together and went
home. Mary felt somewhat reassured, because he was
still so passionate with her. She wished she could have
him. It might be the best way to hold him. If she
gave herself he might love her more. If she only dared
give herself to him, everything might be all right. He
wanted it, she knew that.

Before he went back to school she told him that
some day she wanted to have him. If you leave me,
Winfield, and I have to marry someone else, I'll go
away with you some time. I couldn't give you up
without having you. Don't leave me Winfield. When
you go back to school something might happen. It'll
be another whole month before we see each other. It's
terrible for me, facing the girls. You used to come home
so often. Now you don't. I'm so worried Winfield. And
sometimes I think I might as well be dead.

No, please, Mary. Don't talk that way. I love you.
That's all that's necessary isn't it? Well, there you are.
Now don't be silly. Everything will be all right. Come
out all right. If I don't love you as I used to then the
way I love you now is better, more real. Stable, sensible.
Don't you believe that?

—I'm not sure Winfield. Sometimes I think you
don't love me at all. But I don't dare think that. My

whole life is wrapped up in you. I don't dare even
think. I just have to trust you. If I had the pin it would
be different. The train will be here in a minute. You go
away from me. Another month of hell. It's hell for me.
You don't write often. Once you went over a week, not
writing.

—I was in Detroit then. That's why. Don't you
see? I'll write oftener though. Promise I will. Now don't
worry. You'll be crying, if you keep that up. Aren't you
glad I love you? That ought to be enough. I do. They
kissed each other and Winfield climbed into the train.

Jesus, it's getting serious. Talking about killing
people. She might too. Just crazy enough, do a thing
like that. I got to be careful. Might get my head
knocked off. Her mother would be sore too. I'll have
a hell of a time getting out of this fix. I never saw her
acting the way she did this weekend. Must know I don't
like her the way I did. She feels it, that's it. Just knows
it. Intuition. Woman's intuition. Awful thing that.
Glad I haven't got one too. I wish she'd go out with
some fellow at school there. Then I could be sore. Tell
her I was sore, through with her. Wasn't true to me. She
used to go with the fellows. I didn't care then. Now if
I'd be caring she'd see through it. Got to get something
better than that.

He didn't write to Mary every day as he had
promised to do. For a few days he did and then dropped
into writing once every two or three days. He wished
he had something as a cause to break the engagement.
Not that any other girl had come into his life, but only

that he was tired of Mary and didn't want to marry her. He liked her too much to be deliberately cruel to her and hurt her. He didn't dare tell her outright that he no longer loved her. He wished she would see through it and break the engagement herself. That would be the easiest way for him. His letters were cooler than they had ever been before. He reminded her of little things she had said which had annoyed him at the time. He scolded her and told her she didn't really love him, or she couldn't have done those things. He reminded her that she had started going with him only because she wanted a boy to take her to dances in Benton, and because her aunt had sicced her on, in a way.

—I didn't know then, that you were only playing with me. How can I tell now? If you would do such things you might do something worse to me now. You said yourself, that if those girls hadn't announced their engagements you wouldn't have announced ours. And what Helen Thornton told me about you talking with that girl at the country club may have been true. You acted funny that night. I never would have said such a thing, you know that. And still you expect me to believe that you love me so much.

She wrote back and said all of the things he had said might be true. That didn't matter. She loved him now. She knew herself, that she hadn't loved him at first, but he had loved her and she had grown to care more and more for him. Now that she loved him so madly, why should he talk about those things so far in the past? It wasn't true though, about that girl at the country club. Mary wouldn't admit that she had told that story. It would be too damning.

Finally she wrote him and said, now Winfield if you are always saying you love me, why don't you show it and write letters like the ones you used to send me? Now I have to read the old ones for my happiness. The letters you send now are so cold and you are always scolding. If you don't love me, tell me, please. It would be better to know than be so uncertain. Please write me at once and tell me whether you really love me. Tell me the truth Winfield. I want to know and I deserve to know. If there is some other girl you should tell me. You promised once that when the time came that you no longer loved me you would tell me. Please, in your next letter. I am going mad with things going the way they are. If it wasn't for your awful, terrible mother, we would he happy. But she has just ruined everything.

Here was a chance for Winfield. Mary insulting his mother. He'd have to see about that. Mary couldn't insult his mother. Awful, terrible mother. Means I'm awful, terrible myself. I'm my mother's son. That's just as if she was telling me I was awful. I'll have to call her down on that. That's a direct insult to me, come to think about it. He reasoned in this way, knowing that his reasoning was only a blind to hide the fact that he no longer loved her. He wrote a letter to Mary.

Dear Mary, you have hurt me in your last letter. I never thought you would say such insulting things to me. I see now that all along you have not loved me. You could never call my mother an awful, terrible woman, if you respected me, knowing that she is my own mother. I am surprised and cannot understand why you would deliberately write such a thing to me. It seems that all you want to do is hurt me. And then asking me always whether I love you or not. I show it to you in every way and yet you question. It sounds a little as if you didn't want me to love you, when you write such things in your letters. If you don't want my love let me know. And if you do want it you shouldn't insult me in indirect ways such as slamming my mother. It hurts me to have to write to you this way, but when a man loves a girl there is nothing else to do. I am hurt more than you think. It has killed something in me.

Winfield remembered the letter Christabel had sent him. That was a splendid letter. It has killed something in me, my love for all men. Didn't mean so much perhaps, but it was a good sentence. That would make Mary feel pretty cheap. She would see then. That would be her chance to end things. It has killed something in me. Winfield, after writing the sentence, began to think that something in him was dead. He began to feel, when he reread the letter, that she had hurt him, that she had killed his love, something in him. He felt sorry for himself, after he had written the letter and sent it away. And he knew all the time it was a lie. He didn't mean a thing of it. He had called his mother worse things than that himself. But he felt sorry for himself. Thought the letter was the best thing he could have sent under the circumstances.

Mary answered by telegram, you misunderstand. Wait for explanation. Letter follows. All my love. Mary.

A special delivery letter reached him the day after the telegram came. She was sorry she had called his mother that. She didn't mean to hurt Winfield's feeling. If she had known she wouldn't have sent the letter. If

her letters hurt him she wouldn't send any letters to
him. All she wanted was his love. She was ready to
do anything. Run away with him. Quit school. Work
herself, if necessary, so they could be together. She just
wanted Winfield. Was sorry she had hurt him. Had
cried all night and couldn't sleep. She must have an
answer to her letter at once. She wouldn't be able to
sleep until she heard. Everything I said I take back. I
love you Winfield. You are all I want. I would go away
with you anywhere. Even if we didn't marry. I must
have you. Your love. Please forgive me for everything
I have ever done. I am sorry, but I love you, love you,
love you.

Winfield couldn't help feeling love for her when
he read the letter. If she had only been that way a little
sooner. Then it would be all right. It's too late now to
get on her knees. Doesn't do any good now. She just
made me stop loving her. All the little things she did.
I'll bet she did tell that girl she was only kidding me.
I wouldn't believe her at all. It's a good thing I got the
upper hand. She just had me. Now it's different. But
a girl ought to see that before it's too late. She would
have known she couldn't go on like that. A man would
see through all that, sometime. But that's quite a letter
she wrote. She must be nuts about me. Just makes me
cooler though. Don't like grovelling on the ground in
front of me. Schopenhauer says about women. That's
all they are. Old Schopenhauer knew a hell of a lot
about women. Look at Mary. The worm's turned now.
I wonder what I ought to answer to that? Not much to
say. Write her a cool letter. Won't hurt her too much.
She sees how it is, I guess.

Dearest, I got your letter today and am sorry you took my other so hard. I still love you, but as I said before, something is killed in me, after all you have written and said to me. What we need is to talk the thing over. It's almost impossible to put everything in a letter. But never fear, I love you. It would be better for me, more comfortable, if I didn't, because this way I am constantly tortured by the thoughts of all the things I wrote you about. However, I don't want you crying and carrying on. I love you, that should be enough. Please believe me. Wait until I come home. We will talk it all over. I'm going away to New York in a few weeks to work and we want things to be all fixed up first. I'll be home before long. With love. Winfield.

The letter was almost as bad as the other, but he used dearest again, instead of dear. And he told her he loved her. It didn't sound like love though.

If he should stop loving me, I'd just quit school. I couldn't stick it out here, with the girls talking. They all wonder about the pin now, and the ring too. Nobody asks me, but I know they all know what's up. If I only had the pin. Even if he didn't love me so much. If I had the pin, then nobody would know but myself. He ought to let me have the pin, even if he doesn't love me. And he'll be going away and I won't have it. Have nothing to show that he loves me. It's awful, the way the girls look at me now. I never can finish school here, if he leaves me. If I had that pin. Be nice to have something of Winfield's too. Pin be nice. Something dear to him. And help here at school too, with the girls. I got to get it. If he quits loving me, I'll just run away. Go back home. Go to work. Any place. I won't stay in

this college though. I wonder what Winfield means?
Something killed in me. He says that all the time. Likes
the words I guess. He just is getting cold to me. I love
him and he doesn't love me. If I could be cooler, he
might love me. I can't now though. It's too late now.
That would be his excuse. He would just quit. If I was
cold, he would say I didn't love him and quit. And if
he does leave me, if he quits loving me. I got to have
that pin. Got to have it. It wouldn't hurt him to give
it to me. Just a pin. But it makes a difference here. If I
had that, he could go. It would be awful though. Have
him go. I guess he made me love him when he began
getting tired. I should have run away with him when
he asked me to. Eloped. We could have done it. Get
him married. Everything would be all right then. I held
off too long, that's all.

He went back to Benton once more. This would
be his last chance to see Mary until just before going
to New York. He couldn't go home again until the end
of the semester, after the examinations. There would be
too much studying to do. He had let his work pile up
and would have to study for the whole semester in the
few weeks before examinations. When his school was
ended, Mary would be back in Grand Rapids. They
had planned to meet there, before he went to New York
and say their farewells.

Mary was afraid that, breaking away from school,
and the regular visits home, Winfield would never
come back to her. She felt that once she let him go to
New York he never would come back. He would just
forget her and stay away from her. And she didn't have

the ring or the pin. He would bring these to Grand Rapids before going to work.

He might not come to Grand Rapids after their little quarrel. He might be through with her. He could just as well give her the pin, and the ring too, as far as that was concerned. Right away. He could at least give her the pin, this weekend. There were only six more weeks of school. It wouldn't hurt if she had the pin that short time. His mother would never know either. Mary had to have something to hold him to her. The pin would be the thing.

Winfield's mother cautioned him to be good to Mary. Not to hurt her feelings. She told him again that he had done a terrible thing when he aroused the young girl. Boys should be more careful. It means so much.

Friday night, Winfield and Mary went to a dance. He loved her, being near her. But he knew that it was a different love than his first wild, mad, one. He could see that she had faults, now. He looked at her hair that had seemed perfect. Now it was not even the same color. Her eyes were not bright as he had seen them before. Her hips seemed unduly accentuated, though they were really graceful. Was she a little bow legged? He wondered. She seemed so weak and feminine now. Her lips quivered, uncertain. Her face looked so babyish. This was the girl he had loved. Lips thin too, he thought. Still, nice lips to kiss. She's not a knockout.

He saw her flaws, saw them all, and more than all of them. But going home that night he made love to her again, passionate love, though it was selfconscious love. He watched her, noticed how she kissed and noticed her reactions. She seemed to be affecting a great deal. Those wild kisses were not wild at all. Only put on. She wasn't passionate. She was just trying to make him passionate. He saw through her little game. Wondered if she had always been acting in that way.

She had not always been that way. But tonight she was thinking of the pin. She wanted to get it back. She thought, If Winfield gets very passionate, as he sometimes does, then I can get it back. He would give it to me. If he was passionate he would do anything for me.

She knew he would be that way.

This night she asked him, Winfield before you go back to school give me the pin. Nobody will know. I won't tell anyone. Won't even wear it. Give it to me. I need it more than you do. Do you love me? I've got to have it, that's all. I've got to.

—I can't give it to you.

He recovered immediately. Not a bit of passion in him now. He straightened up in the seat. Cool. Calm. I can't give it you. My mother would notice it in a minute and raise hell. You know that. Wait until after school's over. You got along without it all this time. Ought to be able to wait a few weeks longer.

He didn't want to give it to her. It would mean that he would have all that trouble of getting it back again when they finally broke. It would make the break easier if he kept the pin. He decided he wouldn't even go to Grand Rapids. He would make love to her this last weekend and then go to New York. Sudden like. That was the way. It would hurt her less and they would have no unpleasant fuss. No arguments that

way. Nothing could be done if he was in New York.
Cowardly thing to do though.

Gee, I've acted like a dog all along. Those letters.
Didn't mean a thing. I can't tell her though, right out.
She'd just go crazy. It would be a break, sudden. Better
to have it sort of die down. But it's a dirty trick to run
away. It's a dirty trick to accuse her all the time. My
own damned fault. But I can't help not loving her.

He felt sorry for Mary and sorry that he was such
a cad. But he would have to go on with it. There was
no other way in sight. He was going to New York and
work. No more school, no more Mary. Work now
and a life by himself. He'd have a good time and a
comfortable job in New York. A real job in a fine, old
established firm. A respectable job, as good as any job
in the world. At the very top, such a job. His father
would be glad that he was working, not fooling away
time in school. His mother wouldn't like it. Now that
the engagement was broken she would want him to go
on with school. But that didn't matter. He was going
to New York. It would settle the whole problem of life.
Get rid of Mary, school, parents. All of the things that
complicated life at this time.

Mary didn't press him for the pin, further than she
had. Next day her aunt invited him to dinner at her
home in Benton. The two young people must eat with
her once before they parted for the last time in Benton.
Mary had practically arranged the whole thing.

After dinner her aunt left and Mary and Winfield
sat on a davenport together. They made love for a long
time. Winfield was passionate and yet cool, in a way.
He saw what was happening and yet he felt desire for

Mary. He watched her closely, watched her making love
to him. That might be the last night they would ever
make love. It probably would be. He wanted her to
think well of him always. He wanted her to remember
him. So he tried to be tender and loving. Tried to
say nice things to her, so that she would think of the
night tenderly. And doing this he grew very passionate.
Pulled her tightly to himself and held her, kissing her
hard on the lips. Tongue between her lips, kissing her.
Utmost passion.

She raised herself, pulled herself away from him.
Cool, calm. Take me? Winfield. The pin. Take me. It
won't hurt you to give me the pin. I have got to have it.
It means everything. I know. I see. I know you. Do you
want me? You always did. You can have me. Stupid.
Don't look stupid. I'm offering to go with you. You can
have me. Why, you look foolish. I want that pin.

Winfield couldn't speak to her. He just got up
from the davenport. Buttoned his coat, smoothed his
hair. For a pin? Why Mary? A damned fraternity pin!
It's like a whore. I couldn't take anybody that way.
Paying them. Oh, God, you did that? Never could do
it. You must be crazy, Mary. Pride. Your pride. Want
the pin to show off. I know it all. Afraid of what the
girls say. Afraid. Common. Thought that was the way
to get me? Make me passionate? Ask for the pin? Open
up to me. No, cheapen yourself. God, Mary, you gave
me a fright. You do such a thing.

Mary buried her head in her hands. Cried. Her
light golden hair was tossed about her head, over her
left shoulder. Long mad locks of hair that Winfield had
twined around his neck, had buried his face in. One leg

doubled out, frog leg, on the davenport. Mary crying.
Dress untidy, dishevelled. Mary crying. She hadn't
thought. Whore. Never thought. Wanted the pin. That
was all. Her own self respect. Winfield was cruel. Say
such a thing. True though. Only for the girl. No, that
wasn't true. Wanted Winfield herself. More than he
wanted me. Always wanted him. Afraid of him. Baby.
That was all. Only partly the pin. It was his though. I
want something of Winfield's. He hates me. Hates me.
For an old whore, he said.

Winfield was calmer standing there. He hated
to see the girl crying. It just made him cold. He
wished she would hurry up and be sensible. It was
uncomfortable standing there, and Mary crying like a
fool. Her aunt might come in too. Be awful.

—No use crying Mary. No sense in that. Get up
and wipe off your face. Be all dirty. Powder, tears that
way. Get up. You make me uneasy that way.

Mary had finished with her tears. For she wondered
what Winfield was doing standing there. She didn't
dare look at him. He would see her. She thought she
would cry a little longer. Then get up. Do something,
anything. Have to think quick. Got to do something.
Can't let him leave the house. I'd never get over it. After
this. I was a fool. Simple fool. He might tell people.
God Almighty. Got to think of something.

—Now Mary, you know very well I would have
given you the pin long ago, but I promised my mother
I wouldn't. He accented the *would have* quite distinctly.
Mary noticed. I couldn't do that, because I promised.
She would have known. We don't get along well Mary.
Always quarrelling and arguing. You want a man with

money. I don't want to be rich. We ought to quit while we have got the chance.

Winfield now thought he was doing the manly thing. This was the time. He had told her. The end was here. Mary knew it was the end too.

—Winfield, it was only because I loved you, wanted you. The pin because it's your pin. You like it. I wanted it. That's why. You'll always hate me after this. But I couldn't help myself. I wanted you, Winfield. She began to cry. Bitter tears of pain defeat. The tears touched Winfield, but he had to be firm now that he had started.

—Don't cry Mary. I would only have made you unhappy all your life. I've been mean to you. Said mean things. It'll be better for you. You'll be damned thankful, I tell you. I'm not the man for you, or any girl. I'll never marry. I wouldn't make a good husband for any woman. Any woman would hate me. You hate me down in your heart. I guess I'll never marry. I just make everybody unhappy. I know that. I'll never marry. We've had the best love I ever knew of. Let's go apart and be happy.

If only he never would marry. That would be easier. She could lose him that way. Easier to lose him that way. I've been such a fool, Winfield. But I love you. I do. I want you. Promise me if I have to marry some time you'll go away with me. Up in the woods sometime. Two weeks or three. I've got to have you. You're all I want, ever wanted, ever will want. I may marry for money sometime. May not too. I hate everybody but you. You may come back though. Someday come back. I'll be true to you. I couldn't go with another man.

Couldn't kiss another man. It's just awful. Like I was
dying, Winfield. I believe I am. I feel so funny. You
don't know. I say funny things I feel dead. No feeling
at all. Legs dead. Look Winfield. Arms too. Can't move
them. I believe I'm dying. You are killing me. What I
say to you. I'm dying. I'll scream, Winfield. Stand there
like a fool, you. Stand there. Dying. Are you crazy? See
me. Die. God, you're funny. Killing me I could laugh
at you. Funny, love you. Mary laughed hysterically. The
laugh broke into choking gasps. Painful.

She had been talking, looking up toward the
ceiling. Winfield was afraid. She was hysterical, crazy.
He ought to do something. What could he do? She
sank into the cushions of the davenport. Wept. He
stroked her back, the shoulders, affectionately.

—There, you'll be all right.

He wished he might know she would be all right.
He was worried. She took it so hard. She thought she
was talking sense. She didn't know what she was talking
about. She fell asleep there on the davenport.

He straightened her hair and clothes. Covered
her with a white bearskin rug. Sat beside her worried,
waiting. Jesus, I'd like to get out of this. Get loose.
These damned messes. In New York I'll be away. She
can't pull that stuff on me there. Her mother may
raise hell, or her father. I ought to beat it now. No,
something might happen. Better just wait awhile. See
what happens.

Mary's aunt came into the hallway. Tapped lightly
on the door.

—Yes, he answered.

—Mary had better be going to bed, the aunt said.

Winfield went to the door. He told Mary's aunt that the girl was sleeping, she had been feeling bad. He wondered what to do. The aunt, worried, walked up to Mary, looked at her. Thought to herself, Maybe the children have been up to something. She gave a suspicious look at Winfield. She was reassured. He didn't look as if he had done anything bad to the girl. Just nerves, she thought. School and love.

She awakened Mary.

—Oh, I'm sorry. I fell asleep. So tired. Winfield is going away tomorrow. To school.

She was so composed now. It was a wonder.

—I think I had better go to bed, Auntie. I'm tired. Good night, Winfield. She gave him her hand. Good night. Wait Auntie. I must kiss Winfield good night. Wait for me. Don't go out of the room. I'm all right. Winfield, good night.

She kissed him hard on the lips. I love only you, Winfield. Everything I said I mean. I'll have you some day. It's true, lover. No matter what happens, it's you I love.

—Good night, she said once more, aloud, so her aunt would hear.

Well I got out of that, Winfield thought, as he walked toward home.

About the Author

John Herrmann was born November 9, 1900, in Lansing, Michigan. He grew up in Lansing and later attended George Washington University, the University of Michigan, and the University of Munich. After spending a brief period of time in Paris as part of the expatriate literary circle of the 1920s, Herrmann returned to the United States, where he married fellow writer Josephine Herbst in 1926. Herrmann wrote three novels and over two dozen other publications (novellas, short stories, and essays) over the next two decades, and when he was not writing he often worked as a traveling salesman to supplement his income. His moment of highest literary acclaim occurred in 1932, when he tied with Thomas Wolfe for the *Scribner's Magazine* prize for short fiction. During the 1930s, he became increasingly involved in political issues and workers' rights struggles. Herrmann and Herbst divorced in 1940, and he married Ruth Tate that same year. He served in the U.S. Coast Guard during World War II, and by the late 1940s, honorably discharged, Herrmann fled to Mexico after discovering that the FBI was investigating his earlier political activities. He died April 9, 1959, in Guadalajara, Mexico.